NIGHTSPELL

NIGHTSPELL

LEAH CYPESS

GREENWILLOW BOOKS

An Imprint of HarperCollinsPublishers

Nightspell
Copyright © 2011 by Leah Cypess

The text of this book is set in 11-point Stempel Garamond.
Book design by Paul Zakris

Library of Congress Cataloging-in-Publication Data

Cypess, Leah.
Nightspell / by Leah Cypess.
p. cm.
"Greenwillow Books."
Summary: Sent by her father, the king of Raellia, who is trying to forge an empire out of warring tribes, Darri arrives in Ghostland and discovers that her sister, whom she planned to rescue, may not want to leave this land where the dead mingle freely with the living.
ISBN 978-0-06-195702-4 (trade bdg.)
[1. Ghosts—Fiction. 2. Sisters—Fiction. 3. Dead—Fiction.
4. Kings, queens, rulers, etc.]
I. Title.
PZ7.C9972Gh 2011   [Fic]—dc22   2010012637

11 12 13 14 15 LP/RRDB 10 9 8 7 6 5 4 3 2 1
First Edition

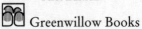 Greenwillow Books

To Mommy & Daddy

NIGHTSPELL

Chapter One

Darri didn't see the ghost until he was upon her, a solid weight that dropped from the branches above and threw her sideways off the saddle. Because he *was* solid, she didn't realize at first that he was dead. She hit the ground with a thud and rolled to her feet, pulling her dagger from her boot. By the time she was standing, she had already thrown it.

The dagger plunged into the man's chest with a thunk, and he laughed at her. He was a large, ruddy man wearing a fine set of riding clothes and a short cape. As he laughed, his body slowly faded, so that even in the torchlight Darri could see the trees through him. Her dagger dropped straight down through his body and disappeared into the dark mass of ferns that covered the forest floor.

Darri's breath twisted in her throat. Her horse—a

battle-trained stallion who could face a mounted charge without flinching—neighed shrilly in terror and reared. The dead man laughed louder. He became solid again, bent to pick up her dagger, and lunged at her.

Darri's body reacted instinctively, whirling sideways as he rushed past her. She was poised to kick the dagger out of his hand, but her mind betrayed her. Terror burned through her chest, and by the time she swallowed it, the moment had passed. The specter's side was no longer unguarded. He turned and came at her again, and the scent of rotting flesh filled the air.

Her attacker jerked suddenly, an expression of surprise wiping the laughter from his face. And then he was gone.

When his hand vanished, Darri's dagger dropped again. With it fell another—the blade that had been hurled into the ghost's back. That one gleamed with the unmistakable glint of silver before it disappeared into the ferns.

Darri took a deep breath and looked up at her brother, who was leaning back in the saddle to recover from his throw. His face wore its usual unruffled expression.

Darri willed her voice steady. It didn't quite work. "I thought the terms of our invitation specified that we bring no silver weapons."

There was a moment of silence, broken only by the wind and the snorting of her horse. Then Varis's face shifted into its second most common expression: resigned contempt, as if he couldn't believe how stupid she was. "We had better keep going," he said. "Retrieve the knives."

Darri glared up at him. Over the past ten nights of riding, her patience for Varis had grown shorter and shorter. "I didn't exactly get off the horse to dawdle."

"Just get back on!"

He sounded nervous now, which Darri counted as a victory. With deliberately sauntering steps, she walked over and handed him the silver blade, then patted his mount's hindquarters. "Don't worry. I'm not going to try and delay us."

He leaned over to slide the dagger into his boot sheath, then straightened. "It wouldn't surprise me if you did."

"That," Darri snapped, "is because you don't know anything about me anymore."

"Nor," Varis said, gathering up the reins, "am I interested."

She flinched despite herself, and suddenly the whole thing wasn't worth it. She should have known better than to start with Varis; he always hurt her, and she never even scratched his imperturbable surface. Darri mounted her horse without another word.

It had been years since she had even wanted a reaction from Varis—four years, to be exact. But being alone with him in this dark, deadly forest played tricks on her memory. It made her feel afraid, as if she was once again a small girl relying on her older brother to protect her.

She had better get past that fast.

She closed her eyes, trusting her horse to follow the path, thinking as hard as she could of sunlight and blue sky and empty plains. Until now, the mental image had kept her just at the edge of panic; she tried to let it fill her inner vision, pushing out the fear.

It wasn't working anymore. Her arm ached where she had hit the ground, and her grip on the reins was so tight that her horse snorted in protest and tossed his head. She unclenched her fingers and tried to breathe, opening her eyes. All around her, the shadows shifted among the tangled trees. She wanted to be home, where the dead were safely hidden beneath the earth, and you could see an enemy coming for miles. Where people rode during the day and slept at night, instead of the other way around.

Despite herself, Darri looked back. Even with the moon nearly full, the forest was so dark it could have hidden a thousand ghosts—or none at all. The brambles leered at them. Hundreds of eyes could be watching them pass, hundreds of twisted, undead things.

Here be ghosts, the maps said, and that was all they had to say about the kingdom known as Ghostland. They were riding toward a castle where, the legends whispered, the dead outnumbered the living. Each of the dead seeking vengeance and nearly impossible to fight. They could kill the living with any weapon they pleased, but only silver or sunlight could harm a ghost.

Varis prodded his horse into a faster walk and scanned the shadows between the thick tree trunks, as if expecting another ghost to leap out from between them. Darri imitated his movement, her shoulder blades tightening. The thought of another attack was enough to tip the balance between pride and fear. She took a deep breath and said, "Do you think it was alone?"

For a moment she was sure Varis wasn't going to answer. Then he shrugged and said, "Probably. If there were two, they would have attacked together."

"Why did it attack us at all?"

Varis glanced over his shoulder at her, long enough for her to see that the contempt was back. "Because we will control their country, one way or another. For all the talk of alliances and marriage, some of them must realize it."

Great. Wonderful.

Callie, she thought, and called up a memory of her sister: Callie with her arms spread to her sides, twirling around and around in the long grass with her small round face tilted back, giggling uncontrollably. The memory was an old one—Callie had been perhaps five years old, Darri eight—but it was the one Darri had fallen asleep to for more nights than she could count.

Except she always woke up to another old memory: Varis sneaking into her tent to tell her the news. She had been eager to see him, thinking he was coming for one of his usual visits, to regale her in whispers with the tale of a daring raid or a successful hunt. Instead he had told her, in calm concise tones, that Callie would be sent to marry the prince of Ghostland. That their little sister was a reasonable price to pay for the one territory on the east coast they couldn't easily conquer.

He had seemed surprised when she erupted from her bedroll, but not too surprised to grab her by the wrist before she made it to the door flap. "Darri. I know it's hard. But no sacrifice is too great."

"This one is," Darri had raged at him, trying ineffectually to free herself. "This is *Callie* you're talking about, Varis, not a herd of horses or a tactical battle advantage. Father can't do this to her. He can't. I'll stop it."

Her brother had looked at her with his blue eyes narrowed, disbelief slowly turning to disgust, and said, "I won't let you."

That was the last time he had ever snuck into her tent.

Now Varis shifted in the saddle, and his voice sharpened.

"I think it would be best not to mention this incident when we get to the castle."

"Because in order to explain what happened, we would have to admit you were carrying a silver dagger?"

His response was another look of cool contempt, and Darri had had just about enough of those. She wasn't stupid, no matter how many stupid things she had done in her rage over Callie's betrayal. Maybe it was time Varis noticed that. She spurred her horse forward to ride beside him, shouldering his stallion sideways so they could both fit on the forest path, ignoring both his raised eyebrows and the branches that brushed along her left arm. "I know what we're doing here, Varis."

"I should hope so. It's been explained to you in some detail."

And he had been repeating it twice daily since they left: the alliance with Ghostland was crucial, especially now that their forces were ready to turn west. They didn't have time to wait for Callie to come of age. Instead it would be Darri who married the prince of Ghostland, and she had better remember her responsibility to her people.

The fact that Darri never argued didn't seem to reassure him at all. Varis was not stupid either.

She shouldn't argue now, she knew; there was nothing to gain. But the words came tumbling out anyhow.

"I stopped listening to the explanations after your first attempt," she said. "They're not going to start making sense because you keep repeating them. Nobody bothered to ride here with Callie when you traded her away. Why do I get treated better than she did?"

"Someone has to watch you," Varis snapped, "to make sure you do your duty. You've made that perfectly clear."

An overhead branch snagged her hair, and she reached up with one hand to wrench it away. The pain in her scalp was welcome; it felt deserved. "Because I love my sister more than I love our father's ambitions. Unforgivable."

Varis's fingers tightened on the reins. "There is nothing more important than maintaining our security. Don't you remember what it was like when we were the weakest of the tribes, when anyone could hurt us at will?"

He knew she did. Neither of them would ever forget the night their mother was kidnapped and killed, the night their two older brothers had died trying to protect her. Callie had been just a baby, wailing for her mother without understanding that she was gone forever. It had been Varis who had wept with Darri, and held her, for night after night as their father prepared for war. And then left her behind to go to war with him.

She didn't want to remember that, or to think about how much he had changed when he came back. How she had closed her eyes to the changes in him, followed his lead, wanted exactly what he wanted . . . until the night she finally realized how far he would go.

Varis drew in a breath, let it out, and—in the moment it took his horse to step over a fallen log—became cool and remote again. "But now you care about nothing but Callie. So you should be happy that the two of you will be together again."

Darri lost control of the reins for a moment, and her horse hit his hind leg on the log and stumbled. She regained her balance and turned in the saddle, this time ignoring the branches that caught at her hair. "Callie will go back with *you*! Once I marry Prince Kestin—"

"She can help you settle in." Varis spurred his horse forward, leaving her with a view of his rigid back and his horse's swishing tail. "Her experience will be valuable to you as you learn the ways of the court."

Darri watched openmouthed as his horse's tail flicked against her stallion's face, making her mount snort and shake his head. That was so like Varis—to assume that Callie would still be loyal, would still devote herself to the Raellian conquest, even after her life had been traded away.

Let him assume it, she thought as she let her horse fall back. Let him assume whatever he wanted. It would make her task easier.

Because regardless of her father's true reasons for sending them to Ghostland, Darri was here for one purpose only: to get Callie out. And not Varis or her father or all the dead men in Ghostland were going to stop her.

Prince Kestin, Callie noted, was brooding. He had been gloomy for several nights now, and it made him look exceptionally handsome—he had the sort of long, intense face that seemed made for deep thought, and always looked a bit incongruous when he laughed. For most of the banquet, Callie had thought that was the reason for the brooding. But now he had taken to drinking, which was a bad sign.

"They'll be here before daybreak," Jano said, materializing in the empty chair next to hers. As Callie turned to look at him, Jano went solid. "I just heard from one of the scouts."

Callie smiled, knowing it wouldn't fool him, and looked down at her plate. So her siblings were riding at night. Day and night were reversed in Ghostland to accommodate the dead, but she wouldn't have thought Darri and Varis would follow that custom until they had to. On the other hand, it was smart that they had given themselves a few days to adjust before reaching the castle. Varis's idea, probably.

Jano followed her gaze. "You've barely eaten a bite all night. Aren't you excited to see your sister?"

She ignored him. He might look like a ten-year-old child, but in truth he was hundreds of years old. Far too old to get away with this type of rudeness.

"The scout said she's not as ugly as we had feared." Jano apparently didn't notice that he was being ignored. He grinned at her, looping one leg over the arm of the chair. "She's wearing breeches, though. And riding astride, like a man."

"All the plains women ride astride," Callie snapped.

"How barbaric. Lucky that *you* were brought up in a civilized country."

A traitorous part of her thought he was right, and was ashamed of her sister in her mannish clothes. Callie looked over Jano's head at Prince Kestin, who was still scowling at his food as if it had offended him.

Darri would be seventeen now, only four years younger than Kestin. Did her father really imagine that would make her a more acceptable bride? True, Callie had been too young, but that was only part of the problem. The real issue was that the Ghostlanders didn't concern themselves with anyone outside their own kingdom. She had spent the last four years in an uncertain status, more an unwelcome guest than a hostage, and in all that time nobody had ever seemed to care why she was there. Even the royalty here married whomever they pleased within their own country, and had never before bothered seeking out foreigners for the sake of alliances.

Not that it was relevant anymore. Not for Prince Kestin.

A commotion erupted near the front of the banquet hall. The Guardian went striding past them, his two swords crossed at his back, the silver one catching the lamplight. The black iron mask on his face gleamed too, not quite as shiny as his sword. All at once the hall was silent. Prince Kestin looked up from his food, his face bleak and still.

Oh, burial plots. Callie shoved her hands under the folds of her skirt to hide their shaking. "You said before daybreak!"

Jano noticed the motion. His teeth gleamed white as he smiled. "Is it not before daybreak?"

Callie bit her tongue to keep from saying something she would regret later. Annoying as Jano was, she couldn't lose her only real friend at court. And to be fair, most ghosts liked to act as if they were above the petty concerns of the living. *Deadheads*, some of the living called them. Usually behind their backs.

But Callie was still too foreign—would always, she knew, be too foreign—to dare say anything negative about the dead. So she just gave Jano a nasty look before turning to watch the spectacle.

Varis strode in first. Her brother hadn't changed much:

tall and powerfully built, with a blunt, roughly hewn face. To her Raellian eyes, he looked underdressed without a sword on his hip. To her Ghostland eyes, he looked underdressed period. He had changed from his riding clothes and was wearing a black silk cape and breeches, his hair bound back in a long, tight braid. The silk meant this was finery, but it was ragged and coarse compared to even the simplest garments worn by the Ghostlanders. King Ais, in his velvet-trimmed robe and elaborately embroidered cape, his hair cut neatly at his shoulders, was clearly not sure whether this was the prince or an advance retainer.

Of all the people in the hall, Callie was certain that only she could tell Varis was annoyed. He bowed from the waist. "Your Majesty. On behalf of my royal father, we extend our greetings to you and your court."

King Ais blinked only once before beginning his formal response—which would certainly be five times as long as Varis's, though it wouldn't say anything more. Callie didn't bother paying attention. She wondered where Darri was.

People were watching her, she knew. Waiting to see how she would react. Wondering if she had truly been civilized—*tamed*, a voice in her mind whispered—or if she would revert to type once she was back in touch with her own kind. Her skin felt stretched tight over her face, and she had to dig her fingernails into her palms to keep herself still.

"Thank you," Varis said, jerking her attention back to the throne. "May I present my sister, Princess Darriniaka of Raellia?"

She had forgotten how fast things moved among her people. How quickly you had to respond among horses and the living. A Ghostlander would have spoken about Darri for at least ten minutes before introducing her. For a painful moment, Callie missed that quickness, and hated herself for being a step behind.

Then Darri walked in, and she banished the thought. That was a weakness she couldn't afford.

Darri, too, was dressed in finery; but unlike Varis, who was simply drab, she looked ridiculous. Her pale pink gown was a cacophony of faded fashions, probably cobbled together from traders' reports of Ghostland dress, and she walked jerkily in the tight underskirt. Her hair flowed down her back like a horse's mane, and her skin was a sun-baked brown. Kestin leaned against the back of his throne, looking momentarily taken aback; then he composed his face into stiff politeness. Callie flushed with shame for her sister.

But Darri wasn't ashamed. She held her head high, her eyes darting back and forth with a hunter's alertness despite the awkwardness of her gait. No woman of the plains would ever cut or bind up her hair, and pale skin was generally a sign of illness. To her own people, Darri had always been strikingly attractive.

For a moment Callie saw the court through her sister's eyes, with its elaborate stone pillars, painted walls, and floor lined with layers of carpet. She tried to remember how it had looked to her when she first arrived. Overdone, probably. Stifling. The women in their many-colored gowns had seemed grotesquely fake, their eyes scarily outlined in black. She hadn't even known, then, that the outlining was makeup. She had never heard of makeup.

But really, she hadn't been thinking about any of that. She had been too focused on the women who were only half-solid, whose gowns she could see right through. She remembered the first time she had seen one of those women wink out of existence, the space she had been standing in suddenly empty. Worse, she remembered the first time she had seen a translucent woman go solid, and realized there was no way to tell who was dead and who was alive. That in this castle, anyone might be a ghost.

She would have given anything, that first year, to hear that Darri was coming. But now she looked down at her gown—violet silk with black lace—and touched her braided hair, and wondered what Darri would think when she saw her.

Darri stopped next to Varis and curtseyed perfunctorily,

an obviously unaccustomed gesture. Instead of focusing on her hands and feet, she looked furtively around the court.

Looking for me, Callie realized, and shrank back against her chair. Last time she had seen Darri, the two of them had been huddled together in a tent, their hair falling over each other's shoulders, her own hopeless sobs mingling with Darri's angry weeping. Callie remembered clearly her sister's fierce whispers: "I'll come for you, Callie. I won't let this happen. I swear it."

She probably still intended to keep that promise. A little late. Sometimes late really was worse than never.

Darri had been slim even at thirteen, but the saddle had burned whatever fat she'd had right off her. Now she was so thin she was almost gaunt, cheekbones slashing across her face. She looked . . . dangerous.

A few of the ghosts had risen into the air so they could see better. Callie winced, watching Darri's face pale, and wished the court would be a little more tactful. But then Darri saw Callie, and her whole face lit up.

Everyone was watching. Callie looked away fast, but not fast enough to miss seeing the way Darri's smile died.

She spent the rest of the formal introductions avoiding her sister's gaze. A part of her was angry: what did Darri expect, and why couldn't she control herself in front of the court? A larger part of her felt guilty, and ashamed, and—irrationally—hurt herself.

Darri probably thought she was rescuing Callie, giving her the chance to escape back to the life she had grown up in. Once, Callie would have been tempted.

But now, all her sister was going to accomplish was to ruin everything.

Chapter Two

Darri made her first social blunder immediately after the welcoming ceremony. King Ais, after a flowery ramble about how much he hoped their countries would be joined in friendship, announced that they would now attend a banquet. An overdressed servant appeared—literally, appeared—at Varis's side to escort them to their table.

Varis jerked visibly away, and the servant looked affronted, so Darri figured it was as good a time as any to be rude. "Where will we be sitting?" she asked.

King Ais frowned and looked at his son—Darri's potential betrothed, the supposed reason for this journey. So far, Darri had not been required to address Prince Kestin, though she had noticed the strong, clean lines of his face and the directness of his gaze. She couldn't help noticing. It was that kind of face. And besides, she would be a fool to ignore anything that might make her sacrifice a little bit easier.

"I'd like to sit with my sister," Darri went on. "It's been so long since we've seen each other."

Varis shot her a furious scowl. In the long, frozen silence, Prince Kestin made a tiny sound that might have been a laugh.

"Of course," King Ais said. "I'll see to it."

The banquet hall was a vast room, crammed with tables covered with embroidered linen cloths, and filled with so many gold and copper dishes that the effect was blinding. Darri had never before seen so many people in such a small space. But of course, they weren't all people; some of them were dead spirits in the guise of the living, moving and speaking as if their bodies were whole, trapped by the abhorrent charade.

It wasn't until they were seated—at a blessedly empty table—that they had enough privacy for Varis to hiss, "You know you were supposed to sit with the prince. What were you thinking?"

"That I'd like to speak to Callie," Darri said.

"Do you really think it's a good idea to insult Prince Kestin within two minutes of arriving in his country?"

"Yes," Darri said, just to see his reaction, "I do."

Unfortunately, at that moment a young woman in a

yellow gown took the seat across from them, and Varis's face smoothed instantly into an expression of bland politeness. The woman tilted her head at them and said, "Guess."

"Guess what?" Varis said, falling right into what was obviously a trap. Darri resisted the urge to kick him under the table.

The woman smiled. She was plump and pretty, despite her pasty skin, with red-tinged hair arranged in knots and twirls. "Whether I'm alive or dead."

Varis flinched, and Darri couldn't blame him. She tried to think of something cutting to say. Nothing came to mind.

Darri had once fallen asleep in long grass and woken to find ants crawling all over her body, wriggling into her nostrils and tickling over her tongue. That had been nothing compared to how she felt now, surrounded by dead creatures whose corpses were rotting below the ground. She kept catching whiffs of decomposing flesh, kept imagining the anguished screams of human spirits bound to lifeless bodies. This was a terrible place, beneath the gowns and smiles and glitter.

And she was going to spend the rest of her life here.

"Stop it," Callie said from behind Darri. "Leave them alone."

Darri turned so fast she almost overturned her chair.

Her younger sister stepped away from the near-mishap primly, without looking at Darri. Her eyes were on the woman, who smoothed back her hair and smiled.

"Oh, come, darling. Why protect them? No one protected you."

"As you made perfectly clear," Callie said. "Though I understand your motives, Lizette. With that hairstyle, only a foreigner couldn't guess in seconds that you were dead. And for quite a while."

Lizette raised one hand to her hair, and suddenly there was no face beneath the elaborate hairstyle; instead there was a skull, shreds of skin clinging to gray bone, a white maggot squirming out of one blank eyehole.

Varis made a sick noise, obviously involuntary. Lizette's mask of a face reappeared. She smirked at him and at Callie, then turned to Darri and said, "I understand you have your eye on our prince. You had better get used to this sort of thing, if you're thinking of marrying him. I'm the least frightening ghost here."

"Really?" Darri did her best to sound unconcerned. She would show these creatures they couldn't cow a Raellian princess. "How did you die?"

A short, absolute silence passed. Lizette tittered and touched a finger to her lips. "Now, now. We've only just met."

Darri glanced at her sister, whose face was beet red; the last time Darri had seen Callie so embarrassed, she had just lost control of a horse. Apparently this was not a question one asked of the dead.

Lizette vanished. Varis made another strangled sound. Callie sighed and said, "It would really be better if you stopped doing that."

Varis clenched his fists on the table. Darri tried to exchange a triumphant look with Callie, who had never been particularly close to Varis, but Callie took a seat without looking at her.

A serving boy came by with wine and a tray of complicated-looking delicacies. Darri took one and bit in. It was overcooked and overspiced. Callie did not take any. She sat with her hands folded in her lap, like someone suffering through a very boring etiquette lesson.

"I asked King Ais to seat us together," Darri said, deciding to ignore Callie's silence. Her sister was in there, somewhere. She had retreated deep inside herself—and who could blame her—but Darri would find her. "He wanted me to sit with Prince Kestin."

"For understandable reasons." Varis spat the words out more viciously than usual. His uncontrolled whimpers had been even more impolite than Darri's forthrightness, and he knew it. "Prince Kestin is the reason you're here. Not that I would expect you to remember that for more than five seconds."

Callie did look up then, not at them, but at the prince's table across the room. When she spoke, her voice was flat. "Prince Kestin is dead."

Darri followed her sister's gaze to watch the prince toss back half a goblet of wine. "Dead?"

Callie put her elbow on the table and propped her chin up on her hand. "The dead can eat and drink. They don't have to, but many of them enjoy it."

"No, I mean—no one told us—"

"He was murdered several weeks ago."

Just a few minutes before, Darri had been thinking him handsome. Thinking it might not be so bad if, to seal an alliance . . . her stomach turned. While she was forcing back her bile, Varis said sharply, "The king's son was killed, and the murderer still has not been brought to justice?"

"Not only that." Callie leaned back in her chair, resting her elbows on the armrests and watching her brother. Her evident enjoyment of Varis's discomfiture gave Darri some hope; she just wished her sister would look at her. "The murderer is protected by law. King Ais has issued a royal decree forbidding anyone to look for his son's killer. Any investigation into Kestin's death is an act of treason."

"Why?" Varis demanded.

"Because in *this* kingdom, fathers love their children." Callie smiled bitterly. "And the purpose of a ghost's existence is vengeance. If Kestin finds out who murdered him, he will kill that person. And then he will disappear."

Varis wrinkled his nose in disgust. "His purpose is vengeance and freedom . . . and his father would rather keep his spirit trapped on this earth?"

Callie dropped her hands to her lap. "Control your prejudices, brother. A third of the people in this room are dead. To Ghostlanders, it doesn't make that much of a difference."

All that did was turn his expression into an outright sneer. "Hard to credit, but I would believe anything of these people."

Darri tried to breathe. If Kestin was dead . . . for the past ten nights, she had prepared herself to be a sacrifice, a trade for her sister's freedom. She hadn't even imagined there could be a way to save herself as well—hadn't let herself imagine it. Because if she had been willing to sacrifice herself last time, instead of dreaming of a happy ending for both of them, maybe Callie wouldn't be here.

But the prospect that opened before her now was so dizzying she could barely think. If no marriage was possible . . . what if she and Callie could ride out of this kingdom *together*?

She turned and looked at Varis, recognizing the intent look on his face, the rigidity of his jaw. He had not missed the implications of Prince Kestin's death.

"Well," she said, and somewhat enjoyed the wariness with which he turned toward her. "If Prince Kestin is dead, there's no reason for either me or Callie to remain here, is there?"

"Of course not," Varis said, not flinching from her gaze. "The sooner we leave this place, the better. We'll stay at least a week so as not to be insulting, but I'll speak to the king shortly about making arrangements for our departure."

That had been *far* too easy—but at least it hadn't been an outright refusal. Maybe he actually meant it. Darri turned to her sister, and her breath caught halfway down her throat. Callie's face was perfectly blank, but her lips were set in a grim line that Darri recognized from long ago.

Callie was not happy about her imminent escape.

Callie glanced swiftly at Darri, then away. She reached for the tray of food, expertly flipped up her flared sleeve so it didn't knock anything over, and kept her eyes on her plate as she chewed on a tiny meat pastry.

I can save you, Darri thought at her. *You can trust me this time.* But Callie didn't look up.

Darri picked up her own pastry and bit into it savagely. Varis, she noted, had not picked his up again after the first bite. Callie, on the other hand, was digging in avidly.

You can trust me this time. But Callie didn't know that. Once, when she had been small enough to sob herself to sleep with her head on Darri's lap, Darri had promised to save her. And failed.

Darri couldn't blame Callie for not believing that this time would be different. But it would. If she couldn't get through to her sister, then Callie would have to find it out along with everyone else.

Callie knew Darri was going to try to get her alone once the banquet ended, so she planned ahead. She munched on candied fruit until half the nobles had staggered to their rooms to sleep. Then she looked across the room and caught Duke Salir's eye.

It needed no more than that. The duke heaved himself to his feet and waddled across the room, his small eyes bright with curiosity. Duke Salir always wanted to know more than anyone else, and frequently did. He had been eyeing the exotic new arrivals, waiting for his chance to pounce, since the moment the banquet began.

"My lord," Callie murmured when he was a few yards away, to give her siblings just a bit of warning. "Would you care to join us?"

Varis's and Darri's heads snapped up, their expressions

for a moment identical. Darri would have been greatly distressed if she knew it—judging from the strained remarks they addressed toward each other, the relationship between her siblings had never recovered from Varis's refusal to aid Callie. She couldn't help feeling a small, mean satisfaction over that.

"Thank you," the duke said, settling himself heavily into one of the high-backed chairs. "I've been looking forward to the chance to speak to Your Highnesses. I am very interested in the lands outside our borders, and have been following with great admiration the exploits of your tribe."

Callie barely suppressed a snort at the lie. In Ghostland, that was the equivalent of announcing that you were interested in the courtship rites of ants.

Varis looked predictably flattered, but as he murmured a polite response, he shot Callie a look of thinly disguised panic. She could easily guess what he was thinking: Was the man he was talking to alive or dead?

Callie pressed her lips together and said nothing. There was no easy way to tell; even the ghosts didn't automatically recognize their fellow dead. Callie had spent months learning the necessary combination of reading clues and not caring. Varis could survive for a few nights.

Besides, informing them that Duke Salir *was* dead wouldn't be doing them much of a favor.

"Excuse me," she said, and slipped out of her chair. Darri half-turned, but not before the duke had addressed a question to her, which she reluctantly turned back to answer. Thinking, no doubt, that she would catch up with Callie later.

A trapped, panicked feeling burned its way up Callie's throat. She forced it down, concentrating on maneuvering her way between tables, and was halfway to the side door of the banquet hall when the room behind her went silent.

It was just for a second—a momentary break in the rhythm of conversation—but Callie had learned to pay attention to the moods of the court, and she knew immediately that something was wrong. She whirled, her skirt catching on a chair edge, afraid to find out what her sister had done now.

But Darri was still seated, her shoulders tense beneath her shiny strands of dark hair, leaning forward in that way she did when she was spoiling for a fight. Varis was seated too, his tired face set in a shrewd, polite expression. Neither of them had seen what the rest of the court had.

The Guardian was striding across the banquet hall toward them. He moved far more easily than should have been possible in that iron casing, as if the black metal was a second skin.

Callie's breath caught in her throat as she struggled

between an urge to run toward Darri and an urge to get out of the banquet hall. In the end, she followed her strongest instinct: to do exactly what the rest of the court was doing. Nothing at all. She watched.

The Guardian's feet hit the marble floor with a heavy, metallic tread. Everyone watched him as he passed, though they pretended not to; they returned to dining and talking, but less ostentatiously, trying not to draw attention to themselves.

Across the room, Prince Kestin stood, his eyes flashing, but he was too far away to do anything.

The Guardian drew his silver sword. He was so fast that not even Varis had time to move before the sword sliced through Duke Salir's throat, just as the duke was tilting his head back to down a goblet of wine.

Wine splattered, Duke Salir vanished, and the goblet shattered on the floor. For a moment the room resembled a painting, everyone in it frozen and silent, all staring at the Guardian. The silver sword was the only real-looking object in the room.

Then, one by one, the courtiers turned away. The low buzz of conversation resumed, a few servants detached themselves from the corners to clean up the wine and glass, and the Guardian sheathed his sword and kept walking.

Toward her.

Callie didn't try to run. She didn't try to keep her face composed either. She had once tried not to be afraid of the Guardian, until she had realized that this particular fear had nothing to do with her foreignness. Everyone was afraid of the Guardian.

Ironically, Callie was probably less afraid than anyone else in this room. She knew what it was like to live with terror so real she could feel it, so paralyzing she had to remind herself to breathe. She had spent so long in fear of *everyone* that the edges had dulled, rubbed smooth by overuse. She was able to watch the Guardian approach with her thoughts blank.

The Guardian stopped several feet away. His face was covered by an iron mask, with two narrow rectangles for his eyes; no way to tell what he was thinking or feeling. Or whether he was about to draw his sword and slice it through her throat.

She glanced, despite herself, at her sister. Darri was on the edge of her seat, alert and coiled. She might as well have been half a world away.

"The duke was commanded to kill them," the Guardian said, so low that no one but Callie could hear. She jerked her gaze back to him. "You should warn them to be wary. Many of the dead do not want them here."

Then he turned and strode away.

Callie stood for another moment, not breathing or moving. From the corner of her eye, she saw a movement she recognized well: Darri sheathing her dagger. As if a dagger could have done anything for her, against the Guardian. As if Darri could do anything in this castle except make everything worse.

She turned, almost tripping over her gown, and exited the hall through one of the side doors.

Once outside, she had to lean against the wall for a moment, and the weakness infuriated her. No one saw except two kitchen girls, but servants talked, even the insignificant ones. She had spent so much time and effort working her way into this court, putting her barbarian heritage behind her, adapting so well that almost no one made catty remarks about her past anymore. She was not going to let it all be ruined in a few nights.

Callie took a deep breath, straightened, and glanced at one of the tall mirrors set into the stone wall. The image was dark and slightly distorted—ghosts didn't have reflections in mirrors made with silver, so all the mirrors in the castle were made of polished steel. The inadequate mirrors were a frequent cause of complaint among the living, and almost all high-ranking living women had unlawful silver mirrors in their apartments. Still, the reflection in the steel, though imperfect, was enough. Callie's makeup was faded, her hair a little frazzled—but no more than anyone else's, this close to dawn. She turned left, heading for the interior of the castle, where there were no windows to let sunlight through and revelry could continue long into daylight.

She found a party in a small sitting room, where a group of young men were playing cards with a cluster of ladies-in-waiting. Lady Velochier, the king's first mistress, was floating above them and calling out hints about what each player held. The hints were mostly directed against the ladies-in-waiting. Lady Velochier had hated the queen, who she believed had ordered her killed; but since the queen had died of natural causes and was now beyond her reach, she directed her animosity at those who had once served her rival.

Callie smiled as she stepped into the room. She liked Lady Velochier, who was funny and sharp-tongued. The merriment in the room was infectious, and she let it fill her along with the scent of wine, washing away Darri's demanding stares and Varis's scorn and the memories of the bare windswept plains she had once called home. No one on the plains had the slightest idea how to have fun. They were probably suspicious of the very concept.

But as she sat, the girl next to her turned and stopped giggling, her blue eyes going very wide. "Oh, Callie!

Whatever are you doing here? Shouldn't you be with your family?"

"She'll be with them soon enough," Lady Velochier called out from above. She tilted her body downward and ran one hand gently over the blue-eyed girl's hair; the girl, Aznette, was her daughter. "Leave her be, sweetling. The poor thing has only a few more nights at court."

"And then it's back to the barren plains," one of the men said. "Let us give you some fond memories to remember us by."

"I'll take charge of that!" laughed another, a handsome duke's son named Ayad who was the biggest flirt at court.

Callie smiled as if she was amused, wondering why she hadn't expected this. The answer was easy: because she hadn't wanted to. "I'd be careful," she told the duke's son. "My departure isn't as certain as all that."

"No?" said Lady Velochier. "Don't they want you?"

Another chorus of giggles, and Callie couldn't hide a flush. Lady Velochier had never turned that sharp tongue on *her* before. It no longer seemed so funny. "The king is a fan of the exotic, is he not?" she shot back. "I think my sister may catch his eye. That would delay us as long as his attention holds—so I would wager a month?"

The giggles this time were somewhat tentative; no one was sure if she had gone too far. Neither was Callie. She felt off-balance, and was trying not to show it.

Lady Velochier sank to the floor and became solid, so that she looked like just another lady-in-waiting. She had been no older than most of them when she died, and she was still extraordinarily beautiful, even if her mouth sometimes pursed like an old woman's. She settled next to her daughter and looped one arm around her; Aznette tilted her head onto her dead mother's shoulder and smiled, closing her eyes.

"I would wager less," Lady Velochier sneered. "Abject terror isn't all that attractive, even if your sister were presentable to begin with. Every time one of us goes a shade translucent, she looks ready to faint."

Callie felt a spurt of sympathy for her sister, something she had been trying to avoid since the moment Darri strode into the throne room. She opened her mouth to defend Darri, and realized just in time what a mistake that would be.

The silence in the room stretched too long as Callie struggled against the desire to do it anyhow. Lady Velochier sniggered in victory and looked over the shoulder of the lady-in-waiting next to her. "Who taught you to play, darling? With cards like those, you should have bowed out long ago."

Aznette giggled, the girl shrieked in protest, and the

room erupted in shouts and laughter. Callie drew her knees to her chest and sat silent, not participating, fighting the ridiculous urge to burst into tears.

You should have come years ago, Darri. It would have been different then.

Now it was too late. Unfortunately, that was something Darri would never understand.

Chapter Three

Varis woke up early the next night and sat bolt upright. For a moment he wasn't sure where he was; the bed beneath him was too soft, and he couldn't hear the wind. Then he remembered, and relaxed his muscles one by one. He swung himself onto the hard stone floor and reached for the tinderbox at the side of his bed.

His brain, which had spent the day insisting he wake up, was now insisting it was time to sleep. He shook off his grogginess while he pulled on some riding clothes.

His servant from the night before had said there would be a hunt tonight. If this court was anything like the others he had visited, most of the important noblemen would be on the hunt, and Varis would get a chance to either impress them or talk to them. Preferably both. Either way, it would help him figure out his next step.

He tucked a dagger into his boot, the weight of it reassuringly familiar, and made his way to the castle courtyard. His steps quickened as the fog in his mind cleared, and he strode confidently through empty halls decorated with dreary tapestries. The passageways were dimly lit, but he had been paying attention the night before and knew which way to go. He was nearly at the kennels when someone stepped out of a half-open doorway and stumbled into him.

Varis leaped away, whirled with his dagger already in his hand, and found himself looking at the most beautiful woman he had ever seen.

Even her heavy makeup and overly ornate costume couldn't detract from her beauty. She had a fine-featured face, with blond hair that tumbled over slender shoulders, sculpted cheekbones, and unusually large green eyes. She smiled at him as he stared at her—a slow, sweet smile that told him she was used to this reaction, bored by it even, but did not object to it from him.

She had to be dead. No one living could be this perfect. For a second, Varis didn't even care. "My lady."

"My name is Clarisse, Your Highness."

Varis smiled. Women generally reacted well to his smile. "And mine is Varis."

"I know." She looked up at him from beneath thick lashes, and Varis struggled to hold onto the smile. Despite his usual confidence, he couldn't believe *she* seemed to be reacting well. "Are you here for the hunt?"

"Yes," Varis said. "Are you?"

"Of course. I love to hunt." She said it with a ferocity that made Varis's heart pound. Then she dimpled at him, suddenly a court lady again. "You plainspeople must hunt often?"

Varis didn't like the disparaging tone in which she said "plainspeople," but he was sufficiently fascinated to pretend he didn't notice. "Yes, of course. But we hunt during the day."

"I can see how that would be easier." The disparagement now bordered on contempt. Varis took a step toward her, forcing her to tilt her head back and look up at him. "But it would hardly be polite to exclude half the court, would it?"

"Half" was probably a wild exaggeration, and he knew she had said it only to see his reaction. He managed not to step back, but suspected from the way her eyebrows lifted that he hadn't controlled his expression. "Hunting at night sounds like a challenge," he said as calmly as he could manage.

"I suppose it does."

"Exactly how I like to start my evenings."

She smiled at him with pleased surprise. Varis played this particular game very well; he did not smile back. Instead he lifted his eyebrows meaningfully, as if acknowledging a shared secret. Ignoring the inner voice that was trying to remind him this wasn't why he was here, he said, "It's something to keep me busy, in any case, while I take a break from conquering the world."

Raellian girls generally responded well to the "conquering the world" line, but Clarisse gave him a look that made him feel stupid. "Is that what you're doing in this country? Taking a break?"

Varis shifted his balance, suddenly battle ready. Her tone was still light and mocking, but he didn't believe for a second that the question was innocent. "You have nothing to worry about. Ghostland is not conquerable; I'm here to make an alliance with your people."

"They're not my people."

He looked down at her more closely, and saw what he should have seen at once: the color on her skin, unlike the waxy whiteness of the Ghostland women; the slightly different shape of her eyes; the sharpness of her features. She looked more like the traders from beyond the mountains than like anyone in this kingdom. "I thought there were no foreigners here."

"There aren't supposed to be. I convinced them to make

an exception in my case." Clarisse grinned, eyes gleaming in a way that made his heart speed up. "So you intend to ally yourselves with Ghostland . . . and then? Will you turn west and cross the Kierran Mountains?"

"Probably."

She stepped back and looked him over more carefully. He couldn't read her expression. "I've crossed the mountains, and I know what they're like. You couldn't ride an army of horses through those passes."

In Varis's experience, foreigners had no idea what Raellians could do with their horses. He folded his arms across his chest. "Why do you care?"

"I don't," Clarisse said, pressing her lips into a straight line. "I don't care." She turned abruptly, her golden hair swinging against her shoulders. "Follow me. The hunt will be leaving shortly, and we wouldn't want to miss it."

Darri awoke to complete darkness and to muffled sounds coming from outside her door. For a moment she thought she had woken too early, and turned her face into her pillow. Then she remembered: if there was no light creeping in around the draperies, that meant it was night, and here, that meant it was day.

Darri groaned and buried her face in the silk pillow. Her eyes were blurry, and every one of her limbs protested the thought of moving. Yesterday the light creeping through the narrow spaces between drapes and walls had kept her tossing and turning for hours before she slept. And that had been after similarly fruitless hours spent wandering the halls looking for her sister.

Then someone knocked on her door, and Darri rolled over and sat up instantly. "Callie?"

"It's me, Your Highness," a voice said. The door opened, letting in the sounds of movement and conversation from the hall outside. "Meandra, your maid? I was wondering if you might need assistance?"

Darri just looked at her, so long and intently that the maid flushed and stepped back, drawing her shoulders together. She's afraid of me, Darri recognized with astonishment, and felt a wave of relief. Surely the dead didn't feel fear.

"Of course," she said, and the maid looked at her wide eyed. She was young and drab-looking, with a round face and brown hair tied back in a bun. "I'm not accustomed to—that is, I can dress myself. But I may need your assistance with other things."

The girl's eyes went even wider; clearly she suspected "other things" was code for something foreign, difficult, and immoral. But she crept into the room and closed the door behind her.

The room plunged back into darkness. A moment later the tinderbox near the door sparked into light. The maid—Meandra—carried a candle around the room, solemnly lighting every one of the five lamps in it. When she was done, the room was as bright as day.

They must go through barrels and barrels of oil. On the plains oil was scarce, and once the sun set people worked in the dimmest light they could manage with—or, better yet, just went to sleep. Of course, that wasn't an option here.

The thought of home sent a wave of hope through her, almost painful in its intensity. For so long . . . for weeks, or truly, years . . . she hadn't thought of the plains as home. The stretches of long grass, the horse races, the hunts and the firelit feasts that followed, the quiet dark nights with the wind beating at her tent . . . every bit of happiness she'd felt had been tinged by guilt, because Callie wasn't there to enjoy it with her.

Ever since her father had announced his new plan, she had been prepared to give it all up. To trade herself for Callie and leave the plains behind, spend her life trapped in a nightmare so Callie could escape it. Until last night, when she had found out that the prince was dead, that there was no reason for either of them to stay. If she handled it right, she and Callie could ride out of here side by side. And once they were back on the plains, Darri would never let anyone take her sister away again.

Keeping her eyes on the floor, Meandra clasped her hands together and addressed the braided rug at the foot of Darri's bed. "I was instructed to ask whether Your Highness would be interested in joining tonight's hunt."

"Yes," Darri said instantly. She swung her legs over the side of the bed before her mind caught up with her mouth. "Instructed by whom?"

The girl dared a glance at her, then hastily returned her eyes to the rug. "Your Highness?"

"Who invited me along on the hunt?"

"The—the court, Your Highness."

Darri forced herself to sound patient. "Which specific person instructed you to ask me?"

"M-mistress Annabel, Your Highness. The housekeeper."

Right. No help there. Darri sighed and slid off the bed. As she started toward the clothes chests lined up along the wall, she said, "Do you know if my sister was invited along?"

"I'm sure she was, Your Highness. But Lady Callie does not enjoy hunting."

Darri turned around and stared, which was a mistake. It reduced the maid to a quivering mass of terror. "She doesn't enjoy hunting?"

Meandra stumbled over a quick protestation that she might be mistaken, it probably wasn't true, she should not have presumed. A few more pointed questions did nothing but increase the ratio of stutters to words. Finally Darri gave up, dismissed her—a bit shortly—and turned her attention to finding appropriate clothes.

Darri loved to hunt. It was the primary form of entertainment on the plains, and even among a tribe of warriors who rode before they walked, she was one of the best. She could use the opportunity to talk to some of the nobles, try to figure out what had happened to Callie to make her so unreachable.

And in the meantime, it would be fun to show this castleful of overdressed courtiers what a Raellian princess could do.

A sudden sound made Callie sit straight up. She could still feel the impression of the couch fabric on her neck and back; she rolled her shoulders instinctively, but they didn't ache, even though she must have been asleep for hours. She had fallen asleep on the couch long after the card party ended, because she'd had nowhere else to go. She was sure if she had gone to her bedchambers, Darri would have been there waiting for her.

The lamps had gone out, and the windowless room was

pitch-black and cold. She had been asleep for a long time. In the darkness, someone had just knocked something over.

"Jano?" she said, ignoring her pounding heart. This was the sort of opportunity he would love. Scaring the living, and especially scaring her, was one of his favorite pastimes.

Reminding herself firmly that she was no longer easy to scare, Callie reached over the arm of the couch, groping for a lamp.

A hand clamped over her wrist. "Don't."

The hand was cold and clammy, but the voice was worse: dry, raspy, and guttural, as if it was being forced through a mouthful of dirt. Callie twisted and went for the lamp with her other hand.

Two seconds later she was on the floor, her head slamming against the far wall; she had been lifted by her arm and tossed across the room. Callie drew her knees up and bit her lip to keep in a whimper.

That inhuman voice rattled out of the darkness: "I said 'don't.'"

Suddenly Callie felt very much like the terrified child she had been when she first arrived in Ghostland. She didn't even think of getting to her feet, or running, or fighting. Something about that voice drained every ounce of will from her. She hugged her knees to her chest and forced her voice through her tightening throat. "What do you want?"

"I am here to do you a favor."

That was better than *to kill you*. But only by a little; Callie was familiar with Ghostland "favors." She took a deep breath, trying to figure out who was doing this. "Lovely," she said. She had learned long ago how well sarcasm masked fear.

"Or rather, to do your siblings a favor."

"Even better," Callie said. "I'm eternally grateful."

The laugh was worse than the voice. "You think you don't care about them? Then you need do nothing when I tell you where they are."

A prickle ran up Callie's spine. In this castle there were places—people—whom it was well-advised to stay away from. Darri would have no way of knowing that.

She tried to tell herself Darri deserved to know what it felt like, but she couldn't make it convincing. Darri was here, after all. She had come willingly to this terrible place, where the dead walked with the living as if they belonged on this earth. And she had come for Callie. Callie pushed herself up from the floor, her mouth set.

"Where," she said, "are they?"

Chapter Four

It didn't take Darri long to discover that being the best rider on the plains was of little relevance on a Ghostland hunt.

When the horns blew in the distance and the riders around her streamed forward, she found herself enveloped by darkness. The foliage overhead hid the light of the moon, and the enclosed torch on her saddle pommel, ingenious as it was, barely lit the area past her horse's head. She couldn't see what was in front of his hooves at all. She hesitated for a moment—a moment too long, allowing the lights of the other saddles to get ahead of her. Then she gritted her teeth and dug her heels into the stallion's sides.

It had been years since Darri had been afraid of falling off a horse. But as her mount plunged through darkness, following the baying of the hounds, fear rose in her throat and lodged there. She had seen it happen—horses losing their footing on uneven terrain, going over, crushing their riders beneath them. Her horse stumbled several times, and with each stagger she nearly stopped breathing. She couldn't prepare for a fall because she couldn't *see*.

Branches whipped out of the blackness at her, slicing at her face and hair and arms, invisible until they hit her. She crouched low over the horse's neck, so low it made her feel even more off balance, but a sturdy branch would knock her to the ground more surely than a misstep. She had never seen *that* happen, because no Raellian rider would ever be so careless.

This was madness. Even if all the courtiers on this hunt were outpacing her, it was still insanity. Shame battled fear, and she felt herself pulling back on the reins despite her best intentions. She had not asked how many people died on a typical nighttime hunt. Maybe the Ghostlanders didn't fear death the way normal people did.

She thought again of the contempt in their eyes, and loosened her grip. Her horse surged forward, his powerful muscles sliding beneath her; then, just as she was leaning into his pace, he stumbled and came to an abrupt stop. Darri, completely unprepared, was thrown forward.

The last time Darri had fallen off a horse without being pushed, she had been seven years old and trying to switch from one steed to another at full gallop. The second horse had pulled a bit too far ahead, and she had fallen flat on her face in the thick prairie grass. Varis had laughed at her, then helped her round up the horses.

Now she pitched forward into darkness, her hands still on the reins, her face scraping against her horse's hide. The world inverted as she somersaulted in the air, and the reins jerked away from her fingers. She landed on her back with an impact that knocked the breath out of her.

But even before her breath was back, she was on her feet and had found the reins. Gasping for breath, her face hot with shame, she clenched them in one sweaty hand. At least there was no one there to see. The sounds of the hunt had faded into the distance.

"Need help?"

Darri swore and looked up. A young boy with slightly crooked teeth was sitting on a horse a few feet away. Only the dim light of her pommel-torch lit his face; his saddle had no light, and his horse was perfectly still. He looked familiar, but she couldn't remember why. He also looked far too young to be along for the hunt. And he was grinning at her in a way that her bruised pride interpreted as mockery.

She bit down the words, *I'm fine*, which were patently

untrue and would only make the smile worse. "I think I can manage," she said. "It will take a little time to adjust to riding in the dark."

"You should have taken one of our horses. They're trained for it."

She turned her back on him. He watched in silence as she swung herself back into the saddle. Then he said, "Callie was the same way. Wouldn't touch another horse until the steed that brought her here died."

She turned sharply in the saddle, exactly as he must have intended her to. The mocking smile *was* worse, but now she recognized him. He was the boy who had been sitting with Callie last night, when Callie had avoided Darri's eyes and leaned over instead to talk to him.

"Who are you?" she said.

He bowed from the saddle. "Jano. Bastard son of Duke Salir the Fourth."

The fat man who had been killed last night had been Duke Salir the Twenty-first. Darri thought she was successful in hiding her automatic revulsion. She was more interested in what this boy could tell her—and in wiping that grin off his face—than in the fact that he should have been buried centuries ago.

"You seem to be having trouble keeping up," the boy went on. "Why do you think that is?"

The hunt was long gone, but that didn't seem to concern him. What had he been doing, a boy who didn't have to worry about falls or chest-high branches, hanging all the way back with the bumbling novice? The answer was obvious, and the absence of a torch only confirmed it.

"What interests me more," Darri said, "is why you are following me."

He didn't even try to deny it. "Maybe your sister asked me to keep an eye on you."

"I doubt it."

"Well, that's smart of you." The first intelligent thing she had done, his voice implied. He leaned forward and stroked his mount's neck. "Why would Callie imagine you would come along on a hunt reserved for the dead?"

"What?"

He gave her the smug grin of a child who had pulled off a successful prank. "Only the dead hunt at night. Do you think the living in Ghostland are suicidal?"

Darri's horse snorted and shuffled his feet; she knew she should calm him, but her attention was on Jano. "I was invited!"

"Oh, really? By whom?"

"I don't know. My maid—"

"Meandra." Jano straightened in the saddle. "She is a very good maid, but about two hundred years ago she made the mistake of having an affair with someone high above her station. His wife was not pleased."

This was not a prank. This was a trap.

Darri touched her heel to her horse's flank just as the boy leaped at her, a reckless leap that would have broken bones if his had been solid. But he was only solid for a moment, just long enough to knock her sideways; then she felt his body fade away, warm flesh turning to a cold fog that sank into her skin. That feeling, as much as the blow, was what made her let go of the reins.

For the second time in ten years, and in five minutes, Darri fell off her horse. This time, when she scrambled to her feet, she was too late. The boy was floating in mid-air, slapping the hindquarters of first his mount and then hers. The horses took off in a spurt of dust, forcing Darri to jump back. She grabbed for the reins and missed, and horsehair whipped across her face in stinging lines. The last thing she saw, before the light disappeared, was Jano's grin as he looked down at her; then, with the torch gone, it was too dark to see anything.

His voice emerged from right next to her ear. "Don't worry about your steed. We rarely lose horses on the hunt."

He was close enough to touch her again. Darri bit down a scream and whirled away. Her breath sounded panicked, and she knew he could hear it. She imagined his smile. "Why are you doing this?"

"Oh, come on. That's rather obvious, isn't it?"

"Don't kill her," a feminine voice trilled. "Yet. We agreed we would kill them all together."

This voice came from behind Darri. She started to turn, then stopped with her foot digging into the ground. She didn't want Jano at her back. But she couldn't see him in the thick blackness. He could be anywhere now, and she didn't know how many of them were closing in around her.

A faintly sour scent wafted past her, and she heard twigs crackling. She turned again, this time in the direction of the sound.

Varis had once told her what it felt like to ride into an ambush, the sudden realization that you were in a trap designed to end with your death. He had said it sharpened every sense. But what use was that when she couldn't see?

She was a Raellian princess. She had no fear of death. She told herself so firmly, but was still glad of the darkness to hide her shaking. "Why?" she said as steadily as she could. "Who are you?"

A torch blazed up in the boy's hand, revealing a golden-haired woman with eyes that shimmered green even in the dimness. Darri spared the woman only a glance before turning to the man who stood next to her.

Varis looked as terrified as she felt, which under other circumstances would have made her feel better. He met her eyes for a second before looking back at the woman, with a sick horror that immediately told Darri what she wanted to know.

"You're dead too," she whispered.

The woman smiled. "Oh, yes. Your brother found that out while he was taking certain . . . liberties . . . with my person. I'm afraid he was quite distressed." She smirked, catlike, and looked at Jano. "You owe me for that, by the way. I can still smell his puke."

"So can I." Jano made a face. "And why should I owe you anything? This wasn't my idea, Clarisse."

Darri looked around, not bothering to be surreptitious about it. They were in a small clearing, surrounded by grim gnarled trees and a darkness so thick it felt solid. The torch cast flickering light over tangles of roots and rocks and brambles. Even if she knew where to go, there was no way she could outrun a ghost who could simply float over all those obstacles. And apparently Varis hadn't thought to bring his silver dagger along on this lark.

She couldn't run. She couldn't fight. She cleared her throat. "Then whose idea was it?"

The ghosts both looked at her, surprised and—she hoped—disappointed. They wanted her terrified. She was, but she shoved it deep and faced them. Diplomacy had never been among her talents, but right now it was her only chance.

"I don't see how that information is of any use to you," Jano said.

"I don't see how our deaths will be of any use to you," Darri retorted. "Unless you're *trying* to give my father an excuse to attack your kingdom."

"That would be fun," Clarisse said. "Nothing keeps you sharp like the constant threat of invasion."

Darri glanced at Varis, who stared at her dumbly, then tried again. "Or are you trying to keep us from taking Callie home?"

"Actually," Clarisse said, "I thought Callie was going to be with you. I guess we'll have to take care of her later."

Rage surged through Darri in a wave of heat, harder to hide than the fear. She forced it down—forced them both down. She had to think.

Jano went red. "I couldn't find her."

"Very convincing, Jano. I'm beginning to suspect you actually *like* your little barbarian amusement. Do you think she'll never find out it was you who killed her siblings?"

Jano brushed twigs out of his hair and scowled. "I don't want her to have to watch. I find it annoying when the living cry."

"Really?" Clarisse said. "I rather like it."

"Sorry to disappoint," Darri said.

"Don't be." Clarisse jerked her head at Jano, who pulled a knife from his belt sheath. A silver knife, which he held gingerly by its wooden handle. "I don't think I'll be disappointed for long."

Wrong. Darri stood perfectly still as Jano approached; out of the corner of her eye, she saw Varis step forward, but neither ghost so much as glanced at him. *I will not cry. I will not scream. I will not disgrace myself.* She would die like a Raellian princess.

Like a Raellian . . .

"Wait," Darri gasped. "If you kill us, won't we . . . come back?"

"That's the way it works," Jano said cheerfully. He put the torch down carefully on a rotting tree stump, then turned back to face her with the knife held low.

If she hadn't already been saturated with terror, that thought would have made things worse. Varis made a strangled noise, and she heard the hiss of steel as he pulled a knife from his boot. If he was fast enough, he would turn it on himself before they got to him.

"If I do come back," Darri forced out, "I'll avenge myself. I'll come after both of you."

"You can try," Clarisse said. "It's a bit difficult to

destroy a ghost. Somehow I doubt either one of you will be any more competent dead than you are alive. And no one will care enough to help you."

"My sister Callie will," Darri said.

There was a startled silence, and then Jano laughed.

"*Your sister* Callie," he said mockingly, "wishes you had stayed with your horses where you belong. Or hadn't you noticed that she's not exactly tagging about after you the way she did on the plains?" He laughed again, probably at the look on her face. His laugh was shrill and childlike, but also triumphant. "Oh, yes, she told me about you. Her beloved older sister, so brave and fierce. Who never hesitated to speak her mind, who once challenged a warrior to save a lame horse, and yet who made not one move to stop her sister from being sent away—"

"That's not true!" Darri shouted, for a moment forgetting her impending death. "I begged him to leave her—I threw myself at his feet, I threatened him—nothing made a difference! What could I have done?"

"You could have offered to go yourself," Callie said.

They all whirled, ghosts and living alike. Callie sat astride a squat roan horse, her gown hiked up over her knees. She had stopped her mount just at the edge of the trees. If Darri hadn't been shouting, they probably would have heard her coming.

"Callie," Clarisse purred. "How nice to see you."

Callie ignored her and looked straight at Jano. "Playing a practical joke on my siblings, Jano?"

There was no way she could believe that. The knife was pointed straight at Darri. Jano looked at Callie, and she looked back, and for a moment the night swallowed up their silence.

"Yes," Jano said finally. "Sorry, Cal, but I couldn't resist. They're such easy targets."

The knife slipped behind his back. Clarisse hissed between her teeth and rose into the air, floating a few feet above the ground. Varis backed away from her, so fast he tripped over an exposed root and nearly fell.

Jano laughed jarringly, but Clarisse kept her eyes on Callie. "They're not the only easy targets here."

Callie narrowed her eyes right back. "No. They're not."

"Do you have silver on you, little girl?" Clarisse's golden hair flared out around her head. "Obviously not, or you would have drawn it by now. What did you think you would achieve by coming here?" She turned to Jano and held out her hand. "Give me the knife."

"Jano," Callie said.

The boy didn't look at her. His eyes were fixed on Clarisse.

Clarisse descended slowly, until her shoes barely

touched the ground. She glided toward Jano. The dead boy didn't move. Clarisse smiled and took several more steps.

Darri threw herself at Varis, colliding into him just as Clarisse turned and struck. Clarisse's blade passed through Darri's hair; she felt a quick, cold tug as a few strands were severed from her scalp, but there was no time to think of that. She rolled in a mound of ferns and mud, and was on her feet by the time Clarisse recovered enough to face her. The steel dagger in the dead girl's hand was long, thin, and straight.

"I knew you had to have a knife of your own," Darri said triumphantly. "I knew you were just trying to distract us."

"How nice for you," Clarisse said, her blade tracking Darri's every motion. "Too bad *you* don't have a knife of your own."

A good point. Darri drew her dagger at last, ignoring Clarisse's scornful laugh. She knew it was useless, but it made her feel better to have it in her hand. Behind her, Varis leaped to his feet.

"Jano. Don't," Callie said. "Please."

Clarisse glanced at her—an obvious opportunity for Darri to strike, so Darri didn't. "Don't bother, Princess. He might have some sentimental attachment to you, but he doesn't dare disobey. Do you, boy?"

"Jano!" Callie said again.

The boy swallowed hard. "I can't help you. Callie, I'm sorry—"

"Don't be sorry," Clarisse snapped. "Do what has to be done. Or do you want to explain your failure to the Defender?"

Jano's hand emerged from behind his back. It was still holding the wooden-handled silver knife. Clarisse smiled like a cat and circled around, pinning Darri and Varis between the two of them. Varis put his back to Darri's, and she felt his shoulder blades go rigid.

"I won't forgive you," Callie spat. "Not ever. I'll hate you *forever*."

Jano threw her a stricken look and vanished. The silver knife dropped soundlessly into a patch of ferns.

Darri whirled, just in time to parry Clarisse's thrust. Varis moved with her, protecting her back. The dead girl laughed and fell back, undismayed. "I should have known better than to count on Jano. Then again, Callie, so should *you*. Did you really think he would have the courage to turn on me? If you came to save your siblings, you should have brought some help."

"I know," Callie said. "I did."

Clarisse looked at her in earnest this time, and Darri lunged. Her dagger hit solid skin, slicing right through the white flesh above Clarisse's lacy neckline. She dropped back, feeling a surge of triumph that died when she realized there was no blood on the blade.

Clarisse glanced down at her smooth unbroken skin, then up at Darri. "That stung a bit," she said. "What was it supposed to accomplish?"

"It was supposed to sting," Darri snapped.

"Well done, then." Clarisse raised a mocking eyebrow. "Now, I believe Callie was in the middle of pretending there's someone hiding in the woods?"

"Not some*one*," Callie said. "And not hiding."

No, they weren't. All at once Darri could hear it: first rustling in the bushes, then distant murmurs, and then—coming swiftly closer—frantic barking.

The hunt was on its way.

"I drew off some of the hounds," Callie said. "They're headed straight here. I'm sure some of the hunters are following."

"I had better make this quick, then," Clarisse snarled, but Callie laughed.

"I don't think so. My sister may not be able to hurt you, but I assure you, she can keep out of your way for quite a while. Long enough for the hunters to arrive—and if that many people see you kill her, the Guardian will hear about it."

For a moment Clarisse's beautiful face was ugly with

fury; and it was that, rather than Callie's words, that gave Darri sudden hope.

Clarisse lifted her arm and threw her dagger. Darri leaped to one side, Varis to the other. Darri heard a *thunk* as the point plunged into a tree.

"See what I mean?" Callie said, but she was talking to empty air. Clarisse was gone.

With a furious snarl and crashing of twigs, a thin brown dog dashed from the trees, nose low, tail streaming straight out behind him. The sounds of the hunt were clearer now, hoofbeats and barks and gleeful shouts.

"We should probably," Callie said, "get out of the way."

Once they had retreated to the thickness of the forest, Callie didn't look at them. She leaned over and stroked her horse's neck, calming him as he strained toward the sounds of the dogs. By then Varis had regained his composure. He whirled on Callie. "Why were they trying to kill us?"

"I don't know," Callie said, not turning.

"How did you know where we were, then?"

"There was a clear trail, if you were looking for it."

Varis glanced once at the tangled darkness around them. "Why were you looking for it? How did you know we were in trouble?"

Callie hesitated a moment this time. "I was warned."

"By whom?"

"I don't know who he was."

"How can you—"

"Thank you, Callie," Darri interrupted him. Varis shot her a glare, which she ignored. "Thank you. That was brilliant."

Her sister sat up in the saddle and looked straight ahead, at the impenetrable darkness of the night forest. "Best I could come up with."

"Why didn't you bring silver?" Varis said.

Callie finally turned and gave him a slow, incredulous look. "You're right, that was stupid of me. My humblest apologies."

Varis didn't even have the grace to look embarrassed. He just stared at his youngest sister suspiciously—suspicious of *what*, Darri couldn't begin to guess—before snapping, "That ghost said someone called the Defender was behind this."

"So she did." Now that Callie was looking at them, Darri could see, by the torchlight, how tight her sister's face was. Not angry, or scared, just . . . *tight*. As if she was holding herself in, away from them. "I'm glad to hear you were actually aware of what was happening. From the way you were just standing there most of the time, it was hard to tell." Varis flushed, and Callie gathered up the reins. "I understand why you would want to be angry at someone other than yourself. And I would love to be that person, just for old time's sakes. But we had better start back to the castle."

"No," Darri said. She found, somewhat to her surprise, that she was on the verge of tears. "We're not going anywhere until you tell us what happened to you."

Callie favored her with a cold look. "What makes you think something happened to me?"

"Because you're not acting like yourself."

"Like *myself*? You don't know who that is. What makes you think you know how I act?"

"Because I remember." Darri stepped closer to the horse, twigs crunching beneath her feet. "I remember you, who you really are. Four years is not enough to change that."

"Maybe not for you. For me, it was a very long time."

"Long enough to make you hate me?" Darri's voice caught, and she had to pause before going on. Callie's face was grim and remote. "I spent every second of those years thinking of ways to save you. That's why I'm here now. I—" Her voice caught again, but this time she forced the words through it. "I love you, Callie."

Callie held still, eyes wide with an emotion Darri couldn't identify. Varis looked faintly disgusted. Darri waited in the rustling silence, her eyes on her sister's face.

Which, after several long moments, shut down. It was

like watching flesh turn to wood: whatever expression had been in Callie's eyes vanished, her lips flattened, and she said with a complete lack of expression, "That's nice. But we really should head back."

She might as well have hit Darri; the sudden blunt pain, the inability to breathe, was the same. Darri folded her arms over her chest and said, "No. I'm not going with you until we talk."

Callie raised her eyebrows, turned her mount around, and flicked the reins. Before Darri had time to react, the horse's tail disappeared between the trees, taking the light of the torch with it. She and Varis were alone in the woods, the shapes of the trees and of his grim face illuminated only faintly by the moonlight.

"I don't think you thought this through," Varis said.

"Be quiet," Darri said shortly.

"I don't suppose you know how to get back to the castle?"

"Of course I do," Darri said, which was an absolute lie. She hadn't been paying attention to the trail, assuming she would be riding back with the rest of the hunting party; and she wasn't used to wooded terrain, especially not at night. She couldn't even tell which direction they had come from. In the moonlight, the jumble of trees and rocks and darkness appeared identical every way she looked. At least the ghosts were gone.

Or seemed to be.

"We're not safe here," Varis said, reading her thoughts. Well, they were rather obvious thoughts. "Those two—creatures—could return at any second. And thanks to you, Callie's not here to stop them."

"Callie couldn't stop them a second time, even if she was here," Darri said. "Were you *there*? She doesn't have silver. Drawing off the hunt was genius, but the hunt is gone."

Varis's eyes narrowed. "The ghost boy vanished when she told him to stop."

Darri thought of the look that had passed between her sister and the dead boy before he disappeared. "I think," she said reluctantly, "that they're friends."

Varis stared at her. "But he's dead!"

"So are a lot of people," Darri said. "It doesn't seem to matter much to these Ghostlanders, does it?"

"Callie is not a Ghostlander."

Darri gave him a look of scorn that she didn't really feel. She hadn't seen it either, even though it should have been obvious from the moment Callie looked away from her across a room full of perfumed nobles. Should, in retrospect, have been obvious even before she saddled up her horse to ride to her sister's rescue. Why had it never occurred to her that Callie might not want to be rescued?

Looking around at the towering dark trees pressing in on them, Darri found that she still couldn't quite believe it. She remembered racing her sister beneath an azure sky, remembered lying with her in the long grass, the two of them imagining pictures in the shifting shapes of the clouds. If Callie wanted to remain in this unnatural land, where she would rarely see a clear swath of sky, where trapped spirits were forced into a foul pretense of life, it was only because she had forgotten. Darri would have to remind her.

And if she couldn't . . .

Darri's jaw tightened. If Callie couldn't be reminded, then Darri would just have to rescue her anyhow.

It wouldn't take Callie long, once she was back on the plains, to remember how much she loved the sky and the grass and the wild winds. The sooner they got her away from the perversions of Ghostland, the easier it would be.

Callie might hate her at first—and what difference did that make, when she seemed to hate her already?—but she would realize, in time, that Darri was right, and be grateful for being rescued. This country was no place for the living.

Jano materialized when Callie was nearly home. Because she didn't want to see anyone, she had circled around the gates and outer yards, and was trotting alongside the remains of the vast stone wall that had once surrounded the back of the castle. The crumbling wall, a relic from a time before the presence of the dead made such defenses unnecessary, was riddled with gaps large enough to ride through.

One moment she saw only the weathered stones; the next, her view was blocked by the laughing form of a young boy in a dark gray riding outfit. Her horse balked, but Callie dug her heels in and kept going as if she hadn't seen him. A moment later he was beside her, racing along the loose stones at a speed that would have been death defying in the living.

"How long are you going to be angry at me?" he asked.

"For trying to kill my family?" She saw a gap and turned the horse with a light touch of her foot. "It may take a while."

He hopped off the edge of the wall, blocking her way. "Oh, come on. I stopped when you showed up, didn't I? Clarisse would gladly have killed all three of you."

"I'm overwhelmed with gratitude." Another nudge of her foot, and her horse snorted and surged forward. Jano went translucent right before the gelding's broad chest would have hit his face, and stood there smirking as she rode through him. Callie slowed down, fully intending to turn around and tell him exactly what she thought of his childish tricks; but before she could start, he was on the horse behind her, squeezing her forward in the saddle with his arms around her waist.

Callie stiffened. He must have leaped back on the wall and swung himself onto the horse as she went by; another move only for those who had no life to lose. "Get off!"

"Calm down, Callie." His arms tightened. "This isn't so bad, is it?"

Back when she had first arrived in Ghostland—after the first wave of shock had passed, but before the desperation and fear had begun to recede—Callie had developed an infatuation with Jano. She had known he was dead, which doubtless would have horrified Darri—she had horrified herself—but she had been so alone. The castle had seemed a craggy dark prison filled with shadowy people and expressions of scorn, and Jano had made everything bearable by making fun of it.

The infatuation was long gone; it was quite ridiculous now that she had grown older than him. He barely reached her shoulder. But Jano, curse him, never tired of teasing her about it. The only defense was to ignore him until he moved on to other pursuits.

But Callie wasn't in her most patient mood, so she jabbed backward with her elbow as hard as she could.

He faded, of course, and laughed as she struggled to regain her seat. She reined in her horse and twisted around to look at him.

"Why," she asked, "did you have a silver knife?"

He went solid again, his arms still pressing into her sides. "They're prettier."

"They're illegal. And dangerous for a ghost to carry. And you didn't need one for my siblings."

He shrugged. "I was told to bring it."

"By whom?"

That got no answer. Callie went straight to her next question. "Who is the Defender?"

His eyes widened. "How did you—oh. Graveyards. Clarisse."

"Who is he?"

Jano swung one leg over the back of the saddle and slid to the ground. "If that's the price of your forgiveness, I'll survive without it." He stared up at her, the worry in his eyes contradicting his perky tone. "Callie, take my advice. Forget you ever heard that name."

The castle loomed over them, dark and craggy. "Since it's the name of the person who ordered you to kill my sister, I don't think I can."

"You have to." He put a hand on her reins; she flicked them away with more force than was necessary, making her horse toss his head in protest. "It's not a name the living were meant to hear. It's dangerous."

Dangerous for him. Callie wasn't deluded for a second into thinking the worry was for her. "Well, if you won't tell me, I'll just have to ask someone else."

Jano swore at her, lengthily and inventively. Callie waited until he was done, then said, "Or we can make a deal."

Only twice before had she gotten the better of Jano. This time, her satisfaction was tempered by the fear in his eyes. She didn't think he was faking it. "I liked you better when you were innocent, Callie."

So had Darri. Too bad for both of them. "Where can I find him?"

Jano closed his eyes, like someone preparing to jump off a cliff. "You don't know what you're getting involved with."

"I will if you explain it to me."

His eyes popped open. Now he looked like someone who had already jumped, watching the ground rush up at him. Not for the first time, she wondered how Jano had died. "I can't."

Callie narrowed her eyes. "I already know he exists. When I go looking for him, I'll be sure to tell everyone I heard about him from you."

"I don't think you would do that."

Unfortunately, he was right. Callie made her voice as hard as she could. "Are you willing to bet your existence on that?"

"I don't see that I have much choice." Jano stepped back. "I've told you enough. More than enough. It's unfortunate that you heard his name, and even more unfortunate that you're too stubborn to be smart about it. But if you develop some brains in the near future, you'll take my advice. Forget what you heard."

Callie sighed. "I assume you're going to follow that dire warning with a dramatic disappearance."

He didn't smile. But he did take the trouble to turn and walk away, not disappearing until he reached the gap in the wall.

Callie's fists clenched so tightly on the reins that her mount nickered and backed up in protest. She took several long breaths, then turned her back on the forest and guided her horse toward the castle.

Chapter Five

The first thing Darri did, when she stepped into the banquet hall the next evening, was look around for her sister: first a quick sweep, then a slower one when it occurred to her how easily Callie would blend in with the Ghostland women. Both revealed the same thing: a roomful of kohl-rimmed eyes staring at her, a few giggling maids floating near the ceiling, and no Callie.

The second sweep also revealed two empty seats at the king's table, on the dais near the back of the hall.

Darri stopped short. "We're sitting with Prince Kestin?"

"We have to." Varis took her elbow and tugged her farther into the room. "We can't ignore him. He's the crown prince."

His voice was firm, but lacked its usual contemptuous

edge. After his humiliating performance on the hunt the night before, Varis had been subdued; he hadn't even pressed the point that it was he who had found their way back to the castle. Nor had he made any mention of the dagger-bearing belt she had strapped defiantly around her gown. Instead of finding it a relief, his restraint made Darri's skin prickle.

She pulled her elbow away from his grasp. "I won't be courted by a dead man."

"Of course you won't," Varis snapped. "I will talk to Kestin and let him know no marriage is possible. But you can't insult him by refusing to speak to him."

"Really?" Darri said, and he turned and looked at her. His jaw twitched. Right after Callie's departure, their father had invited the son of his best commander to court Darri; Darri had refused to say a word to him, had not even acknowledged his presence, until their father threatened to marry her off to a shepherd instead. Then she had suggested improvements to her suitor's riding technique. It had taken a herd of horses loaded with gifts to redress the insult, and Darri had spent the rest of the summer gathering horse dung.

But this time, the consequences of rudeness wouldn't affect only her. They would affect Callie, too.

Reluctantly, Darri mounted the dais after Varis. Only

King Ais and Prince Kestin were seated there, one at each side of the large, square table. Kestin was watching her with his eyebrows slanted; when she met his gaze, his face smoothed over swiftly. Gingerly, Darri took a seat at his side.

The prince leaned over and smiled at her. "Princess Darriniaka. I hope you are enjoying your time here so far?"

"Tremendously," Darri said. "I had a particularly exhilarating time on the hunt last night."

Varis choked on his soup and shot her a warning look. Darri picked up her own spoon and smiled at him sweetly. She knew full well that Varis didn't want to talk about the ambush, or anything related to the deads' opposition to the Raellian presence.

"The hunt?" Kestin leaned back. "You were on—"

"It was very exciting," Darri said. She waited until Varis picked up his spoon again, then added, "Do you know where my sister is? I was expecting to see her here."

This time, Varis managed not to choke, though he did glare at her as he swallowed.

Once again Kestin's eyebrows plunged down, this time long enough for Darri to pin down his expression: he was assessing her, trying to figure her out. Well, that was fair enough. If he hadn't been dead, she would have been doing the same.

Whatever he saw, Kestin seemed to approve. His lips curved upward as he looked down at his own soup without touching his spoon. "Callie doesn't take part in many of the social activities at court. I'm sorry to say that people weren't very friendly to her when she first came here."

"They will be kinder to you," King Ais put in, making it sound like a proclamation. The king was a short man with a long, hollow-cheeked face and a close-cut beard. His eyes were small and tired. "My son will see to it."

Kestin didn't look at his father, but his shoulders stiffened. Darri resisted the urge to point out just how much she didn't care whether the members of this court were friendly to her. She said instead, "I would be grateful for that."

"It will be my pleasure," Kestin said.

A quiver of disgust ran through Darri, but she was able to force a smile. She had been courted many times before, and sometimes—when her father's choices happened to be young and handsome and witty—enjoyed the process. Even when they were old and dull, it hadn't been too bad. She had taken none of them seriously, because none of them had been important enough for her father to force her to marry. And she had known she would never marry anyone of her own choice. Her future was something she refused to think about until she rescued her sister.

Kestin waited until King Ais had turned his attention

to his soup; then he said in a low voice, "Forgive my father's presumption. I do not assume that you will accept my suit."

Across the table, Varis was talking to King Ais; over the noise of the rest of the banquet hall, Darri could only make out the vaguest murmur of their conversation, which meant Varis couldn't hear hers, either. She said, "That's good. Because I'm not going to accept it."

Kestin choked on his wine. For a moment she thought he was angry; then she realized he was laughing.

"Really?" he said finally, putting down his goblet. There were purple stains at the upturned corners of his lips. "And yet I've barely said a word to you. The women here don't find me unattractive, but perhaps on the plains women value different things in a man."

Like having a pulse? Darri just looked at him.

"Truth be told, I would rather wait a few years and marry your sister." The prince flashed a conspiratorial grin, one that probably had a great deal to do with Ghostland women's high opinion of his looks. "I would still be the same age I am now, you know."

Darri lifted her goblet to her lips; upon consideration, instead of sipping the wine, she drained as much of it as she could. Kestin's eyes gleamed—he *knew* the effect he was having on her. Suddenly furious, Darri straightened and looked straight at him. Without flinching, she said, "Yes. I do know. And you should know that my brother won't force either of us to marry a dead man."

Kestin put his goblet down on the table, his grin suddenly gone. Out of the corner of her eye, Darri saw Varis watching them anxiously; but King Ais was still talking, and her brother had no way to intervene.

Kestin wiped off his mouth and leaned forward, his black hair swinging across his cheek. "Are you so sure?"

"Yes," Darri said, but all at once she wasn't. She glanced away from Kestin at Varis. His bloodshot blue eyes seemed small and faded after the impact of Kestin's dark gaze, his mouth grim and uncompromising. He looked at her as if he didn't much like what he was seeing.

It had been a long time since she had truly known her brother, if she ever had. He spent his life fighting and scheming and killing. She had no idea what he was capable of; and, obviously, he hadn't followed through on his assurance that they would be leaving soon. Maybe he *would* wed her to an abomination, if he deemed it necessary.

Then again, he had no idea what *she* was capable of. *You just try it*, she thought at him, and his eyes widened slightly as he met her gaze.

"Don't look so terrified," the abomination said, and she turned back to him. His eyebrows lifted, and he leaned back in his chair; clearly, terror was not what he was seeing on her face now.

"I meant," he said, "don't look so terrified, because it won't happen. There is another option."

She clenched her hand around the cool stem of her goblet, waiting. But before Kestin could continue, Varis leaned over the table and said loudly, "Darri can tell you about the time she ruined a hunt to save her favorite dog."

Darri's fist clenched; she loosened it before she broke the goblet, but kept her lips pressed together. After an awkward moment, Varis coughed and began telling the story himself, and Kestin gave her a small nod that clearly meant *later.*

The rest of the meal passed in a series of awkward conversational forays issuing from the other three people at the table. Darri didn't bother. She had never been much good at pretending, and obviously it wouldn't matter; Varis expected nothing of her, Kestin didn't intend to marry her, and King Ais was a fading power, an old king clinging to his dead son.

When the meal was finally over, Kestin stood with an easy grace and extended his hand to her. Darri looked at the blue silk covering his forearm. Her flesh crept along her hand; she tried to think of something to do, something that wouldn't make her revulsion so evident, but she couldn't. And she couldn't make herself take his arm.

Kestin's mouth tightened, but he merely inclined his head politely and let his arm drop to his side. "I was hoping you would walk with me," he said. "I'd like to show you the castle."

"That would be wonderful," Darri replied promptly. "Would you take me to my sister's rooms? I would love to see where she has been living."

From the corner of her eye, she saw Varis make some sort of movement, but she ignored him; there was nothing he could do to stop this charade.

Kestin's eyes crinkled at the corners, reminding her that he, too, knew it was a charade. But he merely said, "Of course. You must miss her, after all this time."

"Yes," Darri said, and all at once was overwhelmed by how true it was. She missed Callie so much it was like an ever-growing hole somewhere inside her; and now that Callie was so close, it was worse than it had ever been. She turned abruptly from the sympathy in Kestin's eyes, blinking fast to keep herself from tears. The wine had been a mistake; she had forgotten it could have effects other than lightheartedness.

They walked out of the banquet hall, turned left down a wide hallway, and walked up a marble spiral stairway. At the top of the stairs was a round, lamp-lit chamber, from which a multitude of narrow passageways led into the depths of the castle. Kestin turned down one, and Darri followed him. It wasn't until they had passed several closed wooden doors, and the silence was becoming thick and oppressive, that she stopped walking and turned to face him.

"Can we talk here?" she asked.

Kestin stepped back on his heel as he turned, a lithe motion that reminded Darri of Varis. It was the instinctive movement of a trained swordsman. "These rooms are all unoccupied, so we're safe. There's no one who can over-hear us."

Darri gathered her hair in one hand and slung it behind her back. "No one I can see."

"No one you can't see, either." Kestin raised an eye-brow. In the lamplight, his hair gleamed blue-black. "When ghosts become invisible, their presence can be sensed; ironically enough, it's easier for them to hide when they're solid. I'd know if we had any watchers. You'll pick up on the feeling soon enough."

Darri hoped she would be gone long before she had to learn that particular skill . . . a brief, forlorn hope, but difficult to let go of now that she had let it in. She took a deep breath, braced herself, and said, "What is the other option?"

Kestin stepped back to the opposite wall of the hallway and leaned against a red and gray tapestry. This time, there was nothing hidden or quick about the assessment in his gaze; he watched her for a long, considering moment before he spoke. "I have a second cousin named Cerix. He's next in line to the throne after me, and he's alive."

Slowly Darri said, "I don't think a second cousin will seal this particular alliance."

"No," Kestin agreed. "Your father's armies are too powerful for anything but a royal marriage to stop him."

A royal marriage or an army of ghosts, Darri thought; but Kestin must know the stakes as well as—or better than—she did. Her father didn't truly want to test his soldiers by ordering them to invade Ghostland; and King Ais, presumably, didn't want to risk an invasion either. The heart of Ghostland, a three-day ride through gnarled forest, was safe enough; but its borderlands, where forest faded or was cut into field, and where a band of horsemen could ride in at sunrise and be out by dusk, was dangerously vulnerable. A few well-timed raids could destroy a season's harvest, which would be felt even in the deepest, darkest chambers of this invulnerable castle; and the commoners would die in swathes.

So both countries needed an alliance, and a marriage to make it stick.

"I was told," she said slowly, "that your father considers you his heir."

Kestin jerked his shoulders, making the tapestry shift dangerously behind him. "He does," he said, biting off the words. "It is unprecedented, but quite legal."

She rubbed the back of her neck. "Then what are we—"

"But I am not heir yet," Kestin went on. His eyes narrowed. "Until I agree to the coronation ceremony, his choice is not binding, which is where my father's trouble currently lies. I don't want to be king, not anymore. Not now that I'm—" He stopped, lips pressed together, and Darri knew she hadn't succeeded in hiding her reaction. "My cousin Cerix, on the other hand, does want to be king. Quite desperately. And if I were to disappear, he would be next in line."

Darri hadn't the slightest clue what Kestin was getting at. She said, "If . . ."

"If I find out who killed me, and avenge myself, I will cease to be."

"Is that what you want?"

Kestin was very still, but his black eyes blazed. "Yes."

Darri couldn't tear her eyes away from his. She had been raised to understand the importance of vengeance; and she knew, oh she knew, what it was to want one thing so badly that nothing else mattered. She leaned toward him and said, "You want my help."

"I need your help." Kestin leaned forward too; she could see the beads of sweat on his forehead, the sharp creases around his eyes.

Darri lifted her eyebrows. "Why me?"

Kestin blew out a short breath. "My father has forbidden any of his subjects to help me. He wants me as his heir. The dead are backing him because they want one of their own on the throne. And the living are all too afraid to help me."

The disdainful undertone in the way he said "the living" made Darri blink. For a moment she had almost managed to forget that the man in front of her was dead.

Bile rose in her throat. She swallowed it hard and straightened abruptly. "What if you change your mind, at the end? Decide you don't wish to just . . . vanish?"

"If I know who killed me, there will be nothing to decide." Kestin went translucent as he spoke and made a violent gesture with his arm, which went right through the wall behind him. "That's how it is, for ghosts. It's an obsession. As the living desire procreation, so do the dead desire justice."

Darri wrenched her eyes away from that arm, her stomach roiling. The remnants of the wine didn't help at all with the sudden wrenching emptiness inside of her. Because she had no doubt that Varis would accede to *this* plan.

Nothing had changed, she told herself. She had come to trade herself for Callie. She would marry Cerix instead of Kestin, and Callie would get to go home, and it would be exactly as she had planned. Nothing had changed just because she had dared believe, for a short while, that there was a happy ending for both of them.

Kestin's eyes were intently watchful, and something in their dark gaze made her think he sympathized. Which was probably his intent. She looked at his arm, still half in the wall.

"I will help you," she said quietly, "if you promise me that you'll make Callie go."

"Of course. She's not a prisoner. "

"Not *let* her go. *Make* her go."

Kestin's eyebrows slanted, two diagonal black lines on his ash white forehead. He pulled his hand out of the wall and passed it across his face. "Even if she's content here?"

She's learned not to think about the perversion that surrounds her, Darri thought. That's not "content." But of course she couldn't say that to Kestin, and in any case, she had no interest in discussing her sister with the dead prince. "Yes."

Kestin nodded, and Darri drew in a deep breath. This

was good, she told herself. This was exactly what she wanted.

She folded her arms over her chest. "Then we're agreed. I'll help you find your murderer. How did you die?"

He looked up at her in surprise, his hair falling back over his cheekbones. She had guessed it was a rude question, but she didn't have time for him to get around to the subject on his own. She lifted her chin and waited.

Kestin bit his lower lip. "I was strangled in the middle of the day. I didn't even realize I was dead until I woke up in the evening, and found out it was three full nights after I had gone to sleep."

"Who do you think did it?"

"I don't know. It must have been one of the dead, because my guards saw no one pass."

"So whoever it was went through the walls?" He nodded. "What were you strangled with?"

"I don't know. It was gone by the time my body was discovered."

"Can ghosts carry weapons through walls?"

Kestin pressed both his hands against the tapestry behind him. This time, they didn't go through. Instead he ran his fingers over the fabric, making a faint brushing sound. "The older ghosts can; they can make anything they're holding fade with their bodies. The new ghosts . . . it's difficult for us to do anything we couldn't do when we were alive."

He grimaced. "The older we get, the more powerful we become. I can't manage much yet."

We. I. It was impossible to forget what he truly was, a corpse guised in silk and skin. Darri said hastily, "And it happened a few weeks ago?"

He pushed himself away from the wall and took two steps sideways, his eyes remaining on her. "Yes."

Just about the time they would have heard about Kestin's new marriage prospect.

"And your father . . ." She said it experimentally, with no idea how she was going to end the sentence, and recognized the betrayed anger that ignited in the prince's eyes. His father had trapped him in this state, unable to move beyond life, unable to be alive, either.

"We'll keep your father out of it," she said, and his eyes flashed again, but this time it wasn't with anger. He smiled at her slowly.

It was almost easy to tilt her head up and smile back. He stepped toward her, and something in the shift of shadows made his face look suddenly like a skull, white bone and bare teeth and hollow, empty eyes. She caught her breath and looked away from him, down the dim, empty hall. When she looked back, he was no longer smiling. His forehead was creased as he looked down at her.

"Be careful, though," he said. "You're not . . . there are

members of the court, living and dead, who are not happy about the Raellian presence here. Be wary when you talk to people. And try to avoid the Guardian."

His face looked alive again; his skin was bone white, his eyes deep-set and black, that was all. She was amazed when her voice emerged steady. "Who is the Guardian?"

"The Guardian of the Living is his full title." Kestin stepped back and leaned against the wall again. "He tends to make an impression. He killed the man you were talking to the night you arrived."

"I remember," Darri said shortly. "Guardian of the Living? Guarding them from what?"

He laughed. "Isn't it obvious?"

"From the . . . dead?"

Kestin shrugged. "Like I said: the dead are dangerous. Once it became clear that not all of us were going to take vengeance and move on, it was necessary for someone to protect the living. The Guardian took up that role."

"Is he dead too?"

"He's been around for hundreds of years. I would assume so."

"Why the armor?"

"No one knows. So he can carry a silver sword, maybe." Kestin shook his head. "He has absolute power to punish the dead, and nobody would argue with him if he went after one of the living. I don't know how he feels about the presence of foreigners in our kingdom, so it's probably best if you stay out of his way."

"Thank you for the warning," Darri said. "And I will do my best. But right now, I would like to talk to my sister."

"Of course," Kestin said. He turned and gestured down the passageway. "Her room is right down this hall and up the stairs at the end, the first door on your left. I can walk you there, if you like."

She almost said yes. But then he dropped his hand to his side, and she saw the dark red of the tapestry right through it.

"No," she said. "Thank you, but—I think it would be better if I spoke to her alone."

Kestin nodded, expressionless.

Darri turned her back on the prince and made her way through the long, dark passageway and up the narrow, dusty stairway at the end. The hallway here was darker than the one downstairs, with fewer lamps and almost no tapestries to cover the bare stone walls. Whatever Callie's status in this castle was, it clearly wasn't *honored guest*.

Darri's breath burned in her chest. She walked to the first door on the left, lifted her hand to rap on the dark wood, and couldn't complete the motion. She kept thinking of the stiffness of Callie's face, half-hidden in the tangled trees. *You could have offered to go yourself.*

It would have made no difference. Callie was the daughter her father had chosen; she was prettier, more adaptable, more docile than Darri. Besides, as the elder daughter, Darri was more valuable as a marriage partner to the other tribal leaders.

All true. Her father would never have sent her instead.

But she hadn't offered.

Darri dropped her hand to her side, fighting a sick feeling in her chest. For so long Callie had been the only person in her life she didn't hate. She didn't know how she would bear it if it turned out Callie hated *her*.

If Callie refused to open the door.

She turned and walked back to the end of the hallway. A large windowsill was set into the stone wall, the window itself covered with uneven bricks. Darri pulled herself onto the stone ledge and leaned against the wall, heedless of the rough-edged stones that scraped against her back. The shadows pulled themselves in around her as she settled back to wait.

Chapter Six

There was no way to stop Darri from doing whatever she intended to do; there rarely was. Varis, when he finally left the banquet hall at King Ais's side, did his best not to think about what that might be. Ever since Callie had been sent away, Darri had been a thorn in his side, and absolutely impossible to control. Twice she had even tried to ride to Ghostland herself, though each time she had been caught before half a day had passed. It was only sheer luck that she had been stopped by horsemen who had sworn loyalty to their father, and not by rival tribes who would have raped and killed her on the spot. The danger hadn't stopped her from trying, any more than the beatings she had received when she was returned.

Varis wasn't even going to try to stop her. He would

untangle whatever trouble she caused later. With any luck, he could manage that before she caused any serious damage.

Outside the banquet hall, King Ais and his attendants went one way, and Varis went the other. His conversation with the king had been interminable, but he had gleaned one very useful piece of information from it: the name of the man who might be the new linchpin of his plan.

Groups of men and women lounged in the wide hall, leaning against the lush tapestries and steel mirrors or gliding over the white marble floor. Varis approached one woman who seemed, somehow, the most alive. He turned his smile on her.

"I'm looking for Lord Cerix's suite," he said. "Would you mind directing me toward it?" She turned to him with an upward sweep of darkened lashes, and he lifted his eyebrows just far enough to be noticeable. "Or, if you think the way might be confusing, you could escort me."

The woman looked him up and down, and Varis waited, aware of how his simple clothes and wind-roughened skin contrasted with the finery all around him. That was all right. It made him look like a warrior, which was what he was.

"After you go up the stairs, turn left into the hallway with the blue tapestries. It's the last door on the left, all the way at the end of the hall." The woman tilted her head to the side. "I hear that Lord Cerix is interested in speaking to you."

The look she gave him was a clear invitation, and that "I hear" meant she might know something useful. Varis stepped closer to her, allowing his glance to turn admiring; but just then another woman stepped right through the wall, dangling a string of necklaces from her hand. When she turned solid, the necklaces did too, and tinkled loudly as they swung against the wall. She looped her arm around the first woman's shoulders and smiled at Varis.

Varis barely managed a thank you before backing away and heading down the hall. He could feel both women's smirks boring into his back, even as he reached the spiral stairway at the end of the hall and started up it.

But the last door on the left was opened by a servant, who informed him that Lord Cerix was in the castle court-yard watching a dogfight. When Varis scowled, the man laughed and took a swig from his clay jug. "Dogfighting is a popular sport here," he said. "It's because of the dead. They get bored, and develop obsessions to keep themselves busy. The haughty and pretentious ones become artists; the rest bet on blood sports. Long as it's not people they're sporting with, we let them be."

"And how do you make sure they don't start sporting with people instead?" Varis asked.

The man snorted knowingly. "You'll want to talk to Lord Cerix about that," he said. "He'll be a good distance from the castle, so you don't have to worry about deadheads—they don't like being far from shelter, even this early in the evening. Sunrise isn't pretty for *them*." He laughed and drank again. "One of the stableboys can tell you which way to go, if you're that intent on speaking to Lord Cerix. Go down these stairs right here, and then through the kitchens to the courtyard."

The stairway the servant directed him to was far less grand than the one he had come up on: a deserted, somewhat dusty set of stone stairs, with bricked-up windows and sparsely spaced torches. Varis thought about returning to the spiral staircase instead, then shrugged and started down.

He had just reached the first landing when a ghost erupted from the stone wall of the stairway and shoved him.

The blow should have sent him tumbling; but even when his mind was wandering, Varis was always prepared to be attacked. He twisted and rolled as he fell, landing on his feet on one of the steps, grabbing the banister and swinging himself around, one foot already lashing out—

At no one. The thing that had attacked him was not a man. It was a black cloud, a thick smoke, and the stench of death around him was so strong he could barely breathe.

When his foot hit nothing, it threw him off-balance, and he wasn't ready for the next blow. He tumbled down the steps, stone edges hitting his head and back and arms; by the time he reached the next landing, he had recovered enough to leap to his feet, but he was in no shape to fight. He blinked hard before he could see, and then what he saw was a black cloud oozing down the stairs toward him.

Varis drew a silver knife and threw it. It passed right through the blackness and hit the stairs behind it, and the fog kept coming. Varis whirled toward the lower stairway, but he was too late; the thing was upon him, cold and dank and stinking of the grave. He backed up until he hit the stone wall, and the smoke surrounded him, pressing on him.

All at once the stairwell was pitch-black, as if light had ceased to exist. The darkness wrapped around his face, creeping into his mouth, absorbing his terror. This was death itself, coiling around him: the death that crept all through this castle, a faint and rotting miasma.

Now it was upon him, and there was no escape. He was going to be killed by this horror; he would become a horror himself, once the pain and darkness were done. There was nothing he could do to stop it.

And all at once he wasn't afraid.

He had always been prepared to die, for the cause that

was his life. There was nothing shameful in it, no matter what killed him, no matter what he became afterward.

It didn't matter if he had no chance. He was a Raellian. He would fight.

He drew a second silver knife, the ridges of the hilt pressing against his palm, and thrust it into the heart of the seething darkness. The motion was as useless as he had expected, but he used the momentum to roll himself forward and sideways, through the dark smoke and into the empty air above the staircase. He landed precisely on one of the stairs, which was sheer luck, and tottered for a moment before grabbing the railing and spinning himself around.

The dark cloud reared above him. Varis struck into it with all his might, ignoring the way the skin of his arm shrank back from the writhing cloud. He pushed himself away from the railing and plunged the knife farther into the darkness, seeking its heart, closing his eyes as the slick cold pressed against his face.

Something inside the cloud pulled back, and the knife was wrenched out of his hand. Varis's fingers clenched together on the roiling darkness; a dozen clammy tendrils moved against his palm. He jerked his hand back to his side and threw himself backward, half-falling down the top few steps, catching himself on the railing and yanking himself to his feet. Shivers ran up and down his body, under his skin. He drew his last silver knife, the one sheathed at his back, and held it close to his side. The black fog rose over him, and he knew, without the faintest doubt, that he was about to die.

"Stop!"

For a moment Varis was too frozen to react; then his mind grasped that he wasn't dead, and he whirled. The creature called the Guardian stood below him at the foot of the stairs, as still as a black iron statue.

"Stop this," the Guardian said again, his voice a hollow echo.

The black cloud roiled, but Varis still wasn't dead. So the Guardian had some sort of power over it.

The sudden, unexpected appearance of hope sharpened Varis's fear; but this time the fear didn't paralyze him. He swung himself onto the banister and slid down without taking his eyes off the black-armored man or losing hold of his dagger. When he landed next to the Guardian, he turned to face his attacker again.

The darkness spoke. It sounded like a dark wind moaning words; Varis could almost feel the voice rumbling past him. "You should never have brought them here."

"There are many things," the Guardian said very quietly, "that I should not have done. And many things you should not have done as well. It is your actions that place our kingdom in danger, not mine."

The shadow moved then, seeping down the stairs toward them; it passed right under the lights of the wall lamps without becoming the slightest bit less black. "That is true if you count only the living as part of our kingdom."

"The dead were never meant to be a part of it."

"But they are." Halfway down the steps, the darkness reared upward, forming a vaguely humanlike shape. "We of all people know that just because we created them, that does not mean we control them."

The Guardian took a step back, an action Varis didn't like at all. He wondered if he should run. "I'm not a fool. You have forgotten the reason for what we did, and betrayed everything we sacrificed for."

"No," the fog hissed. "I am doing what I must, to defend my people. Do you think I don't know why you brought the foreigners here?"

The Guardian lifted his face and stared at the blackness above him. "Do you think I don't know what you are after? The foreigners are under my protection."

Two darker patches flashed in the fog, where human eyes would have been. They looked, Varis realized, more like rectangular eyeholes than like actual eyes. Silence stretched between the iron man and the black fog, an ominous stillness that Varis recognized well: the endless moment before a long-awaited battle.

"Are you ready, then?" the Guardian said, reaching up very slowly for the hilt of his silver sword. "Are you certain you want to do this now?"

"Not now." The fog swirled and seethed, then went still. "But soon. Soon the dead will outnumber the living, and then I will not need you anymore."

And all at once the darkness was gone. A few smokelike tendrils curled in the air, and then they were gone too, and Varis decided to start breathing again.

After a moment the Guardian let his ironclad arm drop to his side. He turned his head and looked at Varis through the black rectangular eyeholes of his mask.

Varis let go of the banister, wondering if he had jumped out of a stampede and into quicksand. Well, he wasn't dead, so that had to be an improvement. "Thank you."

After a moment the voice echoed hollowly within the mask. "You are welcome."

"What was that thing?" Varis asked.

The Guardian was silent. Varis lifted his eyebrows. "It was not exactly trying to keep its existence a secret from me."

"He," the Guardian said. "Not *it*."

"That was a person?"

"Yes. Or he was, once." The Guardian lifted his hand

and laid it on the back of his neck, a gesture that seemed incongruously human. Raellians didn't wear armor, but Varis had heard it could itch. "He is the defender of the dead, as I am the guardian of the living."

Varis leaned back against the banister. "The dead need defending?"

The Guardian turned and started down the stairs. Varis fell into step beside him. "Even here, the living are not always comfortable with the presence of the dead. Fear of death is the most primal fear there is. There are always factions saying we would be better off without them, or at least with far less of them."

"Those factions must be thrilled with the idea of a dead king," Varis noted.

The Guardian made a sound that, after a moment, Varis interpreted as laughter. "Your being here is not helping matters, of course. Everyone believes your sister will never marry a dead man, which gives Cerix's faction reason to complain more loudly about how the dead are nothing but a burden to the living, and make stirring speeches about why we must return to the way things were before Ghostdawn."

"Ghostdawn," Varis repeated.

"When the spell was created that brings murder victims back as ghosts."

They reached the bottom of the stairs just then. Ahead of them stretched a wide marble hall. The Guardian inclined his head once, then turned and strode away, his iron boots clanging against the marble floor.

Varis watched him for a moment, then turned around and went back up the stairs. He could find Cerix another time. Right now, he had to think.

Ghostdawn.

All the wrongness of this country—and all the things that made it unconquerable—were due to a spell. From the casual way the Guardian had mentioned it, the Ghostlanders all knew it; but he wondered if they had ever thought of the consequences.

Raellians distrusted magic, so Varis had never seen it used. But he had heard enough about spells from travelers to know one crucial thing about them:

They could be broken.

And, he thought as he bent on the landing to retrieve his daggers, wouldn't *that* make things interesting?

Chapter Seven

Callie stepped into Lord Ayad's sitting chamber and was immediately knocked to the side by a drunk serving girl, who shrieked as she raced toward the door and full tilt into Callie. Callie regained her balance by grabbing the doorframe; the serving girl staggered and straightened, but not before spilling the entire contents of her goblet down the front of Callie's gown.

Callie let out her breath in a hiss; the serving girl tossed her goblet to the floor and kept going without bothering to apologize. A moment later a well-dressed man Callie didn't recognize rushed past as well, and they disappeared into the hall.

Peeling the damp fabric of her gown away from her skin, Callie stepped into the room and bent to pick up the still-intact goblet. The stem was slim and brittle between her fingers; she thought, suddenly, about letting it drop to the floor, finding out if it would survive a second fall. She doubted it would. She thought of glass shattering with anticipatory satisfaction, and her fingers slid closer to each other.

She glanced up at the crowd filling the sitting chamber, instinctively checking to see if anyone was watching her. Nobody was—but a head could turn at any moment, and then they would all gape at her, delightedly aghast at her uncivilized outburst. She took a deep breath and placed the goblet carefully on a dainty table, then stepped farther into the room and leaned against the wall, searching the giddy crowd.

There were several parties tonight where Darri's maid might have gone, but Callie was willing to bet the girl was here. This was a very particular kind of party: the men here were all noblemen, while the women were mostly servants.

It was also a party for the living. Nobody would ever be so gauche as to say so, but everyone understood. Even though they all dwelled together, there was an understanding at court that sometimes the living just wanted to be with the living, and the dead with the dead. And so they were in one of the rare rooms on the outskirts of the castle, with large arched windows that would be bright and deadly with sunlight in just a few hours.

Not that Callie would be there by then. She didn't even want to be here now. She would stay only as long as she had to in order to find out how her sister had ended up on a hunt reserved for the dead.

Her search ended with Lord Ayad, who was leaning against the far wall surrounded by at least seven girls, all laughing very loudly at everything he said. One of those girls was Darri's maid. Callie reached up to adjust her braids, then made her way over.

When he saw her, Ayad grinned over the heads of his admirers. "Callie!" he said, his speech slurred. "I'm surprised to see you here. We thought you were holed up in a room with your kinsmen, discussing horse droppings and how best to cook them."

The serving girls erupted into peals of laughter. Callie smiled tightly. "Sentha could tell you if that were true."

One of the serving girls, a tall thin girl with a crooked nose, stopped mid-laugh. "I am no longer your sister's maid."

"Really?" Callie said mildly. "I thought that was your assignment. You certainly complained about it long enough."

Everyone now watched Sentha, who flushed bright red. Callie couldn't tell if she was pleased or annoyed by the attention; perhaps both. "Long and effectively. Someone took pity on me."

"She must have been a *very* good friend," Callie said, putting one hand on her hip.

It was a moment before the other girls noticed that Callie had said something disparaging about her sister; another moment before they giggled approvingly. Into that laughter, Callie added idly, "Or a very bored ghost."

"The latter," Sentha said. Her flush had faded and her voice was merry. "Do you know Meandra? She's one of the dead who paints—she's spent the last year or so perfecting the shadow of a leaf on her latest creation. She needed a break, so she decided to have some fun scaring the foreigners." She lowered her voice, tilting her head conspiratorially. "Do you know if she succeeded? I haven't heard the story yet."

"I'm sure she did," Callie said, brushing a stray curl away from her face. "It wouldn't take much effort."

"Did you hear what Prince Kestin told Lord Sazon?" Another girl leaned in. "He said that when he saw Princess Darriniaka, he finally had a reason to thank the man who killed him."

Callie bit the inside of her mouth and joined the giggles, forcing herself to wait until all the girls turned back to Lord Ayad and he to them. Then she announced that she was thirsty and left them, making her way to one of the servants in charge of drinks. He bowed and reached for a goblet.

"I don't want wine," Callie said curtly, and the servant blinked at her. Other noblewomen were habitually rude to servants, but not Callie; she had spent her time here being as unobtrusive as possible, trying to make no enemies. But what had that gained her? She glared at the servant, who glared back at her—just for a moment, but it was a moment longer than he would have dared glare at a real Ghostland noblewoman—before dropping his eyes.

"I'm looking for Meandra," Callie snapped. "Tell me where her rooms are."

Callie was very familiar with the third floor of the castle, where the rooms were smaller, the hallways dingier, and the stones dustier than the rooms of the true nobility. Until she ventured into the servants' quarters, though, she hadn't realized just how low in the castle hierarchy her own section was. Here, at least the halls were lined with tapestries, even if those tapestries were faded and out-of-date. She felt a familiar sense of resentful humiliation, and gritted her teeth against it. That was the last thing she had time for now.

Ten minutes after leaving the party, she finally turned

a corner into a narrow hallway lined with frayed rugs, started toward a dark wooden door—

And her sister sprinted past her, hair flying. Darri whirled and stood, arms crossed, in front of the door Callie had been headed for.

Callie stopped short. "What are you doing here?"

Darri tilted her head to the side. "The same thing you are, I expect."

"You followed me?"

"Of course." Darri smirked openly. "I was watching your room. I saw you leave." She took a tiny step forward. "I watched your room for hours. And not once did anyone come to see you. No wonder you don't want to leave this place, where you have so many wonderful friends."

For a moment Callie couldn't speak. Guilt and gratitude and anger coiled in her stomach, forming a painful knot. "You've been sitting outside my room all night?"

"I have nothing more important to do." Darri uncrossed her arms and pulled her shoulders back. "You're the entire reason I'm here."

The anger exploded out of the knot, hot and simple, and Callie welcomed it. She stepped forward. "I didn't ask you to come. And this isn't the time for this conversation. I'm here to—"

"Find out more about who ordered the attack. I know."

Darri looked over her shoulder at the closed door. "It wasn't difficult to figure out who you were looking for at that disgusting party. And I had no maid when I woke up this evening."

Callie moved swiftly, putting herself in the narrow space between Darri and the door. "She's not your maid. She hasn't been anyone's maid for hundreds of years."

Darri turned around and looked down at her. "If you're not going to come in with me, will you step out of my way?"

"There's nothing you can do here, Darri."

Their eyes were only inches apart. Darri's were dark and hard, and Callie's heart twisted. She had always hated having Darri angry at her.

"I said," Darri snapped, "step out of my way."

Her heart twisted harder, and then something snapped. Callie lifted her chin. She was shorter, she was younger, and Darri still thought of her as a child; but ever since the moment Darri had stepped into the banquet hall, without any idea of what she was walking into, Callie had felt like *she* was the older sister. "Don't tell me what to do, Darri. You have no idea what I've been through, or what I know. I'm the one who can handle this. You're just getting in over your head."

Darri went red with fury. "Over my head? Because I

haven't become a sniveling courtier who turns her back on her own family? Because I'm just a Raellian barbarian?"

Well . . . yes. Callie clenched her fists at her sides. "Is that what you think I've been doing? I've been through terror and hopelessness and come out on the other side. And yes, I'm a part of this court now. It was the only way I could survive."

The anger vanished from Darri's face. She said, so softly Callie could barely hear it, "And you blame me."

"No," Callie said, and her own anger drained away just as fast. "Not anymore."

"You should blame me." Darri gave Callie a stricken look. "You believed me, when I said I would save you. And instead I let them take you away."

And suddenly Callie was back on that horse, her hands trembling so hard she could barely hold the reins, looking over her shoulder at her older sister. Watching the stretches of grass grow longer and longer between them, not quite believing that Darri wasn't following her.

She turned away, but Darri grabbed her chin and pulled her head back, forcing her to look into her eyes.

"I should have stopped them. It doesn't matter that I couldn't, I still should have, and if you hate me, Callie, I understand. I failed you. It's my fault, everything that's happened to you."

"No," Callie whispered. She jerked her head free. "Darri, don't you see? The reason you were the one who failed was because you were the only one who even tried."

"I'm here to do more than try. This time, Callie, this time it's different. I'll be the one who stays, and Varis will take you back. They have no use for both of us. You can go back to the plains—"

Callie felt dizzy with panic. "Into the arms of my loving family? Do you think I want that?"

"We always knew we meant nothing to Father," Darri said. "We were never going to let that stop us. Nothing has changed. Everything will be the way it was going to be, before—you'll be married to one of the warriors, and you'll have your own tent, your own horses. You'll have your own *life*, and when it ends, your spirit will ride the wind. You won't spend your life and your death buried in a castle, in darkness, surrounded by monsters."

"Instead you will?" Callie whispered.

"Yes," Darri said. "Gladly. All I want is to save you."

If she cried, she was lost. Callie struggled against the tears, forcing her eyes wide, clenching her throat. She waited so long that Darri started to move forward again, and Callie held up both hands to stop her. "Darri, wait. I'm—I appreciate it." It sounded terribly inadequate, for what Darri had just offered, but she couldn't think of what else to say. "But you have to believe me. You can do no good here."

"I'm not here to do good," Darri said flatly, and shoved Callie to the side. Callie had been braced for that, ready to fight, but she should have saved herself the trouble. Her sister was *strong*.

Well, Darri had been living on horseback, while Callie had spent her time in long gowns and gossipy parties. For an unguarded moment, shame tickled her—a reminder of what it would be like to see herself through her own people's eyes. A hint of what it would feel like if she went back.

Not that it mattered. She would never go back.

Darri glanced over her shoulder at Callie, clearly surprised at how easy that had been, then turned back to the door.

"Hold on a second," Callie said. "You can't just knock on the door and expect—"

Darri leaned back and kicked the door open. It hadn't been locked, and the force of her kick slammed the door to the wall with a thud.

The girl in the room glanced up at them and disappeared at once.

"See?" Callie muttered.

Darri leaned against one side of the doorframe and put a foot up on the other. "So what?" she said. "She's invisible, but she's still here. I doubt she's interested in finding new living quarters, or giving me a chance to look through her belongings."

"That's your great plan, then—to wait her out?"

"Yes," Darri said.

Callie looked at her sister's face and sighed. "She'll do it, you know," she addressed the emptiness in the room. "She'll literally stand there for days."

"But she has to eat, doesn't she?" The voice that spoke back out of the emptiness was sharp, with a commoner's accent but not a hint of servility. "Whereas I do not."

"We just want to talk to you," Callie said.

"Alas," the voice murmured, "I do not want to talk to you."

"That's a shame," Darri said. With one smooth movement she pulled open her belt pouch, dipped into it, and flung out her hand.

Callie heard Meandra scream before she saw the flashes in the air and realized what Darri had done. The scream was so loud it nearly drowned out the tinkling of dozens of coins hitting the floor.

Callie had seen those coins a million times before she left the plains. They were minted in the Green Islands and favored by merchants because of their stable value and small size.

They were made of silver.

Meandra was visible now, crouched on the deep blue rug near the bed, screaming. An angry red welt showed where one coin had hit her cheek.

"Darri!" Callie gasped.

Her sister strode into the room, bending to scoop up one of the coins as she went. She grabbed Meandra by the hair, wrenched her head up, and made as if to slap the coin to her neck. The scream became shrill and terrified.

Darri's hand stopped with deadly precision an inch from the maid's throat. "Who is the Defender?"

"Don't kill me!" the dead girl shrieked.

"They're coins, not knives. They won't kill you. They'll only"—Darri paused—"hurt you."

"I can't tell you—"

Darri's smile froze Callie's blood. Barbarian, she thought. She would really do it. She would do anything.

"Are you sure?" Darri said. Her hand moved. Callie couldn't see if she touched the coin to the maid's skin or not, but the movement ripped another scream from Meandra's throat. And right on the tail of the scream, a phrase.

Darri let go of her hair and stepped back. "Thank you."

Meandra looked up at her, sobbing, the welt an angry red on her round face. Callie flinched slightly as Meandra looked past her sister at her.

"Let's go," Darri said, and strode back toward the door, leaving the deadly coins scattered on the floor.

Callie had to scurry to keep up with her. "That was not smart."

"I got my answer, didn't I?" Darri flung over her shoulder. "So the Defender is the leader of the dead. Very interesting. Do the living know that the dead have their own leader?"

"That's not important right now. Darri, stop!"

Her sister obeyed so instantly that Callie, who hadn't expected compliance, almost ran into her. She took several hasty steps back.

"You don't know what you just did." Even though the hall was deserted, Callie instinctively lowered her voice. "The prohibition against silver weapons is as old as Ghostdawn."

Darri shrugged, turning to face her. "Coins are not weapons."

"You just proved otherwise, didn't you?"

"So what are they going to do, sneer at me more obviously?"

Callie jabbed her hand downward. "The Guardian himself punishes those who bring silver weapons into the castle, and his decisions are never questioned. Don't you understand what it means here, to carry a weapon that could murder a ghost and steal his chance for vengeance? A ghost could never come back to haunt you!"

Darri pushed her hair back over her shoulder. "Neither could anyone, in the rest of the world."

"But we're not used to it."

"We?"

Callie let out her breath in a hiss and pulled her shoulders back. "We. I belong here now, Darri."

"No."

"Yes!" Callie felt tears in her eyes, heard them in her voice, and knew there was no stopping them. She went on, heedless of the humiliation, as the first few tracked down her cheek. "I don't blame you for what happened to me, all right? I know there was nothing you could have done. But there's nothing you can do *now*, either. I can't go back." She looked away. "I belong here."

Darri stepped around to the side, so that she and Callie were still face-to-face. "Do you? Or do you try to fit in, night after night, minute after minute? Afraid to step out of line lest you be called a barbarian. Ashamed of where you come from. That's not belonging."

"It is to me! And that's not how it is!" Dimly, Callie was aware that she was contradicting herself. The air felt like it was choking her, and Darri's circling made her feel like prey. "Leave me alone, Darri! Don't you see? That's all I want from you. I like it here! I won't leave."

"Can't," Darri said.

"What?"

Her sister's face was oddly intent. "Just before. You said you *can't* go back."

Callie didn't like that expression. "It's the same thing. Can't, won't—I'm staying here, Darri, whether you like it or not."

"Fine." Darri shrugged abruptly. "Have it your way. I only want to help you."

"You want me to need your help. And I don't. Not anymore."

"So you've said, again and again. So this is the last thing I'll offer." Darri smiled, but it wasn't a smile. "Take this. It might be useful."

And she threw the silver coin at Callie.

Callie screamed and dodged. The coin whizzed past, mere inches from her face, and hit the wall. It slid to the floor and landed with a dull clink.

The two sisters stared at each other. Darri's face was white. "You're—"

Callie didn't want to hear it. Before Darri could finish the sentence, she went invisible and ran down the hall, cutting a large arc around the tiny silver coin nestled in a crack in the stone.

Chapter Eight

In all her years at court, through all the parties and banquets she had attended, and despite all the teasing she had endured from Jano, Callie had never gotten drunk. But there seemed no time like the present to start.

Or to find out if ghosts *could* get drunk.

After leaving Darri's horrified expression behind her, she made her body solid again. The older ghosts flickered in and out of visibility without a thought, walking through walls and even shifting appearances as if their bodies meant nothing at all, but Callie—like most of the newer ghosts— still hated feeling like she wasn't there.

She wandered the halls, seeking oblivion. Finally she found the type of party she had never, until now, dared step foot in: a party of the dead.

The dead withdrew to the depths of the castle for their own private parties, affairs marked by barbed comments about centuries-old feuds and long conversations about the obscure hobbies with which the ghosts filled their endless time. There was nothing to exclude the living, except the occasional rumors of the penalty exacted from anyone alive who tried to impose themselves. If you tried to join the dead, it was said, they would welcome you with open arms. They would make you one of them.

But I already am one of them, Callie thought, with an anguished bitterness that had not dulled in five weeks. And now it wouldn't be long before everyone knew it. Maybe that was for the best. Though she had invented dozens of logical reasons for keeping her death a secret, she now knew that all she had really wanted was to hide it from Darri.

The party was in a large, dimly lit room, crowded with long couches, square card tables, and silent servants carrying trays of delicacies and pitchers of wine. It was far less raucous than the party she had attended earlier: a musician floated near the ceiling playing a plaintive, dissonant melody on his lute, and the ghosts sipped wine and murmured, fading in and out, their laughs low and throaty.

Lamps gave enough dim light for Callie to make out a familiar figure lounging on a couch in the far corner. Feeling drunk already—by association, and by the sense of *not caring* that was spreading through her—she headed across the room, ignoring the startled and scornful glances she drew after her.

Raellian foreigner, Jano had said to her long ago, after she had committed a far less obnoxious social blunder. *Doesn't know where she's not wanted.*

Wouldn't that include this entire country? Callie had snapped at him, her misery finally breaking into anger. That had been the first time she had surprised Jano, and soon afterward he had stopped being just her tormenter and become her friend.

Of course, Jano—for all his childishness and casual spite—was far less intimidating than the ghost she was approaching now.

Clarisse didn't look up until Callie was standing right next to her couch. Then she tilted her head, her golden hair spilling over the light blue upholstery. "Callie. Should you be here?"

"Probably not," Callie said. "I'm looking for the Defender."

The murmur and rustle of cards stopped short; even the music went silent, for a startled moment, before the musician jerkily restarted his melody. Callie looked up and saw that every face was turned toward them, cards lying ignored on the tables, goblets and forks lowered. Dozens of dark eyes glittered at them, unnaturally alight in the dimness.

Callie still didn't care. The feeling was dangerously liberating; she was almost enjoying herself.

"Well, well." Clarisse leaned back with the smile of someone settling in to watch a theater play. "Where did you hear *that* name?"

"From you," Callie said, not bothering to hide her smugness. Clarisse's smirk all but begged her to knock it down. "You got a little careless while my sister was outfighting you."

The smirk didn't budge, but Clarisse craned her neck to observe the masses of party goers openly watching them. Many had gone translucent, the lights of the lamps flickering through their wavering forms.

No one living should know that name. So they were demonstrating their deadness. They were *afraid*.

"Child, you should stay out of matters that don't concern you." Clarisse crossed one ankle over the other. "The living aren't supposed to know about the Defender. You can either forget what you know, or we can solve the other part of that problem."

Callie resisted the urge to tell her just how *not* frightening that threat was. She met Clarisse's mocking green eyes and said flatly, "They're my *kin*. I can't forget."

Something deep and bitter flashed across Clarisse's face. "You can try," she said. She drained the rest of her goblet and held it high. A servant rushed over from the corner to refill it.

Callie clenched up inside. There had been a time when she had envied the effortlessness with which Clarisse fit into the court, somehow making her foreignness an asset instead of an embarrassment. She claimed to be a princess from somewhere to the west of the Kierran Mountains; no one believed her, but it didn't much matter. When Callie had arrived at Ghostland, Clarisse had been there for less than a year, and had already been working her way methodically through the hearts of high-ranking noblemen.

"As kin go, yours are not bad," Clarisse said, swishing the wine in a slow circle. "Your brother, in particular. He interests me."

"Why?" Callie said bluntly.

The dead girl tilted her head to the side. "Indeed. A good question."

She said it with complete seriousness, and Callie wasn't sure what that meant. What she did know was that if Clarisse thought it would annoy enough people, she really would go after Varis. Her apparent goal ever since Callie had known her had been to make as many enemies as possible, usually by entangling herself in dozens of conspiracies at once, supporting opposite factions simultaneously, helping people one minute then turning and destroying them the next. Her dalliances with increasingly powerful men, culminating with Prince Kestin himself, had only given her the power to destroy more plans and facilitated her ability to make herself hated.

Callie had not been very surprised when she died. The fall from her horse could easily have been engineered by one of the many people she had angered. But when Clarisse's ghost hadn't made an appearance for two years after her death, everyone had assumed the fall was an accident after all. Most of the ghosts returned only a few nights after their murders; the longest she had ever heard of was a week. Obviously, Clarisse had been somewhere else all this time.

"I doubt *you* interest *him*," Callie said finally. "There is that whole you-tried-to-kill-him problem."

"Hmm. Perhaps I'll see if I can make him forget that."

"We're Raellians," Callie snapped, then wished—too late—that she hadn't said *we*. She flicked her skirt away from her legs; it was still uncomfortably sticky from the wine that had spilled on it earlier. "Raellian bedtime stories are about blood feuds. They don't *forget* when people try to kill them."

Clarisse sighed. "Then I suppose I'll have to find a way to make it up to him."

And that, Callie decided, was just about enough of that subject. She sat on the other end of the couch, as far from Clarisse as she could get. "Tell me about the Defender."

Clarisse took a sip. "You know what's odd? I can't think of a single reason why I should."

"If you don't," Callie said, "I'll tell the Guardian—"

"—that I tried to kill you?" Clarisse stretched her arms over her head. "There are other things you should talk to the Guardian about first. He hasn't told you anything at all, has he?"

"Why should he tell me anything?"

"He's the reason you're here." Clarisse sat up, curling her legs under her, and smiled at Callie. "He advised King Ais to accept your father's offer to send you."

"Why?" Callie demanded.

"You should ask him."

Callie put one hand down on the couch cushion; the embroidered velvet felt cool and smooth beneath her palm. "I'm asking you."

"And maybe I'll answer you. Some other time." Clarisse took another sip and made a face. "I miss good wine."

She lifted one hand to cover a yawn and vanished. The goblet landed on the couch, spilling red wine all over the light blue cushions.

Callie remained where she was, aware of the dead

watching her. The wine stain spread jaggedly over the cushion, seeping in, a dark purple patch that no one would ever get out. She touched it with her finger, which came away wet; she lifted that finger to her tongue, and tasted delicate acridness.

She remembered the first time a ghost had vanished from right beside her; remembered her instinctive shudder, the horror that had whipped through her. She had just seen that horror reflected in her sister's eyes, and she understood it completely. Once, a long time ago, she would have found herself repulsive too.

Callie was no longer that girl—that Raellian girl. She didn't have to think of herself the way a Raellian did. She didn't have to be ashamed that Darri knew. It didn't matter what Darri thought of her.

And her thoughts stopped there, as if they had crashed painfully against a rock barrier. Because it did matter. It mattered so much, and yet there was nothing she could do to change it.

If not for Darri, she thought bitterly, she could have been wholly a Ghostlander. She had no clues to her murder, no idea how to seek out her killer; and she hadn't, in truth, been trying all that hard. In time the part of her that thirsted for vengeance would have withered, become something she could ignore, just as all the ghosts did. Nobody in

Ghostland would think any less of her. Jano would think more of her. She could have followed her strongest instinct and done exactly what the rest of the court was doing: pretend she was alive, pretend so hard that she would come to believe it. Most of the time.

Most of the time would have been enough. Even the living weren't happy all of the time.

But she couldn't forget, and she couldn't pretend, now that Darri knew.

You're the entire reason I'm here.

Guilt writhed through her. After all those years and all her sacrifices, Darri had come to Ghostland and discovered what Ghostland had made of her sister. Now that she knew, she would never look at Callie without reservation again.

Callie picked up the goblet, drained the few dregs still sloshing at its bottom, then held it up and waited for a servant to come by. She could do a little pretending, at least, while Darri wasn't there to stop her.

Chapter Nine

His sister wouldn't come to her door; not an unexpected outcome, but an annoying one all the same. Varis lifted his fist to pound on the dark wood again, then thought better of it. He lowered his hand and glanced down the long, dimly lit hall.

It had been a night and a day since Darri had walked out of the banquet hall with Prince Kestin. Varis hadn't seen her since then, but had been told by a servant that she was holed up in her room, refusing even the food that was left outside her door. Apparently she was refusing his visit as well, even though he had been knocking and calling her name for several minutes.

Varis sighed and stepped back. No doubt it had finally dawned on his impetuous sister that he had no real intention of leaving Ghostland anytime soon; that despite Kestin's death, their father's plans still required her to spend her life in this castle.

She had a right to her grief, and there was nothing he could say to make it better. If she would listen to anything he had to say, which she wouldn't. She had made it quite clear that she hated him.

It had been a long time since he had cared. He spent most of his time now riding out to battle, and when he returned there was admiration in the eyes of the other warriors and adoration on the faces of the women and children. He had seen no reason to visit the tent of the one person in his father's camp who would greet him with irrational hostility.

He felt a pang of sympathy now, but that was only because the two of them were so isolated here, and because soon she would be gone forever. Far too soon to patch up everything that had gone wrong between them, even if he'd had the time or inclination to try.

So he turned to go, and found himself staring at the dead prince of Ghostland.

Prince Kestin inclined his head. He was wearing a ridiculously elaborate outfit, purple and gold with an excessive amount of ruffles. "Your Highness," he said, with a polite half-bow. "I was wondering if your sister was available for a walk."

"She isn't here," Varis said. He had promised Darri that he would put a stop to this macabre pretense of a courtship; he could, at least, do that much for her. "In any case, I wished to speak to you about her."

"To make sure I didn't think I could still marry her? She made that clear to me on her own."

Varis flushed. "I apologize for any rudeness—"

Kestin smiled, with a bit of an edge. "What makes you think she was rude about it?"

Varis did not enjoy being toyed with. On the other hand, he had no interest in quarreling with the dead prince. Yet. So he merely smiled politely and fell into step beside Kestin as they started down the hall toward the central staircase.

"I've been meaning to ask *you*," Prince Kestin said, glancing at him sideways, "how the two of you ended up on the ghost hunt."

Varis shrugged; now that the Guardian knew about them, there was probably no point in keeping the attacks secret anymore. "I was invited by a dead woman named Clarisse."

The prince's reaction caught him by surprise. Kestin stopped short, his face stark white. For a moment he stared at Varis, his eyes dark holes in his face; then he turned away, his shoulders knotted.

"Your Highness?" Varis said cautiously.

"You're sure it was her?" Kestin's voice was clear and steady, though he wouldn't turn to show Varis his face. "No, never mind—don't bother to answer that."

Varis stood, not sure what to do, until Kestin swung back to him. The dead prince's face was perfectly composed, no trace of redness or wetness around his eyes . . . could ghosts make those signs vanish?

"Forgive me, Prince Varis," Kestin said. "Before she died, Clarisse and I were . . . very close."

Varis had fallen in love only once—a long time ago, and with a girl so obviously inappropriate it made him blush to remember it. The girl had allowed him to court her, and had made the correct responses, but had never loved him back. He still remembered the moment he had finally realized that, the abrupt transformation of fond memories into humiliating ones. He looked at the stricken expression on Kestin's face and said nothing.

The dead prince turned away. "There are things I must attend to. We can finish this later."

Varis watched him go, then turned and continued down the hall. Spirits, but things were tangled in this castle. He wanted the space and quiet of his room so he could work it all out. It was time for him to make his next move, and that would have to be carefully planned.

But when he finally opened his door, wanting nothing

more than to drop onto the bed and let the world go away for a while, he found Darri waiting for him.

She was sitting cross-legged on his bed, wearing a dark green dress and an expression that suggested she was no happier to be in his room than he was to find her there. Varis considered ordering her to leave and imagined her reaction. He sighed heavily and closed the door behind him.

"I need your help," Darri said.

It had taken every ounce of willpower Darri possessed to walk into Varis's room; when he wasn't there, she took a breath of relief and turned back toward the hallway. Then she stopped, one hand on the door, staring out at the long, dim hall.

It felt so familiar, as if she was looking at a cloudy night sky instead of dusty tapestries, as if she was thirteen years old and her sister ten. The only real difference was the empty ache inside her. She'd had hope, the night before Callie was taken away from the plains; even after all her plots and histrionics had failed, she had believed her sister could be saved. If only Varis would help.

And she had truly thought he would.

So she had gone to him and she had begged. It had taken half the night for her to realize that he wasn't even considering helping her. He was humoring her request while he tried to talk her into accepting what had to be done.

She had sworn then that she would die before she ever asked her brother for help again. But then again, it wasn't *her* that had died.

Her heart felt frozen solid, while her mind was a whirlwind: it kept returning to Callie, to what Callie was, to the translucent figure that had fled from her down the long dark hall. She had barely been able to take a complete breath since that terrible moment when she had thrown those coins at her sister. All those years of planning and hoping and longing . . . and after all that, she had arrived too late. Her sister was dead.

Her sister was worse than dead.

They would never be together again, never ride across the plains; never laugh together infectiously, or lie together under the stars and trade whispers until sleep overcame them. Even her memories of her sister would be tainted now, forever overlain by the translucent horror in that stone hall. And it was her fault. She should have fought harder, better, to keep Callie at her side. She should have found a way to come here sooner, before . . .

She bit the inside of her mouth, hard, until she was no longer in danger of crying.

It made her hate Varis even more, for his part in allowing this to happen to their sister. It was that hatred that made her shut the door and go sit on his bed. She knew that if she left, she could never force herself to come back.

Her plans were shattered; there was no escape for Callie. But at the very least, Darri could save Callie from what she was now. *If I avenge myself*, Kestin had said, *I will cease to be.* She would help Callie gain her vengeance, help her spirit tear free of its unnatural chains and become one with the wind.

The door swung open, and Darri straightened, the breath freezing in her throat. Varis stopped in the doorway, surprise wiping his face blank. That reprieve lasted for only a second; then he sighed loudly and leaned against the doorpost.

She had been prepared for his expression of resigned irritation. It pricked her pride all the same, and she had to force out the words she had come to say. They left a bitter aftertaste on her tongue.

Varis folded his arms over his chest. "You need *my* help? For what?"

"To find out why we're being attacked."

He dropped his hand to his side. "Ah."

The dismissiveness contained in that syllable could have irritated a far more patient person than Darri. "Don't you want to learn what the Defender wants from us?" she snapped. "We don't know where the next attack will come from. We don't know how to defend ourselves." *We don't know if he's already succeeded in killing one of us.*

Callie couldn't have died much before Kestin, not if nobody in the castle knew about it yet; which meant that she, like Kestin, had died just about the same time that King Ais invited a new pair of foreigners into the kingdom. Callie's death, Kestin's death, the attacks on the Raellians—those three things had to be connected. All Darri had to do was unravel the motives behind one of them, and she would have her answer to all three. She hoped.

Varis didn't move from the doorway. "I have my own ways of looking into it."

Darri gritted her teeth. "Believe it or not, I can help you. I know things that you do not."

He tilted his head back, looking amused. "Such as?"

Darri hesitated. With just a few words, she could knock that skeptical expression right off his face.

But she couldn't betray Callie to Varis. Not even after all that had happened—and no matter *what* happened. The battle lines between them had been drawn far too long ago. She bit her lip.

Varis unfastened his cloak and tossed it into the room. It landed over the back of a chair. "I'm a warrior, Darri. People have tried to kill me before. I've learned not to over-react to it."

"They tried to kill your *sisters*—" Darri broke off. The sense of futility was so familiar she could barely breathe. "You would have cared once."

Something flickered on his face—or, more likely, in her imagination. For a moment he looked like the brother she'd once had, who had wanted to protect her, who had cared what she thought of him.

Then he stepped toward her, his mouth grim, and the illusion vanished. But something was still wrong. Darri remained on the bed, even when Varis made an irritated gesture toward the door.

He was lying. Much as she hated her brother, wanted to think nothing good of him, she knew him too well to believe it. He was a perfect Raellian, and her people didn't forget. Raellians were taught that it was worth years of effort to avenge the slightest wrong. Varis would never let an attack—on himself *and* his family—go unpunished.

Darri pushed off the bed and stalked across the room. She shoved the door closed, then walked around Varis to face him.

"We're going to take vengeance on all of them," she said. "Aren't we?"

Varis's eyes narrowed faintly. Darri raked a hand through her hair, yanking through its tangles so hard it hurt.

"That's the reason we're still here, even though Prince Kestin is dead," she said. "If we can't form an alliance, we'll find a way to conquer all of Ghostland. That's why it doesn't matter to you which specific Ghostlander was behind the attack."

Varis smiled at her blandly. "You're very imaginative, sister."

But Darri, following her own train of thought, felt herself go pale. "It's not *instead* of an alliance, is it? Conquest was always Father's plan. You would have had me marry Kestin if he was alive, to lull them into thinking we wanted peace. And then attacked anyhow."

Varis looked uncomfortable, and Darri knew she was right. Her brother wouldn't have liked that plan, but he would have gone along with it if their father commanded it. She took a quick stride forward, so that there were only inches between herself and her brother. "That's why we're being attacked; because some of the dead know why we're here. They're defending themselves." His pale blue eyes looked down into hers. "You could have warned me."

"I wanted to," Varis said. And then, just as something fragile within her leaped into hope: "I would have, if I thought you could be trusted."

"You're the one who broke the trust between us," Darri said, so viciously that she almost expected him to step back.

Instead he shook his head, a sad, disappointed movement that made her want to hit him.

"Darri—" Varis began, but it ended in a choke. He pitched forward and slammed into her.

A sharp sizzle of pain ran across Darri's neck. Her skin recognized *knifepoint* a moment before her eyes took in everything else: the ghostly shape that had exploded from inside the door onto her brother's back, pushing him forward onto her. And the long dagger jutting through Varis's right shoulder, the tip of which had grazed the side of her neck.

Darri ducked under Varis and rolled to the side, just in time to avoid the thrust of the second blade. She kicked up as she rolled, connecting with the weapon in the now-solid hand. The dagger flew across the room and hit the wall, and Jano's ghost tackled her.

She was ready. This time she wasn't alone and unprepared in a dark forest. Darri thrust her legs upward with every bit of strength in her. Jano's body turned to mist, but not fast enough; not before she had kicked him, sending him flying over her head. His hazy form went right through the bed board and halfway into the mattress.

Darri moved with the force of her kick, rolling over and onto her feet with an effort that wrenched her back. Blood dripped down the side of her neck, but not enough to concern herself with. She shot a quick glance at Jano, caught in a tangle of translucent boy and opaque bed, then raced across the room and scooped up the dagger she had kicked out of his hand.

Jano floated right up through the bedspread and went solid. "What do you plan to do with that—tickle me?"

Darri ignored him and slid to a stop in front of her brother. Varis had pulled himself into a sitting position, leaning against the closed door, blood spreading across his upper arm. He met her eyes and nodded. Darri stepped behind him, grabbed the hilt, and pulled.

She grunted with the effort, but Varis made not the slightest noise. The dagger pulled through his flesh with a sucking sound. Varis immediately tore off the blood-soaked sleeve and wrapped it tightly around the wound, twisting the ends under his armpit with a deft one-handed motion. Then he stood up.

Darri felt that standing up was taking stoicism a step too far. She shook her head at him, and he grinned faintly. The two of them strode side by side into the center of the room, facing Jano.

"That was a wasted effort," Jano said. He stood on the bed with his feet braced wide apart. "You do remember the way things work here, right? You can't use those against me."

Darri passed the clean blade to Varis, who reached his uninjured arm across his chest to take it. "We know," she said. "But now *you* can't use them against *us*. I invite you to try to attack us unarmed." She grinned, every muscle tense and ready, and felt Varis's identical readiness beside her.

"Or you can run along," Varis added. Blood still seeped through the silk of his sleeve, but he appeared to be in no pain at all. Darri, who had been knifed once, knew that couldn't be true. "Isn't it past your bedtime?"

Darri tried to catch Varis's eye; when he wouldn't look at her, she looked around the room, trying to figure out where his silver dagger might be.

"You Raellians are such a disappointment," Jano sputtered. His face had gone beet red, which only made him look more like a child. "Even from barbarians, I expect some capacity for thought. You really believe I can't attack you?"

"Do you have ghostly powers we don't know about yet?" Varis managed to sound like he was sure of the answer to that question.

"Idiots." Jano moved so fast his hands were a blur. "I have *another dagger*."

The blade flew straight across the room. Darri grabbed Varis's wrist and yanked, pulling him downward. The third dagger sliced past her arm, leaving a sharp line of pain and a trail of blood. But instead of hitting the door, it made the distinctive sound of a knife striking flesh.

"Ouch," Clarisse said behind them.

Darri whirled. Clarisse stood in front of the door with the hilt protruding from her chest, sticking incongruously out from the lace that lined her bodice.

Clarisse sighed, reached up, and pulled the blade out. It came smoothly and soundlessly, without any gush of blood. Clarisse frowned down at the rip in the front of her dress, and a moment later it was gone.

Darri glanced over her shoulder at Jano, who was so insubstantial she could barely see him. There was no way she and Varis could fight both of them—not when Clarisse had a weapon. Darri struck out anyhow, aiming her bloody steel blade at Clarisse's wrist. At the last moment she changed direction and struck instead at the weapon in Clarisse's hand.

Clarisse didn't fall for it. She drew her hand back, and Darri's blade sliced uselessly through the air. Darri staggered, off balance for what could have been a fatal moment, then whirled in a circle and threw.

Clarisse lifted her other hand and flicked her fingers. Darri's dagger hit hers and sent both crashing to the ground, along with a thin swath of violet silk cut from Clarisse's sleeve.

Clarisse blinked at the fallen daggers, then let out an aggrieved sigh and folded her arms across her chest. "Right," she said. "I keep forgetting that doesn't work anymore."

Darri stood panting, legs so taut they shook. She wanted to dive for the two weapons lying at Clarisse's feet, on the off chance she could snatch them before the dead girl did. But that moment when Clarisse had avoided her strike, when Darri had been off balance, her entire right side undefended—that moment *should* have been fatal. Clarisse could easily have stabbed her before she recovered.

Instead of lunging for the daggers, Darri regained her breath and said, "Why are you here?"

"To finish what we started," Jano snarled—at Clarisse, not at her.

"Oh," Clarisse said, glancing up at him. "That plan's been changed. Sorry, Jano—did I not tell you?"

Jano glared at her, fists clenched at his sides. "Then what are *you* doing here?"

Clarisse brushed an invisible speck of dust off her sleeve. "I'm here to talk to Prince Varis."

Jano and Darri both looked at Varis, who was crouched on the floor in readiness to attack. He rose slowly to his feet, like a snake uncoiling, his eyes fixed on Clarisse. "Why?"

Clarisse's gaze dropped, and her voice softened. "Because I couldn't stay away."

Varis snorted a laugh, then winced and pressed his hand to his shoulder. Clarisse looked at the dark blood soaking through the white silk and lifted an eyebrow. "Shouldn't you have that bound?"

"Thank you for pointing it out," Varis said through gritted teeth. "I haven't had the leisure just yet."

"Then I'll leave you to it." She knelt smoothly to retrieve her dagger. "When you're done . . . can I assume you know where my old rooms are?"

"Yes," Varis said shortly.

Clarisse held her smile and his gaze. Then she stepped around Varis and held a hand out to Jano, who was now standing at the foot of the bed. "Let's go."

Jano folded his arms across his chest. "Why should I listen to you?"

"Because," Clarisse said patiently, "it will be easier than fighting me."

"I'm hundreds of years older than you," Jano spat. "What makes you think you can fight me?"

Clarisse considered for a moment. Then she smiled, but her teeth weren't teeth; they were fangs, long and white. Her figure blurred and changed; her fingers lengthened, sharpened; her hair loosened from its coils and formed lashing tendrils.

Jano stumbled back, and Clarisse landed on his chest, throwing him to the ground. She crouched over him, still wearing her rose-colored gown, a horrible mixture of human and beast. The sight of her—of the thing she had become—made bile rise in Darri's throat. She swallowed hard, feeling it burn its way through her body.

Clarisse's hair writhed around her head, whipping at Jano's face. She snarled, a purely animal sound, and tore at his throat. Jano's body turned to mist, and Clarisse's fangs hit the floor. She snarled again as Jano rolled out from under her and leaped away, the slashes on his face disappearing as he straightened.

Clarisse rose to her feet, and by the time she was standing she was human again: tapered fingers, finely boned face, blond hair falling neatly around her cheeks. When she smiled, her teeth were small and straight. Only her eyes still glowed, so brilliantly green it was as if they were lit from within.

"Spirits," she said breathlessly. "That's my favorite part of being dead." She whipped her head around to look at Varis, lifted her eyebrows at the horror on his face, then looked back at Jano. "Can you change your body that much, little boy? Because if you can, a fight between us might be fun."

Jano stared at her, eyes wide, lower lip jutting out. Then he shot through the air to the door, going through part of Darri's body like a fetid chill. Darri shuddered but didn't move, not even when Clarisse walked right past her.

At the door, Clarisse turned; and Darri couldn't help stepping back before she saw that the ghost's face was still human in appearance. Clarisse slipped the dagger into her flowing sleeve, gave the room in general a satisfied smile, then walked through the closed door.

When they were finally alone, Varis let out a long breath. "Help me wrap this wound more tightly."

Darri waited until she was sure she could move without trembling, then crossed the room to her brother.

Several strips of linen cloth and one hastily concocted poultice later, Varis said a curt thanks and got to his feet. Darri dropped the remaining cloths when she realized that he was heading away from his bed. "You're not actually going to see her, are you?"

"I am. She has information that I want. And she's no longer trying to kill us."

"You saw what she—what she can—what she is!"

"I'll handle it."

Darri folded her arms across her chest, and her brother laughed. "Worried about my welfare?"

"At least take a silver dagger."

He moved his hand as if to press it to his shoulder, then changed in mid-motion and dropped it to his side instead. "And let you see where I keep them? Not likely."

"Them? You have more than one?"

He looked annoyed and tried to step around her. Darri slid in front of him and looked up at his closed-off face.

"Varis. I need a weapon that will work against the dead. *Please.*"

The word scraped against the inside of her throat, and emerged harsh and angry; but Varis hesitated, his eyes narrowed.

"It's not that that I'm not willing to die," Darri said fiercely. "But if I die here, I'll be worse than dead. Don't let that happen. Don't leave me helpless against them."

Varis bit his lip, and Darri knew she had him. Just a moment ago, they had stood shoulder to shoulder against a pair of ghosts. They had done it without thought, without any need for discussion; because they were kin, and that would never change.

No matter what Callie thought.

Darri stood her ground, knowing there would never be a better time, and finally Varis heaved a sigh. He turned his back on her and spent a few moments unlocking one of the clothes chests. When he stood, he had a steel dagger in his left hand, which he held out to her hilt first. "Try to wait as long as possible before you make me regret this."

Darri crossed her arms over her chest. "I have daggers, Varis. A number of them, in fact."

"It's silver," Varis said.

She blinked. "It doesn't look like silver."

"That's rather the point."

She took the weapon and touched a finger to the blade. Flecks of dull metal came off on her skin. "It's coated?"

"Prescient of Father, wasn't it?"

She turned it over in her hand. A few more flakes fell to the ground, but there was still no silver that she could see. "Is that the plan?"

"I beg your pardon?"

She looked up at her brother. His eyes were cool and opaque again, on guard against her. That was almost a relief. "Is this Father's plan? Silver weapons disguised as steel?"

Varis adjusted his bandage. "Don't think so much, Darri. Just take it." He strode past her and out the door.

Darri scowled and slid the dagger into her boot sheath. When she straightened, she was smiling grimly.

She hadn't lied to Varis; she *did* need a weapon to defend herself against the dead. She had merely neglected to mention that she might also need it to attack one of them.

I'll avenge you, Callie. Even if it's too late to save you. I'll do the one thing I can.

She left Varis's room without looking back, the cold metal in her boot growing gradually warm against her skin.

Chapter Ten

Varis did not, in fact, know the location of Clarisse's rooms; but at the bottom of the spiral staircase, he directed a crisp question to a cowed-looking servant, who told him which way to go. As Varis turned to start back up the stairs, the servant added, "But her death was accidental, Your Highness. Her rooms are unoccupied."

So people still did occasionally die by accident in this castle; Varis had been beginning to wonder. Although Clarisse, obviously, was not one of them. He folded his arms across his chest. "Why haven't they been cleared, then?"

"Prince Kestin ordered them left alone, after her death. He hoped she would come back." The servant bit his lower lip nervously, but Varis kept his eyes trained on him, and the man kept talking. "When she didn't, no one had the heart to approach him about . . . changing the arrangements."

He hoped she would come back. What a sick place this was. Varis turned his back on the servant and strode on down the hall.

Clarisse's bedroom was large and sparsely furnished: a bed, a single ornate table with three chairs, and a few rather grimly colored tapestries. Clarisse wasn't in sight—which did not, of course, mean that she wasn't there. Varis closed the door behind him and walked slowly around the room, taking it in. Looking for . . . he wasn't sure what. Something that would help him understand what Clarisse was plotting and why.

Hanging on the wall beside the bed was a painting of a young family, dressed simply but—judging by the material of their clothes—richly. The man had an angular face and a small, peaceful smile playing at the corners of his mouth. The woman was on the border between plain and pretty, with reddish-brown hair and sharp, dark eyes. She looked as if she didn't quite belong in her stiffly embroidered dress. A young girl sat on the woman's lap, looking bored.

The portrait was masterful, but marred by an uneven rip right down the middle, separating the man from his wife and child. It had been ripped and then glued back together on a separate sheet of parchment, so that the original pieces fit together jaggedly.

Behind him, someone drew in her breath. Varis turned to see Clarisse watching him from the doorway, her arms wrapped around herself, tracing her bare shoulders with her fingernails. She was now wearing a dark green gown with a daring neckline, her hair arranged in intricate loops and coils at the base of her neck. Even with the memory of the snarling beast-woman fresh in his mind, Varis blinked in admiration.

How could she possibly be *dead*?

"I'm so glad you came," Clarisse murmured, but the sultriness in her voice seemed rote. She was looking, not at him, but at the painting.

Varis was trained to recognize weakness. He took a seat on one of the ornate chairs. "Who ripped the portrait?"

Clarisse leaned back against the doorpost. "I did."

"And who glued it back together?"

"I did that, too." She let her arms drop to her sides, still looking at the painting rather than at him.

"I see." Varis leaned forward, resting his elbows on his knees, ignoring the burst of agony from his right shoulder. "And why did you do that?"

Her lips twisted. She strode into the room and stood in front of the bed. "That's not really what you're here to ask me, is it?"

"I came because you invited me," Varis pointed out.

"You would have refused the invitation if you thought you had nothing to gain from it."

"Maybe," he said, mimicking her earlier tone, "I couldn't stay away."

She laughed and smoothed her skirt down with her hands. The look she turned on him made it suddenly difficult to breathe. "You know, I'm rather glad I didn't kill you."

"As am I." Varis got to his feet as well; not a planned move, but an instinct. His muscles were coiled tightly, expecting an attack. Clarisse leaned back with both hands on the bed, clearly waiting for him to walk over, but he only stepped to the side. "Why *did* you try to kill me?"

She smiled at him and traced a finger along her collarbone. So obviously deliberate—yet somehow, that didn't stop it from working. "I was following orders."

"I'm aware of that. Why does the Defender want me dead?"

"It doesn't matter. He no longer wants you dead, and more importantly, I no longer want you dead. I have . . . other uses for you." She pushed herself away from the bed. "I just proved that, didn't I? I saved your life."

"Even if you hadn't shown up, Jano couldn't have killed me."

"*I* would have killed you," Clarisse said, as if explaining the obvious to a very simple child.

"Really. And how would you have done that?"

She moved without warning, a flash of green silk and golden hair; but he had known how she would react, and by the time she reached him he was already turning, moving out of the path of her lunge. She recovered in an instant and turned, but by then he had his dagger out, its edge at her throat.

Her green eyes went wide and startled. Then she laughed and moved forward. The dagger went right through her slender throat; she went translucent as it passed through, then became suddenly solid with both arms on his shoulders, pinning him up against the wall. She was surprisingly strong, but not half as strong as he was; he could have thrown her across the room without much effort. Instead he met her eyes, mere inches from his, matched her quick-breathed smile, and slid his other dagger lightly across the back of her arm.

She screamed and flung herself away from him, clutching at her arm. A thin red line ran across it. She was not breathing at all now, and her beautiful face was contorted with fury.

Varis held up his second dagger. "Looks like steel, doesn't it?" he said. "I could have used it first, against your throat. You would have been dead before you knew what was happening."

For a moment he thought she was going to attack him again, silver dagger or no. Then, with an evident effort, she composed herself. "Ingenious," she said.

"We use it to coat the hooves of mounts carrying suspected spies. Then when we catch the spies, we pour the molten metal over them. Slowly."

"I am suitably impressed by your barbarian ferocity." Clarisse let go of her arm. The wound was gone, her skin unblemished by blood. "What other tricks did you bring with you, Prince Varis, for fighting the dead?"

So that, Varis thought, was why he was here. "I brought weapons to defend myself only," he said. "We did not come here to fight the dead. We are here to seek an alliance."

She laughed. "You Raellians have no more interest in alliances than we do in sundials. Come, Prince. You tell me your secrets, and I'll tell you mine. Doesn't that sound like a fair trade?"

"It does if we reverse it. I want to hear your secrets first." He gestured at her arm. "Let's start with your last trick. Can all ghosts do that?"

"No." She traced her finger along her arm, and all at once there was no arm, just two yellow bones hinged together. Then, almost before he could be sure he had seen them, they were once again covered with smooth white skin. "Only the older ghosts can change their forms, and only the very oldest ones can do it with such precision. It takes time, usually, for the dead to free themselves of the memory of life."

"But you haven't been dead that long," Varis said.

"I've wanted to be able to change my shape for quite a while. And what I want, I usually get." She glanced swiftly at the portrait, then away. "Besides, I've always had a talent for accepting reality."

Varis slid his dagger back into his boot. "And what," he said quietly, "is the reality?"

"That this body doesn't truly exist." She ran her hand down her side. "Or rather, what does exist of it is currently feeding worms." For another of those split seconds, her arm was gone, and this time he couldn't see the bone for the plump white insects coiled around it. "Yet I can eat food I don't need, I can cry tears I don't have, I can blush if I choose to. I feel that I have to breathe, except when I remind myself that I don't. The power of a mind, freed from its body, is rather incredible. The trouble is making it do what *you* want to do, instead of spending all its time trying to pretend it still is inside a living body."

"I was under the impression," Varis said, "that the pretense of life is exactly what most of the dead want."

"Your impression is correct." Clarisse walked toward

him, her feet making no sound on the wooden floor. "They do a good job of it, don't they? Most of them even fool themselves. They think they're happy because they get to act alive. They shut out of their minds the fact that they're dead and trapped and fading every second of their existence."

Varis clasped his hands behind his back. "And you don't?"

"I don't." She rested both hands on the back of one ornate chair, leaning forward. "I don't need to pretend. I can embrace being dead because I chose it."

He found that he was entirely unsurprised. "You died on purpose."

"Of course. You honestly think any of these buffoons could have killed me?" Clarisse tossed her hair; it floated about her shoulders in a cloud. "Once I realized what Ghostland was, everything I did was aimed at giving them a reason and an opportunity."

"Why?"

She shrugged, but there was nothing casual about the expression on her face. "It's a very useful thing, sometimes, to burn your bridges behind you. While they're there, you know you can cross back over them. After all, I could always sail back over a sea, ride back through the plains, climb back over the mountains. There's no way back from death. And once something is impossible, you don't have to think about it anymore."

"Did you know you would no longer be a sorceress?" Varis asked.

She blinked in surprise, which made him feel disproportionately pleased with himself. "How did you—"

"When Darri attacked you," Varis said, "you wiggled your fingers."

Her eyebrows shot up. *"Wiggled my fingers?"*

"Very elegantly," he assured her.

"Thank you." She was silent for a moment, watching him. Then she let go of the chair and straightened. "I didn't know. Sorcery has never been commonly practiced in this kingdom, so there was no precedent. But it turns out that spells designed for living minds don't work very well with dead ones." She made a face. "It did give me a head start, however. I already understood how powerful my mind was."

Varis stepped back and leaned against the wall. "You know about magic, then." He slid both his hands behind him, against the smooth wood. "Do you know what kind of magic was required to make the dead begin coming back to life?"

"Not entirely." She pulled out the chair and sat on it. "It would have required more than one sorcerer to add his

power to it, that's for certain. And spells so powerful need
sacrifices. Willing sacrifices, usually. With unpleasant consequences for those sacrifices."

Varis nodded. Clarisse leaned back, propping her elbows
on the back of the chair. "But spells must be channeled
through human minds. There is someone in this castle
whose existence fuels the spell and gives it power."

Varis strove not to change expression, and knew he
wasn't succeeding. Clarisse tilted her head to the side
and brushed a stray strand of hair away from her eyes.
"Wouldn't you like to know who?"

"I would," Varis said. "But I have a feeling you're not
going to tell me."

Her smile widened. "I might have, if you'd asked
politely. But now I think it's your turn to tell your secrets."

"Not quite yet," Varis said softly.

He expected anger, but instead she gave him a brilliant
smile. "I understand. Why don't you let me know when
you're ready?"

It was a clear dismissal. Varis hesitated, then pushed
himself off the wall, careful to use only his left arm. Her
smile widened—then widened a bit too much, her gums
and her flesh fading away from her teeth, leaving the clear
impression of a skull beneath her smooth skin.

Varis turned his back on her and walked out of the

room, muscles so tense that his injured shoulder burned with pain. Behind him, the chair scraped against the floor, and she laughed low and mockingly. He could feel her eyes on his back, and still smell the faint spicy scent of her perfume; but mixed with it, definite as a warning, was the stomach-turning odor of rotting flesh.

Chapter Eleven

Callie planted the idea carefully, so no one would know it came from her. She pretended to get drunk at a party and flirted outrageously with Lord Cerix, who was usually willing to flirt with any woman in his general vicinity. Cerix was truly drunk, enough so that he began one of his typical rambling monologues about the dead. Those had been amusing to the dead, once, before it became clear that some of the living were listening and not laughing at all.

Callie had never found them amusing, and her tolerance hadn't increased now that she *was* one of the dead. But she forced herself to remain still, even to giggle occasionally, for an interminable half hour before she got a chance to make her point.

"They drag us down with them," Cerix announced,

snapping his fingers impatiently for a servant to bring him another goblet. "They have no right to live alongside us, to benefit from our labor, when they contribute nothing. When they're a pack of cowards who shouldn't even be here, who cling to their existence at the cost of justice. We will never stand for a dead king. Not even if we have to break the ban on silver and fight for the way things should always have been."

Callie spared a moment to wish someone would murder Cerix before he had time to die of natural causes. It would be amusing to watch how he would deal with becoming one of the people he despised.

But Cerix had stopped talking, for what was probably supposed to be a dramatic pause, and she seized her opportunity. "Have you shared your views with my sister?"

Cerix lowered his goblet, and blinked at her. "Er . . . no. I haven't had the opportunity."

"You should arrange for the opportunity, then," Callie said sweetly. "You're a fine hunter"—a statement only Cerix could believe—"and so is she. I think she would be quite impressed by the quality of your falcons." She waited a moment, to make sure Cerix was following, then added, "I think the gloom is getting to her, and to my brother as well. It's difficult to grow accustomed to the lack of sunshine."

"A lack we owe to the presence of the accursed dead,"

Cerix growled, and was off again. Callie waited until a few other people had stopped to listen, then slipped away and left Cerix to his audience.

Just a few days ago she would have stayed at the party a while longer, laughing and observing and enjoying herself, pretending she wasn't dead. It was so easy, sometimes, to feel alive, as if being dead was nothing more than a word. She was fourteen years old. She should be allowed to feel alive for as long as she could manage it.

But the memory of Darri's wide, stricken eyes was still more potent than the carefree ease of the other ghosts. It made it impossible to forget what she was. There was a part of her, now, that cared nothing for peace and joy, that wanted only vengeance; and it was getting harder and harder to ignore that part. Thinking of Darri made her feel guilty for wanting to ignore it. So she left the party and made her way to the banquet hall.

She scattered the rest of her remarks casually around court, comments about how much she had missed sun-shine when she first came here, how much longer this fine weather could last, how beautiful the lake was during the day. After only one night, Lord Riald—the smartest of Cerix's supporters—sidled over to Callie and asked if she thought her siblings would like to go falconing.

"They would love it," Callie said, then pretended to

think twice. "But wouldn't that be an insult to Prince Kestin? He wouldn't be able to come along."

The hunt was set for the next day, which didn't give her as much preparation time as she would have liked; on the other hand, it gave Darri less time to do something drastic. Callie borrowed a lure from the master falconer, one of the few people in the castle who genuinely liked her—his entire existence was his birds, and Callie had taught him some new training tricks—then stole a horse while the stable master, who had not appreciated her advice on technique, wasn't looking. She set off immediately after sunset.

"You don't seem at all excited," said a voice behind Darri. "I thought you plainspeople loved to kill things."

Darri whirled, making the falcon on her gloved wrist spread its wings for balance. Swearing inwardly, she waited for it to settle and fold its wings back in, then glared at Clarisse. "I suppose the last hunt made me a bit nervous."

Clarisse flicked a blond curl out of her eyes. "Well, that's just silly. It will be bright daylight soon."

Darri looked at the sky, which was light gray bruised with pink. "I'm under no illusion that it's only the dead in Ghostland I should be nervous about."

Clarisse laughed. She wore a deep blue riding gown that made Darri wonder if she had planned some way to be able to accompany them. Darri fervently hoped not. "Very good. Although the dead *are* more likely to be a murderous lot. We think of it as doing the living a favor."

"Thank you for sharing that." Darri turned her back on Clarisse, and was just in time to see two men trotting out of the mews carrying a closed litter between them.

She blinked. The litter was little more than a box suspended between two poles, but it had been decorated in obvious haste with purple and gold ribbons and an ornate gold chain. The windows were completely blocked off with heavy black curtains.

While Darri gaped, the litter drew up next to her, and the men knelt so that it hovered just over the cobblestones. The door swung smoothly open to reveal Kestin sitting cross-legged inside. He was wearing what passed for a simple riding habit in Ghostland, complete with ruffled sleeves and an embroidered over-tunic tied at the waist with a yellow sash.

"My lady," he said, inclining his head. "Would you care to join me?"

Darri couldn't tell which of them he was speaking to. She opened her mouth, then closed it. Whether she answered him or not, there was a good chance she would end up looking stupid.

"No thank you, Your Highness," Clarisse said. "The

prospect of being stuck in a dark box all day is rather unappealing"—her dimples flashed as Kestin's face grew taut—"no matter how welcome the company."

He regarded her for a moment before replying. "I am pleased to hear it, as I was actually speaking to Princess Darriniaka."

Clarisse stepped closer to the litter. "Kestin—" she said, and the familiarity in the word jolted Darri. She blinked, and suddenly the grimness of Kestin's face wasn't anger at all, but something far deeper.

"Enough," Kestin said, his voice soft but final. "You've waited years to speak to me. You can wait another few hours. You know where to find me, if you decide to bother."

Clarisse's lips parted; but just as she was about to respond, a group of horses clattered into the courtyard. Clarisse whirled, and for a moment, the blank intentness of her stare matched that of the falcon on Darri's wrist. Then she turned, a bit too hastily for grace, and sauntered away.

Darri blinked after her, then looked at the first of the riders, who she guessed must be Cerix. It was the first time she had seen her substitute husband-to-be, but she couldn't make out his face beneath the wide-brimmed, lace-trimmed hat he was wearing. He was talking loudly and dramatically to his retainers . . . she made out a line about "the beauty of sunlight, which the dead have stolen from our lives" . . . all of whom had expressions of studied politeness on their faces. Darri couldn't imagine why Clarisse seemed wary of him, unless . . .

Kestin made a small sound, and Darri turned her attention back to him. He was watching Clarisse go, his fingers curled tightly over his knees. Then he inclined his head to Darri. He looked tired. "My lady?"

Darri, who shared Clarisse's opinion, said hastily, "My bird—"

Kestin waved a hand. A servant wearing a leather glove appeared at Darri's side, and she reluctantly allowed him to take her falcon. The bird shuffled, feathers rustling, then settled back into its unmoving stance.

Darri spent a second trying to think of another reason to refuse, but couldn't come up with anything. Kestin waited, his face resigned and patient. The carriers of the litter looked resigned but not at all patient, and finally, taking pity on their knees, Darri climbed into the litter. She settled on the cushions next to Kestin, bending her legs awkwardly to make sure her knee didn't touch his. The servant swung the door shut, enveloping them in darkness, and the litter lurched upward.

Darri thought, too late, of another excuse. "Won't two people make the litter too heavy for them?"

A lantern flickered on in Kestin's hand, and he set it carefully back in a holder on the wall before looking at her. The light played along the long planes of his face as the litter swayed forward. "I don't have to weigh anything if I don't want to."

"Oh."

The corners of his mouth quirked upward. "Don't worry, you'll get out before the hunt starts in earnest. But I appear a little less pathetic if I'm not in the litter alone."

His whole face came alight with that half-smile; it lit up his eyes and sharpened the soft angles of his face, making him look intensely vital and alive. Somehow, that made it worse.

She thought of Callie, then banished the thought: this was no time to break down. She settled herself more firmly on the cushions. "I can't say I expected you to be here at all, Your Highness."

"No one did." Kestin folded his hands in his lap. "Cerix arranged this expedition as an insult to me. I'm sure he's stewing over how I've turned it on his head."

By staying cooped up in a litter hidden from the sunshine? Darri had her doubts, but she nodded. "Why am I here, Your Highness?"

"To annoy people," Kestin said. He gave her a sly, conspiratorial wink.

"Which people?" she said coolly. "Your father, Cerix, or Clarisse?"

His expression soured at the last name, and Darri almost wished she hadn't said it. But the look of wary respect that followed was worth it. "All three, actually."

"Efficient," Darri noted approvingly.

That brought back the smile. He drew his legs up, looping his hands around his knees. The litter tilted from side to side as the carriers began walking, and Darri dug her fingers into the cushions. "Mainly Cerix, though. Which brings me to the other reason you're here: so we can talk about how to find out if he killed me. Has he favored you with his attentions yet?"

Darri felt as if she had been punched. Since she had found out her sister was dead, she hadn't thought about her bargain with Kestin, except to wonder about the connection between Callie's death and his. She hadn't thought much about anything except the horror her sister was trapped in, and how Darri could get her out of it.

But why should she feel guilty? Trading Kestin's vengeance for Callie's escape no longer made any sense; there was no reason for her to think about Kestin. No reason for her to marry Cerix, or stay in Ghostland at all, now that Callie was . . .

She struck down the feeling that rose in her, but not fast

enough; not before she recognized it for what it was. She had felt it before, on the day her father formally announced which of his daughters would be sent to the land of the dead.

It was relief.

It was a tiny, whimpering feeling; it was nearly swamped by her overwhelming grief and rage. But it was there, and it made her face heat up with shame.

"So he has spoken to you," Kestin said, misinterpreting her flush.

"No," Darri said. "I can't say I'm particularly looking forward to it."

"And I can't say I blame you." Kestin's arms tightened around his knees, and he looked down at the floor, his dark eyes shadowed. "I need for you to talk to him; he had more to gain from my death than anyone. But don't underestimate him. He has a following among those who hate and fear the ghosts. The harmony between the living and the dead in this castle is not as stable as we thought, and he has taken advantage of that. My death, and my father's insistence that I inherit anyhow, were his opportunity."

Darri nodded. Kestin hesitated, biting his lower lip, then looked up at her. The way his chin-length hair swung over his cheekbones made a traitorous part of her flutter, followed by a surge of revulsion. "I'd guess you can handle him."

"I hope so," Darri said coolly, "since the plan is for me to marry him."

Kestin smiled ruefully. "I don't much like that part of the plan."

Darri shrugged.

He leaned back. "Who would you marry in your own lands? Is it up to you?"

"It's up to my father," Darri said. "He would probably pick the son of another powerful tribe, to bind them to us more closely."

"Weren't you afraid he would choose someone you hated?"

Darri laughed. "He wouldn't have risked it. It would be too likely that I'd insult the man badly enough to cause a civil war."

Kestin shook his head. "It still seems odd to me. It's one of the benefits of being what we are; in Ghostland, even the nobility choose whom to love."

And he had chosen Clarisse. Which just went to show, Darri supposed, that choosing on your own was no less likely to end well than having your marriage arranged by others.

Kestin took a deep breath. "When I said I didn't like that part," he said softly, "what I meant was that I have a better idea."

Darri said, as coolly as she could, "Which is?"

"Well," Kestin began, then stopped. He swallowed, reached behind him, and held out a folded piece of parchment.

Darri stared at the parchment as if it was a live snake. It fluttered jerkily with the movement of the litter. "What is it?"

"You can't read?"

"Do I look like a scribe?" she snapped.

Kestin gave her a surprised, faintly horrified look; clearly, he had suddenly recalled that she was a barbarian. Darri suspected it was a pale imitation of the looks she gave him sometimes, but it made her bristle all the same. She snatched the parchment out of his hand. "What does it say?"

"It's an offer of betrothal."

Darri froze. The paper felt thick and rough under her dry fingers. For several long moments the silence was broken only by the muffled sound of hooves outside—and, for Darri, by the pounding of her heart. The litter felt suddenly very small, without enough air for both of them to breathe. If he'd had to breathe.

Kestin looked at her carefully and, with an obvious effort, laughed. "Am I that monstrous to you?"

Darri tried to rearrange her expression. She wouldn't

have thought the prince of Ghostland would care about a foreigner's prejudices—but she'd heard a note of hurt only half-hidden behind the laugh. She couldn't meet his eyes, and she couldn't manage a lie.

The litter jerked to a stop, then started again; outside, one of the carriers cursed. Kestin leaned back and passed a hand over his face. "It would be in name only. You wouldn't ever have to touch me. I will take vengeance on my killer, and then I will disappear. If we were married first, that would leave you as queen of Ghostland. You could take a consort and give birth to a new heir to the throne. Your son would come before Cerix in the succession."

Relief vanished as fast as it had come, and breathing was once again difficult. "You would do that just so I won't have to marry Cerix?"

"And because I care about my country. I don't particularly want to see my cousin rip it apart." Kestin shrugged, but his voice was strained; Darri wondered how it felt to be torn between a need for vengeance and a sense of duty. Her own loyalty to her country had been left by the wayside long ago.

Then again, her country hadn't ever needed her the way Kestin's did. The Raellians, after all, had Varis.

Kestin shifted and lifted his eyebrows at her. "Besides, I suspect it would foil your brother's plans as well."

Indeed it would. As queen of Ghostland, she would outrank Varis. She grinned despite her near-panic and dropped the parchment into her lap. The litter tilted slightly to the side. "You could marry one of your own people to get around Cerix," she pointed out. "You don't need me."

"But I think you would be a good choice." Kestin stretched his legs out; she shifted her own closer to the wall. "I don't know anyone else who could cut through all our courtly tangles. You would do whatever has to be done, regardless of consequences or who tried to stop you."

It had been so long since she had heard that particular intonation that it took her several seconds to realize what it was: admiration. A blush worked its way up her cheeks. She tried to think of something to say, but couldn't get her throat to work. Ever since Callie had told her she was useless—the words *You're getting in over your head* still whispered constantly through her mind—some part of her had begun to fear it was true. But Kestin was right. She *would* do whatever had to be done, except she would do it to save Callie. And she would do it even if Callie was the one trying to stop her.

Kestin watched her closely. The litter swayed around them, and every time it did, the cushion slid farther out from under her. "In time," he said, "you might even lose your fear of . . . of us."

He made it sound like a question, and she couldn't bring herself to refuse to answer. The blush felt permanently attached to her face now. She pushed the cushion away with one hand, settled herself on the wooden bottom of the litter, then turned back and looked at him. He wanted someone who would cut through courtly tangles, did he?

"I thought you wanted to take vengeance and disappear," she said flatly. "What does it matter whether I lose my fear of you or not?"

"The rest of the dead will still be here," Kestin said. "Even if I disappear. And besides, what if I never find who killed me? I'll have no choice but to continue . . . being this."

"You could end your own existence," Darri said. "With silver. Or sunlight."

He looked up at her sharply, his eyes so black that she was suddenly afraid. She sat very still.

"I would never do that." He leaned forward, and she pressed her back hard against the wooden slats. "If I find my killer, nothing will stop me from taking vengeance. But being killed by silver or sunlight is different. Those deaths don't allow us to move on; they merely end us." He shook his head. "I wouldn't choose that. Even if what I am now is something that was never supposed to be."

"You still wouldn't be what you are now," Darri

whispered. "You wouldn't be frustrated by the urge for vengeance, and trapped among the living. You would be *gone*. Wouldn't that be better?"

He smiled bitterly. "Are you happy, Princess Darriniaka? Or do you miss your sister and hate your brother and feel alone among your kin? When you are unhappy, does your unhappiness make you want to end your life?"

"Of course not. But I'm *supposed* to be alive. You're not."

"And yet I am." He leaned back, and closed his eyes. "Saying I'm not supposed to be here doesn't change that, does it? It doesn't make me want to . . ." The side of his mouth twisted upward, though he didn't open his eyes. "Die. For lack of a better word."

Darri drew in a deep breath, trying not to make it too loud. His eyes snapped open, but whatever had been in them that frightened her, it was gone. He looked tired and lonely. "Would you just end your existence, if you were me?"

"I would," Darri said fiercely. "When *I* die, I want to be free of this life. Not stuck in an endless imitation of it, without the ability to grow and change, to walk in daylight or bear children."

"Well." He leaned forward suddenly, his hands sliding down over his knees, almost touching her. "You can scorn me, if you want, for being willing to accept less. But you're not me, and it's not your decision to make. If it horrifies you so much, then help me avenge myself."

"I intend to," Darri said, a little stiffly.

"I'm glad." Kestin took a deep breath. "If you accept my offer, you know, you could be with Callie as well. I don't think she truly wants to leave."

Not didn't want to; couldn't. It was a moment before Darri could breathe again, and she only managed it by meeting Kestin's eyes, letting their intentness draw her mind from her sister. "Would such an arrangement really be recognized under your laws?"

"There is precedent. My father, at least, would be loath to contest it. Especially since your position as queen would ensure our safety from your father's armies."

Which was, of course, the real reason for this proposal: not her own strengths, but her father's. It was the only reason anyone had ever courted her, so Darri wasn't offended. If anything, she was flattered that Kestin had bothered to pretend otherwise.

The litter turned sharply, and Darri slapped her hands down on the floor to keep her balance. "How," she asked, "would Clarisse react to this? I don't think she'd like it."

"Don't you?" Kestin said. "I don't think she'd care."

His voice frayed on that last sentence, and the bewildered loss on his face made him look almost like a child. Darri recognized his expression; it must have been how she looked, that first night at court, when Callie looked away from her as if wishing she wasn't there.

How could a ghost feel grief? But he did, he clearly did; it was right in front of her, in the blankness of his stare and the tightness of his mouth, and the sympathetic tug she felt all through her body.

"I'm sorry," she whispered, meaning it, not knowing whether she should mean it.

Kestin blinked once, twice, then drew himself up and composed his face. Darri knew what an effort of will that must have cost him. She watched with admiration, something else she shouldn't be feeling for a ghost, and almost— almost—reached out to take his hand. Just a simple gesture of comfort, nothing more.

She couldn't do it. But she wished she could.

"I'll think about it," she said finally, placing her palm flat on the parchment.

They sat in silence as the litter jolted along the path. Darri kept her hands tightly folded around the parchment in her lap, wondering when the ride would end and she could step out into the sun; while beside her, Kestin stared straight ahead into the darkness he could never escape.

Varis brooded as he rode, casting dark looks at the litter his sister shared with Prince Kestin. He admired the prince's courage in riding out in sunlight; it was a bold move, a statement that he had not left the living behind and could still serve as their leader. Varis wondered if the prince was going through the motions of courting his sister in order to make a similar statement, or if it was just Kestin's method for keeping her away from Cerix's attentions.

The second-in-line to the throne rode directly in front of Varis, flanked by two lackeys, and all three were also glowering at the swaying litter. They probably didn't have political considerations in mind, though; the litter, all the way in the front, was slowing everyone down.

Varis didn't mind. Sunlight spilled over the edges of the clouds, warming his skin and turning the foliage into shimmering designs of interlocking green and silver. He hadn't realized how much the lack of daylight had been wearing on him. His shoulder throbbed dully, but his heart was light. He had nothing to do until they reached the lake, so he could afford to simply enjoy the breeze and the sunshine and the smell of the earth. Moments like these, even back on the plains, were becoming rarer and rarer for him.

"Your Highness?"

Not to mention shorter. Varis turned to the gangly, red-haired man who had dropped back to ride at his side. Beneath his ridiculously wide-brimmed hat—Ghostlanders' skin was, of course, unaccustomed to sunlight—his face was oily with sweat.

"Lord Cerix," Varis said, nudging his horse to the side of the path. This was an opportunity he had been waiting for, so he squashed his annoyance. "I hope you're enjoying the ride?"

"Quite." Cerix adjusted his hat, the lace on his sleeves rustling in the breeze. "Although it is unfortunate that I am deprived of my true reason for coming, which was the company of your beautiful sister."

"She was looking forward to it as well." Varis noted that Cerix's attendants were glancing nervously over their shoulders at them. "Perhaps the two of you can ride together when the hunt begins." It was a safe enough offer; there was no doubt in his mind that Darri would be half-way across the hunting grounds before Cerix had managed to so much as don a falconing glove.

"I certainly hope so." Cerix sat back in the saddle. "It must be disheartening for her, having come so far, to find her intended dead. But as I'm sure you've realized, there are other options."

Varis had a momentary image of how Darri would respond to a proposition from Cerix. The thought was cheering enough to help him overlook the would-be prince's presumption. "I thought there might be."

"Indeed." Cerix's lips skewed sideways, into what was probably supposed to be a sly smirk. "She may find herself queen of this kingdom after all."

This was, in theory, why Varis was even talking to Cerix; but the fact that the suggestion had come so soon annoyed him. At least it answered the question of whether Cerix had arranged for Kestin's death. This pompous fop was too stupid to have planned anyone's assassination.

But that didn't mean he didn't have associates who were smarter than he was. Ahead of them, one of Cerix's men had slowed his pace, subtly nudging his horse sideways. It wouldn't be long before he was right next to them on the path.

Which meant Varis didn't have time for subtlety. Luckily, he was fairly sure that handling Cerix wouldn't require it. "I thought King Ais had proclaimed Prince Kestin his heir."

Cerix made a dramatic motion with his hand, making Varis's horse snort nervously. "King Ais is deluded if he thinks his subjects will accept a dead king. We suffer the dead among us because we have no choice, but their decaying presence is a blight upon our kingdom. We will never allow them to try to take the place of the living."

It was always disconcerting to discover that you shared opinions with someone you had no respect for. Varis smiled thinly. "Do you think Kestin's death was arranged by the other ghosts, to place one of their own on the throne?"

Just then the retainer pulled up alongside them. The horses jostled each other, even though the trail was wide enough for all of them. Varis's mount whinnied.

"Lord Riald," Cerix said, inclining his head. Then he focused again on Varis. "It is not beyond consideration. The dead are so self-important, with their brooding and dark secrets, as if the living could never fathom their plans. But nothing stays secret for long. There are murmurs and whispers, if you know how to listen. The dead are plotting something."

"Something," Varis murmured, "like selecting one of their own as king?"

"That's part of it. But their design is darker than that. They wish to put themselves above the living, to make us dependent upon them. To destroy us, that they need not be reminded of what they have lost." He jabbed his finger at Varis, who resisted an urge to draw his dagger and slice it off. "It is what they've always wanted; if not for the presence of the Guardian, they would have overwhelmed us long ago. But now, with the prospect of a dead king, they are growing bolder. There is no limit to how far they would go. And similarly, there must be no limit to how far *we* would go to stop them."

Varis nodded and waited. But as Cerix opened his mouth, Lord Riald said, "You understand that we can say no more at this point."

Varis cursed silently. Out loud he said, gravely, "Of course not."

Cerix looked disappointed, and Varis resisted the urge to swear out loud. If he had pushed a little, Cerix might have been stupid enough to tell him everything, even against his follower's advice.

The horses picked their way along the path. Up ahead, the murmurs of the other riders mingled with the plodding of hooves. Lord Riald looked past Cerix at Varis. "Perhaps," he said, "we could hunt with you and Princess Darriniaka together this afternoon, and find an opportunity to talk?"

"That should be possible," Varis lied. Now that he had gotten a good look at Cerix, he had no intention of letting the would-be prince anywhere near Darri until it was absolutely necessary. "It would be better if I spoke to my sister first, however."

Cerix's face twisted in annoyance. "I am sure she would welcome the company of a living man, after being forced to spend an hour cooped up with a ghost. I am surprised, Your Highness, that you permitted it."

Spirits. Alliance or no, Varis couldn't imagine marrying

his sister off to this buffoon. Darri would probably slit his throat within two days of the wedding.

Though if she did, Cerix would come back for her.

His internal amusement died as swiftly as it had arisen. Ahead, the trail narrowed; he used the excuse to pull in front of the other two horses, before he forgot himself and said something impolitic to Cerix. Or, more likely, did something.

If it was necessary, he told himself, Darri *would* marry Cerix. If his father's plan worked, then after the wedding they could do whatever they liked: kill Cerix, replace him with a Raellian, or simply declare the marriage nullified. The celebration itself was the important thing. If it came to it, he would tell Darri everything, and even she would understand what had to be done.

Or it would have to be made clear that it wasn't up to her.

A task he didn't look forward to at all. Darri was a problem, in more ways than one. Ever since her tantrums upon Callie's departure, the two of them had lived in an icy state of mutual avoidance. On the ride to Ghostland that had been impossible, and her obvious disdain had begun to grate on him. They had been close once, before she had become so small-minded and irrational.

Perhaps if he promised her that Callie could leave . . .

He found himself nodding as the trail widened again and he reined his horse in, waiting for Cerix and Riald to come up beside him again. She would do it, in that case; she would go along with their father's plan, no matter how base and treacherous she thought it was. Much as she would hate to admit it, Darri was a lot like Varis. She had decided to make her goal the welfare of a single person rather than an entire nation, but that didn't mean she was any less ruthless about it. And he could use that to his own advantage.

Because as distant as they had grown, there was one thing about his sister he knew without a doubt: to save Callie, Darri would stop at nothing.

Chapter Twelve

When she finally stepped out of the dark litter, which by then was uncomfortably hot and stuffy, Darri breathed deeply and, for no particular reason, laughed aloud. The litter rested beneath the heavy foliage of three trees, and a thick black canopy had been set up to further block the sun. Beyond the canopy, though, the bright blue sky was half-covered with feathery white clouds, and the wind raced along the top of the lake, making the silver-blue ripples dance. Darri stepped out of the shade and felt the sun warm her skin.

Kestin, stepping out of the litter after her, gave her a quizzical glance from the shadows. Darri grinned at him, and after a moment he grinned back. Every other person in their party took note of the interaction, including Varis, but

Darri was too heady with sunlight to care. She stretched, her cramped muscles uncoiling, clean fresh wind sweeping through her hair. All she needed was a horse beneath her, and for just a few moments life could be perfect.

"Will you have your man bring my bird?" she asked, not caring if it was rude.

Kestin gave her an unreadable look—envy? disappointment? disapproval? She turned quickly away, knowing she shouldn't care what he thought. If only she could invite him to ride with her—

The unbidden thought made the entire sky less bright. He couldn't ride with her because he was trapped in his death. How could he bear being cut off from sunlight and freedom? And how much worse it must be for Callie, who had grown up in daylight, racing across the plains . . .

The servant with the falcon was standing over her; how long had he been there? Darri jerked herself back to the present and took the bird. The falcon turned its head and looked at her, its bleak eyes never once losing their fierce glitter. Another servant brought her horse, which was wearing a Ghostland saddle with a pommel-torch—unlit, of course, and therefore nothing but a rather ridiculous-looking inconvenience. Darri frowned, then decided she wasn't going to care.

She didn't join the party of nobles flying their birds near

the shore of the lake—something she would doubtless hear about from Varis later. But that was *later*. Right now the grass bent ahead of the wind in dark green waves, making the whole shoreline shimmer. The stretch of empty space between the lake and the woods looked almost like the plains back home. Darri wheeled her horse and galloped straight across the grass, the falcon's jesses slapping against her wrist. She flung her arm out, releasing the bird into the sky.

The falcon caught a wind and soared, jesses dangling beneath its outstretched wings. It spiraled up into the air, higher and higher, as if it would never stop—and then, with heart-stopping suddenness, folded its wings and plummeted.

Darri raced after it. She was fiercely glad that it had gone in the direction of the rocky foothills to the north of the lake, leaving the hunting party even farther behind.

She was less glad when she reached the spot where the falcon had dropped and found herself facing a cluster of thickets. She pulled her horse up, waiting. After several moments, she swore under her breath and dismounted, not terribly surprised that a Ghostland falcon would be too ill-trained to bring back its prey. All the same, returning without the bird would reflect badly on her own skills—in Varis's eyes, certainly, and probably in Kestin's as well. She looked around at the sky, and then, guided by instinct, at the thickets.

There, caught in one gnarly branch—a shiny black feather.

Darri caught her breath. No falcon would follow prey into the bush; someone must have been standing here and carried it in. She swung off her horse, hobbled it swiftly, and, with a grimace, pushed her way into the thicket.

Several scratches and torn-out hairs later, she found herself at the mouth of a cave, an irregular crack in the hillside that slanted down into the earth. A prickle of foreboding added to the itch from the bristles clinging to her clothes. She stepped into the cave and let out a low whistle. Nothing happened.

Something cold touched the back of her neck. Darri shrieked and looked up just in time to catch the next drop of water in her eyes. Dripping fingers of stone hung from the ceiling.

She hissed between her teeth, still looking up. In the faint glow from the bush-covered entrance, the stalactites looked like eerie wax candles, and her skin felt dirty where the water had touched it. She whispered, "Callie?"

Her sister stepped out from behind a thick column of rock. Darri's falcon was perched on Callie's ungloved wrist, a hood drawn over its eyes; its claws pierced deep into her skin without drawing blood or eliciting any sign of pain. Darri shuddered. Her sister's eyes followed hers and widened. For a moment she looked embarrassed. Then her face went blank, with no expression on it at all.

Darri wasn't sure what her own face revealed. The last time she had seen her sister, Callie had been translucent, the stones of the wall showing clearly through her body. But Callie looked solid now—solid and familiar and alive. Darri was grateful to her for that.

Darri took another step into the cave and said, "How did you know my falcon would be the first to come here?"

"You were always first, on every hunt," Callie said. She moved closer to the mouth of the cave, and Darri saw that she was holding a lure, which she must have used to draw the falcon toward the mouth of the cave. "I haven't forgotten. And I think anyone else might have hesitated before walking into such an obvious trap."

"I did hesitate," Darri said with dignity.

Callie laughed, but it wasn't the laugh Darri had been waiting to hear; it was joyless and tired. "I'm sure. Anyhow, even the living here don't like open sunlit spaces; and Varis, I assume, still thinks hunting without arrows is an inefficient waste of time. I knew you would be the first to ride in this direction. Did any of them follow you?"

"No."

"Good. We have some time." Callie moved even closer. Darri managed not to flinch away from her, until she noticed how careful Callie was to avoid the few small patches of sunlight. Then she couldn't help herself. She stepped back.

Callie acted as if she hadn't noticed. She took the lure from the falcon and flung it out through the cave mouth. Deftly, she unhooded the bird and let it loose. The falcon let out a cry that sounded eerily like a human scream and flew out into the sunlight.

"They'll come eventually," Callie said. "Varis, if no one else. We should go deeper into the cave."

Darri glanced once at the thick darkness swallowing up the faint light, and then at the ghost who wanted to lead her into it. "You arranged all this just to talk to me?"

"And so you could see where it happened."

"Where it—"

Callie gave her a tired smile. "The lake you're picnicking at is where I died."

The words fell like rocks. Darri swallowed hard and said, inadequately, "I'm sorry."

"That I'm dead?" Her sister's voice held a challenge. "Yes."

"And that I'm still here?"

She had never lied to Callie. Even if this wasn't really Callie. "Yes."

Callie made a sound somewhere between a laugh and a sob. "You can barely stand to look at me, can you?"

Except it *was* Callie. She sounded exactly the same. Darri thought of Kestin in the litter, swallowing his grief, and willed herself to do the same. She looked straight at her sister, consciously imitating Kestin's forced composure. She kept looking as the seconds stretched into a thick silence, until her skin had almost stopped crawling.

Callie wrapped her arms around herself. "Thank you. But you don't have to pretend. I know how you feel. I was hoping you could bear it long enough to help me."

No need to ask with what. Warmth rose in Darri's throat. Despite everything, Callie still needed her; Darri could still take care of her, still save her. Even if they would never ride out of this country together the way she had planned.

The warmth turned into an ache, and she breathed around it, forcing back her sense of loss. There would be time to mourn later, when things were simpler. She drew in the next breath, waited for the knot in her chest to loosen, and said, "How did it happen?"

"I was at the lake." Callie rubbed her forehead. "I used to go there often, just to look across the water. To see a stretch of sky. I didn't tell anyone; they wouldn't have understood. I didn't think anyone knew."

Darri reached for her, almost involuntarily, but Callie stepped away. Darri drew her hand back. "What happened?" She stopped, flushed. "I mean—"

"I know what you mean. I don't remember. One second I was standing there, and the next thing I knew I was floating above the lake's surface." Callie hesitated. "I . . . I don't want to remember that. It was several nights after my death, and it was dark; I wondered why so much time had passed, but not why I was floating. *That* part felt normal. I dove into the water, and it didn't feel cold to me. I had no trouble breathing. Because I wasn't breathing at all. Then—" Her voice wavered, and Darri's heart cracked. "Then I saw my body."

"Callie—"

"Don't," Callie said.

Darri turned away, so Callie wouldn't see her face. Shadows shifted on the rocky ground as an outside breeze ruffled the bushes, but the breath of air didn't reach inside the cave.

When Darri spoke, she was surprised at how even her voice was. "Someone must have hit you on the head from behind and then thrown you into the water. Who was it?" She said it a second before realizing it was a stupid question.

If Callie knew who had killed her, she wouldn't still be here.

Callie drew in a breath. When she let it out, it sounded like a sob. "It must have been one of the living, because it was daylight. But I don't know who. I don't even know if they intended for me to rise afterward. Many people didn't think a foreigner could come back as a ghost." She hesitated, then said in a flat voice, "I hoped they were right. That if I died, I would stay dead."

Darri faced her sister. Callie's round face was very still, her eyes large and dark in the dimness. She looked so alive. "Who would have wanted to kill you?"

"I don't know, but I don't think it was because of anything I did." Callie lifted her chin. "I think it was because of whatever Father's planning. The reason you're here."

"I don't know what Father is planning," Darri said. "But I'm here for you."

"It's too late," Callie whispered. "I'm sorry, Darri."

Darri dragged her feet forward, pushed her hand through the still air, and closed her fingers around her sister's hand. Callie made a tiny jerking motion, but didn't pull away. She looked down at their linked hands, so that all Darri could see was the top of her head, the unruly frizz of her blond hair.

"It's not your fault," Darri said fiercely. "And it's not too late. I can still save you from *this*."

Callie lifted her face, blue eyes wet. So ghosts can cry, Darri thought, and all at once it was impossible not to think about what she was holding. Her sister's dead hand.

She pulled away; she couldn't help it. Callie's lips parted, but before she could speak, they were interrupted.

A loud rushing sound filled the cavern, as if an invisible waterfall was crashing down around them. At the same time, cascades of white misty forms shot down from the stalactites on the cave's ceiling, falling in endless gentle sprays.

Ghosts, landing all around them.

For an awful moment, Darri thought her sister had led her into a trap. Callie's form shimmered like the lake surface, her face as white as the gleam of sunlight on water. The ghosts swooped around them, but—to Darri's intense relief—came nowhere near them. One and all, they landed behind the larger stalagmites, or in the shadows cast by the irregular rock formations. When the air was clear again, the cavern looked as it had before. Darri stared at her sister. Callie, who had gone solid again, looked nearly as spooked as Darri did.

Of course, she also looked as *alive* as Darri did. Everywhere in this country, appearances deceived. The cavern was silent as a grave, but Darri's skin crawled at the thought of all those dead eyes upon them. Her fingers itched for her silver dagger, but she thought of how her father's honor guard preceded him everywhere, and then stood like statues awaiting his arrival. These ghosts, invisible and silent, were preparing the way for someone else. She forced herself to stand still.

Clarisse slid down the longest stalactite and flew through the air in a graceful arc, landing lightly at the far end of the cave. She moved toward them in a smooth, seamless motion that made Darri think of waves of grass rippling in the wind. The edges of her body were blurred and slightly whitish, and her hair floated behind her in a streaming cloud of gold, even though there wasn't a breath of wind in the cold damp air.

"What are you doing here?" Clarisse demanded, and there was something too smooth about her voice as well. "This is *our* place. You don't belong."

In the shadows of the cavern, things stirred and muttered in what sounded like agreement.

Darri's hands shook. She was seeing the dead for real now, stripped of the guises and pretenses they put on for the living. Clarisse, despite her familiar face and form, looked less human than when she had been attacking Jano with fangs and claws. And the murmuring all around them sounded more like howling wind than like human voices.

I knew, Darri thought helplessly. I knew they were worse than they appeared.

"We were not aware of that," Callie said, and Darri looked at her sister with a sensation like glass breaking. Was Callie, too, worse than she appeared? She looked the same, small and brave despite the ridiculous clothes and bright makeup. Even the expression on her face, fear trying to hide behind defiance, was familiar.

"Yet here you are," Clarisse said. "I'm afraid we can't allow it."

The murmur swelled in hideous anticipation. Clarisse smiled, and Darri got the impression that her teeth were filed into points. When she looked closely, they weren't, but she stepped back all the same.

"What makes this place yours?" she asked, needing to say *something* challenging.

Clarisse's eyes fixed on her. "That's a stupid question, Princess. Our bodies are buried beneath the earth; beneath the earth is where we belong. Here we can be truly dead, can discover the powers our minds possess when they have no bodies to concern themselves with. Even the Ghostland living are not ready to discover what we can do. The older dead all come here eventually, to stand guard." Her lips snapped shut, but words kept coming through. "And now you are here. Alive. Foreign. We do not permit it . . . unless you've come to join us?"

The nonexistent wind ricocheted among the rocks, harsh and eager. Darri couldn't speak. She could barely breathe.

Callie snorted. "Not that this isn't very spooky, but if you're all that powerful, how is it you don't know that I've *already* joined you?"

The murmuring stopped as if cut off by a knife. Clarisse jerked her head to stare at Darri's sister.

"How?" she demanded.

"Drowned," Callie said.

The two ghosts faced each other for a long, silent moment. Darri was uncomfortably aware of just *how* silent it was. She knew they were surrounded; she had seen the shadows, heard the whispers. But now she could not hear a single breath except her own.

"Well, then," Clarisse said. Her voice was suddenly brisk, and the fuzzy edges of her body sharpened back into clearly defined lines. Her hair fell heavily against her shoulders. "This is more complicated than I thought."

"So it appears," Callie said.

Clarisse smiled at her, baring straight-edged teeth. "Well beyond me."

"We can simplify it," Callie said.

"By walking away? No, I don't think so. He already knows you're here. He'll decide what to do with you."

"He?"

But Clarisse had already turned and swept into the darkness at the back of the cavern. The air behind her shimmered vaguely, and a faint unreal sound, like the shadows of sighs, followed her into the blackness. Darri turned to the cave entrance and found it blocked by a wall of bones, skeletons crushed together into an impassable barrier, their empty-eyed skulls leering at her.

Callie looked at Darri and rolled her eyes. Feeling vaguely comforted by that, and also knowing that she had no choice, Darri stooped and pulled the disguised silver dagger out of her boot. It was a comfortable weight in her hand as she followed her sister and Clarisse over the slick, dimly lit stone and into the pitch-black passageway beyond it.

Varis found Darri's falcon in front of a cluster of bushes, happily ripping apart the corpse of a field mouse. A quick examination told him the falcon hadn't killed the mouse by itself, and from there it was fairly easy to find the entrance to the caves.

Varis let his own falcon go with faint regret, the motion making his injured shoulder clench. That was two birds sacrificed to whatever crazy ruse Darri had dreamed up this time. No matter how many years they spent in captivity, falcons were never really tamed. They would go wild in the blink of an eye, as easily and completely as if they had never sat on a man's arm or had their food given to them in cut-up pieces. Neither of these birds was ever coming back.

He hobbled his horse next to Darri's and wrenched the torch from the saddle pommel before pushing his way through the bushes. Once his eyes adjusted to the dimness, it took him only a few seconds to make out the faint trail of footprints on the rock floor. He followed them to where the cave bent into darkness. Faint glittering specks were scattered on the damp rock, barely discernible even when he lit the torch, but good enough. He smiled grimly.

The smile flattened into a hard line as he followed the trail deeper into the dank darkness of stone and earth. Where in this unnatural place was Darri going?

Chapter Thirteen

The farther they walked into the labyrinthine passage-ways, the more Darri felt the dead gather around her, filling the air with sibilant whispers that seemed imagined rather than heard. Her skin crawled, but she kept walking.

It was the hardest thing she had ever done. The death around her was thick enough to choke on; so clearly inhuman, so clearly *wrong*. Hundreds of human spirits, trapped forever beneath the earth, misshapen and confused by their unnatural confinement. She kept glancing sideways at Callie, who complicated what should have been clear. Her younger sister seemed no different. But Callie was a part of something twisted and evil, no matter how badly Darri wanted to forget that.

Invisible fingers stroked against her skin, worming

around her ankles and neck. Darri bit back a scream, knowing it was probably only her imagination—which wasn't helped by the way Clarisse insisted on floating several feet above the ground, body glowing with a faint white light. Darri tried to tell herself it looked silly, but it was hard to find anything amusing. Finally her unease got the better of her.

"Not to interfere with the mood you're trying to create," she snapped, "but could you just walk?"

Clarisse looked over her shoulder, hair floating about her face. "Why? Do you find this frightening?"

Darri chose not to answer.

"It's an easier way to travel," Clarisse said, "for those who are no longer made of earth."

"Is that what they're calling it these days?" Callie said.

"I should be asking *you* that, shouldn't I? You're more recently dead than I am."

Callie said nothing, and Clarisse moved suddenly back to float beside her. On the other side from Darri, fortunately, or Darri might have either screamed or attacked her. Or both.

"So," Clarisse said conversationally, "how long have you been dead? And why didn't you let us know?"

"It was a struggle," Callie said dryly. "You know how I hate keeping things from you."

"Don't you think Jano will be hurt that you've kept it from *him*?"

"He tried to kill my family. We can consider the score settled."

Callie's voice had an edge that surprised Darri. Even Clarisse shot Callie a startled glance before going on, in a marginally more sober voice, "How do you like it so far?"

Callie looked sideways at Darri, then away, too swiftly for Darri to react. "I don't," she said.

"You'll become accustomed to it."

"I don't intend to have time for that," Callie said.

"One of those, are you?" Clarisse shook her head reprovingly. "That's not the right attitude."

"What is the right attitude?" Darri cut in, knowing it wasn't smart. "To float around making cryptic pronouncements and vague threats, pretending you like being dead?"

"Of course I like it," Clarisse said, eyes widening. "Death is immortality." She smiled and ran her hands over her hair. "I thought it would be nice to give it a try."

"It's not a *try*," Darri said. "There's no going back from what you are."

"I don't want to go back." When Clarisse let her hands drop, her hair was glowing, adding more light to the dance of shadows along the walls. "You won't want to go back either, once you know the secrets of the dead."

That was directed at Callie, who jerked her shoulders and said, "Nobody's seen fit to let me in on the secrets of the dead."

"That's because they don't know you *are* dead." Clarisse came to a stop and swirled slowly in midair to face them, her gown flaring out and settling against her legs. "But now that I know, I'm happy to complete your education."

Darri stopped too, so suddenly it threw her off balance; her foot went out from under her and she sat down hard on the slippery ground. The dagger flew out of her hand and clattered to a stop several yards away. Her face flushed as she scrambled to her feet, but Clarisse was too focused on Callie to take time out for mockery.

"Your people say death is freedom, that dead spirits join the wind, no longer human but more free than when they were alive. You say we are the trapped ones. I say you are *wrong*. What is the value of being part of the wind, just another breath of air among thousands? Of no longer being you?"

Darri's muscles were clenched so tight they trembled, but Callie merely sighed. "Assuming you have a point, could you get to it soon?"

"My point is that you shouldn't be so ready to throw away your existence. You're dead now, and truly one of us. You no longer have to think like a Raellian."

"Even the Ghostlanders," Darri snapped, "want vengeance, don't they? Don't *you*?"

"Of course I do." Clarisse looked at her with such focused fury that Darri fought the urge to step back. Then Clarisse's face smoothed out, and she smiled. "But I can control it. And when the man who killed me dies, it will become easier to ignore."

"You *know* who killed you?" Callie said. Darri glanced at her. The rapt attention was gone, and Callie was now staring at Clarisse with genuine horror. "You know, and you haven't done anything about it?"

"It wasn't easy," Clarisse said smugly. "I remained down here for two years, out of sight of my murderer, until the urgency of the desire passed. I devoted myself to serving the Defender, to learning to control the powers of the dead."

"The reason we *have* those powers," Callie said, "is to avenge ourselves!"

"You're such a child." Clarisse shook her head almost fondly. "Do you truly think all the ghosts in this castle are here because they failed? There are many of us who hold off the desire for vengeance, who fight for our existence. It's not easy, being dead. But it's not so easy being alive either. Is it, Callie?"

Darri waited for Callie's response. When none came,

she looked sideways at her sister, and saw Callie's throat working.

"It's not the same," Darri snapped, almost spitting out the words. "Just because some of you want it, that doesn't make it right. You shouldn't exist, not any of you. This was *done* to you. And if you weren't lying to yourselves, not one of you would believe your existence is worth it."

"But we do believe it." Clarisse slid her fingers through her hair. "All of us, even those who aren't strong enough to take what they desire. Tell the truth, Callie. What do you really want—to keep your body and your mind and your daily pleasures, or to cross the line into a darkness you don't know? Now that you're dead, are you really no longer afraid to die?"

There was a moment of silence. When Callie finally spoke, her voice was shaky. "Of course I'm afraid. But that's a weakness. To be controlled by fear."

It sounded like a question, not a statement. Darri tensed all over, and Clarisse rolled her shoulders languidly.

"And being controlled by someone else's reasons for allowing our existence—is that not a weakness?" Clarisse shrugged. "Do as you will. But nobody controls *me*."

"Nobody?" whispered the darkness around them.

Darri screamed, then felt hot shame wash through her. Even Clarisse looked startled. Callie flinched, but recovered swiftly and turned, eyes darting among the shadows. Following her gaze, Darri saw it come to rest on a patch of darkness that seemed somehow deeper and blacker than the rest.

"I know you," Callie said.

The voice came, not from the place she was looking at, but from behind them. "I assure you, you do not."

Despite firm intentions not to, Darri shrieked again. Callie's face went white, but she spun and said evenly, "I mean that I've met you before. You sent me to save my siblings when Clarisse and Jano were trying to kill them."

Darri could not force herself to face what her sister was talking to. She tried, but the sound of that raspy voice sent an irresistible, uncontrollable fear over her, as if she were still a child trying to believe there were no monsters hiding in the dark.

She managed to turn her head slightly, but could not bring herself to look over her shoulder; and because of that, she saw Clarisse's face go slack with shock when Callie spoke.

A number of things suddenly became clear. The silver dagger in Jano's hand, when he attacked them on the hunt. Clarisse, sneering, "What did you think you would achieve by coming here?"

You sent me to save my siblings.

She spun around. In front of them, the blackness was not deeper but rather more blurred, moving and shifting. A moment ago her stomach would have tightened with terror; now her fear was swamped by rage. She saw in front of her, not a monster, not a ghost, but something much simpler. Her sister's murderer.

"Why would you do that," she said, "when you were the one who told them to kill us?"

The darkness drew itself upward. Darri's breath ran through her, swift and cold and clear. "You didn't send Callie to save us. You sent her so she would be killed with us. That's why Jano had a silver dagger. To use on Callie."

"No," Callie said. "He didn't know—" She stopped.

"No one knew you were dead," Darri agreed grimly. "Except the person who killed you."

Callie made a sudden, jerking motion, but no sound.

"It had to be done," the darkness whispered. "You are, all of you, more dangerous than you know. You are pawns in the hand of someone much more powerful than yourselves."

"When haven't we been?" Darri said. She moved two steps to the side, so that she was standing next to the dropped dagger. Darri had never yet killed anyone, but she had grown up on stories of killings brave and true;

the *yet* had always been there, just waiting for a reason. "My sister," she said, very quietly. "You took my sister from me."

"She's still here," Clarisse said. "Don't you understand? We mean different things when we say 'dead.'"

"My sister is *dead*," Darri snarled, and she knelt and rose the way she had been taught. If you did it right, you would never be off balance. She did it right. The dagger was in her hand, ready to be thrown.

Clarisse shouted a warning. Darri threw.

The dagger struck *something*, point first. It made the wrong sound, though, piercing something softer than skin, and all at once the cavern was filled with light.

A man stood before them, the hilt sticking out of his chest. His form was more blurred than Clarisse's, but he was undeniably a man, and a rather unremarkable-looking one: black hair, pale skin, a long face, and an aquiline nose.

Darri had nothing else silver on her, but she balanced on the balls of her feet, ready to fight, *eager* to fight. The Defender looked like a man, and that sent a wave of relief through her despite the silver dagger jutting harmlessly from his chest. She could fight him. Even if she was bound to lose, she could fight him. She couldn't fight a shifting nonentity of darkness.

The man took hold of the dagger, pulled it out of his

chest, flipped it around, and offered her the hilt.

Darri hesitated, her instincts screaming at her to take it.

The man smiled at her. "Did you never wonder," he asked, in a quite normal voice, "*why* silver hurts ghosts?"

"I've spent the last couple of nights around dead people," Darri said tersely. "My sense of what's questionable may be a little off."

"Ghosts can't bear the touch of silver because I made them that way," the Defender said. "A safeguard, built into my spell to keep them from being unkillable. The safeguard does not apply to me."

The silence was broken by Callie. "*Your* spell?"

"Of course." The man's smile widened—but it looked, all at once, nothing like a smile. Nothing like a human expression, for all that it was on a human-looking face. "I created the spell, and was the first person brought back from death by its power. I am older than you can imagine, and more powerful. Age does not hurt me, nor silver."

"Nor sunlight," Callie whispered.

Darri, somehow, was no longer in a fighting pose. She didn't know when that had happened. Instead of returning to it, she reached for Callie's hand, and was surprised when her sister accepted her grasp. Callie's hand was small and cold and trembling.

"Why kill me?" Callie asked. "Why wait four years and then kill me?"

The Defender made an irritated gesture and said nothing.

"Why *drown* me?"

"The spell is bound in the earth of our country. That's why it only works within the borders of this land." The Defender grimaced. "I thought it might not work on water. I know better now."

Darri drew back in disgust, but Callie didn't flinch.

"Then why are you doing *nothing*?" Callie shouted. "I'm here now. You have a silver dagger in your hand. Why not kill me *now*?"

Darri should have been proud of her sister's bravery. But she knew, despite Callie's defiant tone, that this wasn't a challenge. It was a plea.

"Killing you now would accomplish nothing," the Defender said.

Now, but not on the hunt. The difference, then, must be that now Darri knew her sister was dead.

Darri opened her mouth, then closed it, the taste of unsaid words bitter on her tongue. *You could kill me too. Then no one would know.* She should be willing to die, if it would set her sister free. She owed Callie that.

The words wouldn't make a difference. The Defender must already be aware of the possibility. Just as her father had always been aware that he could have sent his older daughter instead of the younger. Even if she had said to him, "Send me instead," it wouldn't have changed anything.

So she had told herself, night after night, as she woke from dreams of her sister being devoured by darkness. It was true, but the truth didn't help. She still should have said it.

This time I'll do better, she thought. But before she could draw in breath to speak, Callie whispered, "I can't take vengeance on you. I can't do anything to you. I'm looking straight at you, and I know you killed me, and there's nothing I can do about it. Do you know what that's *like*?"

"I'm sorry," the Defender said. He sounded sincere.

Callie choked out a sob. Darri gripped her hand, feeling more helpless than she ever had in her life.

"I'll be unavenged forever," Callie said, with such despair that even the Defender frowned.

"You'll grow accustomed to it," he said. "They all do, in time."

The sound that came from Callie this time was almost inhuman; not ghostly, but the cry of a wounded animal. She tore her hand from Darri's grip and threw herself bodily at the black-haired man.

The light vanished. In the darkness, Darri heard a thud, and a shriek. And then, as she made her way across the now-empty ground and knelt beside Callie, the broken sounds of her sister's sobs.

Varis had just reached the end of the glittering gray trail when he realized that someone was following him.

He covered his torch immediately and stood still. He heard nothing; the silence was so intense it was practically a sound, more terrible even than the darkness. That meant either that the other person had stopped as well, or—

"Darkness doesn't mean much to ghosts, you know," Kestin said.

—or hadn't been making any sound in the first place. Varis uncovered his torch just as the prince rounded a curve in the passage behind him. Despite himself, Varis's first reaction was not wariness but relief; relief that he was not alone, here in the darkness and silence beneath the earth. "You can see in the dark?"

"So it seems." Kestin smiled. "Every day I discover a new advantage to being dead."

Varis couldn't tell if the statement was meant to be bitter or not. He chose to believe it was, because that was less disturbing. "Your Highness," he said coolly. "How did you get here?"

"I wanted to find out what your sister was up to, so I had my men bring me in my litter. And I ordered everyone else not to follow me on pain of death, which gives us perhaps half an hour before they follow me anyhow. So we shouldn't stand around talking." Kestin moved closer. The torchlight flickered over him, but he cast no shadow. "How do you know where to go?"

Varis hesitated, but couldn't think of a reasonable lie. He gestured at the ground, where flecks of steel glittered when the torchlight hit them.

Kestin raised his eyebrows. "Ingenious. The steel is coating silver, I assume?"

"Of course not," Varis said. "That would be a breach of our agreement."

"Of course not," Kestin echoed, without the slightest trace of sarcasm. "Why did you stop walking?"

"The trail ended. Either the metal powder ran out, or she sheathed her dagger."

"I doubt your sister would do something that stupid. There are ghosts everywhere in these caves."

Varis looked around nervously, then tried to cover it by drawing his own silver dagger with his left hand. He had been carrying the torch in his right, despite his injured shoulder, in preparation for doing just that. "But Darri wouldn't know about them. Where are they?"

"You won't see them. These caves are where the older ghosts go when they grow tired of being among the living. Most of them have forgotten what their bodies look like."

Varis's left hand tightened on his dagger, and Kestin said, "They can, however, still be killed; that dagger will make them nervous. You should probably put it away before I call them."

"Before you what?"

"It's up to you, though." Kestin shrugged and, without appreciably raising his voice, said, "Tell me where the foreigner went."

A sound like wind rushed past Varis, though there was no wind. Kestin nodded and walked past Varis into the darkness.

Varis almost turned and went the opposite way. He felt ice cold down to his bones. The wind had stirred shadows that slid past the walls, wavering over the curves and cracks in the rocks. He swallowed hard, looked straight ahead, and followed the dead prince. He did not sheathe his dagger.

Kestin didn't look back, and Varis did not try to move up beside him. They walked in silence down several turns in the passageway, through a large cavern that seemed full of malevolent awareness, and finally came to an open area surrounded by surreal rock formations. There Kestin stopped, and Varis kept moving until he stood beside the dead prince. His grip on the dagger was so tight his fingers hurt. He would be the happiest man alive on the day he rode out of this cursed land.

"Where are we?" he asked.

"Beneath the castle by now, I suspect." Kestin sounded distracted. "There are ways to get into these caverns from the castle. None of the living know that. Even the newly dead aren't told."

"Then how do you know?"

"I'm the prince of the dead." Kestin trailed his hand along an outcropping of rock. "Have you not realized yet how powerful I am? Do you think any ghost could command the elder dead as I just did?"

A soft sound swirled around them, suggestive of mirthless laughter. Kestin chuckled. "I suppose that explains why you would come here with me, alone and surrounded by the dead. I thought it foolishly brave. But you didn't realize how dangerous it was, did you?"

Varis changed his mind: the day he *conquered* Ghostland would be the happiest of his life. "I don't see my sister."

"They're in the shadows."

"Then why—"

"I'm not sure why. I suspect it's just your usual flair for the dramatic. Isn't it, Clarisse?"

Despite what was obviously his best effort, his voice choked a little on her name. As he said it, Clarisse stepped out of the shadows, so beautiful she looked unreal. It was a moment before Varis noticed both his sisters trailing behind her, Darri's face even more sullen than usual, Callie's eyes red and swollen.

"Hello, Your Highness," Clarisse said, slowly sweeping her lashes down. "Imagine meeting you here."

"I know this is where you've been," Kestin said. "And you must have known I wouldn't allow foreigners to wander through these caves alone."

"Of course." She smiled. "But I wasn't talking to you."

Awkward silence filled the air between them until Varis broke it by turning to Callie. He noted that Darri's dagger was in its sheath, and wondered what had happened to convince her to put it away. "What are you doing here?"

His sisters exchanged glances. Callie said, "I wanted to talk to Darri without anyone knowing."

"Anyone," obviously, meant him. No one else could possibly care that two foreigners were talking to each other. Varis stepped away from Kestin. "And you had to come all the way down here to do it?"

"That wasn't their doing, I'm sure," Kestin almost snarled. Anger radiated from him palpably as he stared at Clarisse, but Varis doubted it was because of their presence in the caves. "What were you thinking, Clarisse? You know they shouldn't be here. They're alive."

Clarisse sat on a raised rock outcropping, using one hand to sweep her skirt around her legs and away from the ground. "Actually—"

Darri cut her off with no attempt at subtlety, and with a frightened look at Varis. "How did you find us?"

"Your dagger leaks," Varis said, unable to hide the smugness in his voice. Her eyes narrowed, and he said, "It was a reasonable precaution. I knew you would do something foolhardy, and apparently I was right. What were *you* thinking? Or is it naïve to assume you were thinking at all?"

"Clarisse," Darri snapped, "decided we should go looking for the Defender."

"And we found him," Callie added. At the very end of the sentence, her voice broke. She stepped backward, toward the edges of the cavern, so that the light didn't touch her face.

"The Defender," Varis repeated, and looked sideways at Kestin. The prince didn't notice. He was staring at Clarisse with his jaw clenched.

"It was a very informative encounter," Clarisse murmured, and the timbre of her voice pulled his gaze back toward her. She was looking straight at him, as if Kestin didn't exist; and she was, clearly, enjoying herself.

Varis turned to his sisters, noting the tight grimness of Darri's face. That expression never boded well, but for the first time in his life he knew how she felt. Until his own encounter with the Defender, he had thought it was stupid, the way she kept fighting even when she couldn't possibly win.

"I think," he said, "that we should get out of these caves."

"That *would* be a good idea," Clarisse said, crossing her ankles. "Of course, I'm the only one who knows the way. But perhaps if you ask nicely . . ."

"Don't be an idiot," Kestin snapped. "The dead will show me the way out."

She lifted an eyebrow at him. "Not if I don't want them to."

Kestin stepped back on one foot, as if preparing to draw a sword and lunge. "Why would they listen to *you*?"

"At the moment," Clarisse said, "I am the second most powerful ghost in existence."

Kestin didn't lunge. He stood completely still, staring at her with wide, dark eyes. Her tone was so cool and uncaring, as if she were talking to a stranger—or an enemy—that Varis couldn't help a pang of sympathy.

Kestin's voice was a strangled whisper. "Did you ever love me at all?"

"Do you still care?"

"I shouldn't have to." His hands knotted and unknotted. "You shouldn't *be* here."

She shrugged and looked away, leaving Kestin standing like an abandoned child in the center of the cavern. Darri took a step toward him, then stopped short. Her throat convulsed.

Varis didn't like that. He could feel the dead watching them, and he liked that even less.

"Did you know," Darri said, glaring at Clarisse, "that the Defender was going to kill Prince Kestin?"

The silence was long and frozen. Kestin's mouth worked for a moment. When he spoke, it was once again to Clarisse, not Darri. "Is that true?"

"It is," Clarisse said lightly, but *she* was speaking to Darri. The tension between the three was tangled enough to choke on. "He killed both of them. Congratulations on figuring that out. Have you figured out why yet? Or why you're here?"

Both of *who*? But Varis knew better than to ask. It was an odd feeling, to be excluded from a circle of knowledge, deemed not important enough to be given information. Darri must feel like this all the time.

"The Guardian," Callie whispered from the shadows, "was the one who brought me here. Not the Defender."

"But he brought us here for a reason," Varis said. "And that reason has something to do with the Defender. I think the two of them are on the verge of war."

"How perceptive." Clarisse rested her hands on her knees, stretching her shoulders back. "Except it's gone a bit farther than *the verge*. And it's not just them who are at war; it's their followers as well. The peace between the living and the dead is about to be broken." She laughed softly. "I would bet on the dead, if I were you."

Kestin drew in a breath, took another step toward her, then turned and strode instead to the other side of the cave. Just before he reached the shadows, he whirled again. "The peace is strained, yes. But not to the breaking point. If war was imminent, someone would have told me."

"Do you really think so?" Clarisse's eyes glinted. "You may be the prince of the dead, their long-awaited hope, but don't think they trust you completely. You're too new. You have too many ties to the living."

"We *all* have ties to the living." Kestin sliced his arm downward. "Friends, family, neighbors. The living and the dead live side by side, interconnected. We have for centuries. That's not going to change."

"Kestin," Darri said, and the familiar way she said his name made Varis's eyes narrow. But Kestin just looked at her, his eyes pitch-black against the shadows behind him.

"Think about it. If you're their long-awaited hope, what is it they're hoping for? As the first dead king of Ghostland, you are either a large step forward in the power of the ghosts, or the spark that ignites a conflict between the living and the dead. A conflict the dead would probably win. Either way, the Defender gains from your death."

Kestin reached out a hand, touching the rock wall as if to steady himself, though the rest of his body hadn't moved. "How could the Defender know my father would insist that I inherit? *I* didn't know. . . ."

"Your father had no choice," Varis said. "Not with Cerix as second-in-line. Haven't you ever wondered why Cerix is still alive, when so many of the dead must itch to make him one of them? The Defender probably commanded that he be left alone, just to ensure your father's choice."

"*Did* he?" Kestin asked Clarisse. "Is that why you haven't—"

"It's not why," Clarisse said sharply. "I follow orders only when it suits me." She stood abruptly, her skirt falling in folds against her legs. "But yes, Prince Varis is correct. The Defender commanded the dead to leave Lord Cerix alive."

Varis felt an irrational surge of pride; irrational because he shouldn't care what a dead girl thought, and also because it wasn't him, really, who had figured this out. It was Darri.

Darri, who knew things he did not. And had no real reason to share them with him.

He met his sister's gaze through the wavering torchlight, and felt again the sense of kinship that had made him give her the dagger. Well, the dagger had been partly a trick, but even so. Perhaps he shouldn't have been so quick to reject the thought of working with her.

"*Why?*" It was an anguished whisper; the dead prince was as still as a statue at the edge of the cave. "Why me, and why now?"

Clarisse shrugged. "You could always summon him and ask."

"Would he come?" Kestin said bitterly. "If I'm just a figurehead?"

"An important figurehead," she said, in a tone that was meant to sound soothing—but, judging by its mocking edge, not to actually *be* soothing. "The Guardian and the Defender both have a nostalgic respect for monarchy. It's one of the Defender's few weaknesses."

Kestin turned away; just a jerk of his head, but it put his face in shadows. Clarisse watched with her lips pursed. Varis did not recognize the expression on her face, but he knew it was neither love nor sympathy. She opened her mouth, and Darri interrupted swiftly, "His weaknesses?"

Clarisse shrugged. "Even immortal creatures have

weaknesses." Her lips flickered upward, briefly and bitterly. "But yes, Kestin, you could call him. And he might come. If you ask for his protection, he will certainly come."

"And then I could look at my murderer and be unable to do anything about it?" Kestin whipped his head around to face them and took two quick steps into the torchlight. Callie, still in the shadows, made a small whimpering sound. Varis looked over at her sharply, but he still couldn't make out her expression. She was so still and silent he had almost forgotten her; but she had always been that way, soft and weak and forgettable, especially in the face of Darri's fierceness.

"Do you still want to do something about it?" Clarisse pushed her hair back from her face with both hands; in the torchlight, her features were unearthly. "I would have thought you might have started enjoying your existence again, by now. Especially since you know I'm here to share it with you."

Kestin flinched as if she had hit him, and Darri's breath hissed between her teeth. She started toward the dead girl. Varis, recognizing her intent expression, grabbed her by the upper arm and pulled her to a stop. She shook him off, but didn't continue her advance.

Kestin glanced swiftly at Darri, then glared at Clarisse.

"You think that's what would resign me to this half-existence? The company of someone else who should be gone?"

"Then what would resign you to it?" Clarisse said softly.

"My duty," Kestin said. "To Ghostland."

Clarisse drew her hands down the back of her neck, letting her hair fall around her face again. "If you were interested in your duty, you wouldn't be running away from it. That you even considered allowing Cerix to take your place doesn't speak very well of your concern for your country, my dearest."

He flinched again, but this time he lifted his chin. "A ghost's first duty is to seek out his murderer."

Clarisse's eyes gleamed. "And now that you've found him?"

Kestin took a deep breath and drew his shoulders back. "Now I think it's time," he said, "that I accept my position as heir."

The air moved suddenly around them, little wisps and shimmers that made Varis's skin creep. In the shadows, the walls looked like they were dancing. Of course . . . the dead had been waiting for this. For Kestin to give up on vengeance, and become what they wanted him to be.

And now that he knew the Defender had killed him, he had no choice but to give up.

So much for marrying Darri to the king of Ghostland. Varis strove not to let his frustration show. There would be no royal wedding now . . . unless he could manage to spur Cerix into trying a coup. He would have to first figure out the chances for a coup's success, then decide which of Cerix's advisers would be amenable, then suggest Darri and the Raellian alliance as a goad. It was a stretch, even for him, but he might pull it off. . . .

Even if it meant placing both his sisters in the middle of a succession crisis. Chances were that at least one of them would be killed by the time the dust settled. That in itself wasn't so bad—any Raellian should be willing to die for her people—but if Darri was killed here, she would come back as one of *them*.

"When will you have the coronation?" Varis asked.

"I'll tell my father as soon as we get back," Kestin said, still watching Clarisse. "Knowing him, the coronation will be in just a few nights. He's been waiting a long time for this." He turned his head at last; it wasn't clear if he was speaking to Varis or Darri. "You will attend, won't you?"

"Of course," Varis said. "We wouldn't dream of leaving before then."

Now both his sisters were watching him, their eyes wide. He smiled at Darri reassuringly. His father wouldn't like this; he would be disappointed, and make that crushingly clear, when he learned how little Varis had managed to accomplish. But deep beneath the earth, in a place his father had never been, beset by complications his father could never have imagined, it didn't matter. Or at least, didn't matter enough.

"After the coronation, though, there is no further reason for us to stay." He met Prince Kestin's shadowed eyes. "We'll return to our own land the evening after. And we'll be taking Callie with us."

Chapter Fourteen

Kestin's coronation was a full-night affair. The celebration would begin at dusk with a play, to be followed by a banquet and dancing. Only at dawn, when all the celebrations were finished, would the coronation ceremony itself take place. According to castle lore, that custom had been instituted so that most of the nobility would be too drunk or exhausted to try to kill their new king.

Callie was determined to enjoy it. If there was anything the Ghostlanders knew how to do, it was throw a party; both the living and the dead waited months for celebrations like these. Two months ago, Callie would have been prepared to spend the evening doing nothing but having fun. There was, she told herself, no reason this evening should be different. No purpose in setting herself apart from the rest of the dead, who would be every bit as light-hearted as the living.

She was going to have to spend centuries emulating those ghosts, learning how to live—to pretend to live—with what she was. She might as well start now.

She spent a full hour on her appearance, donning a high-necked green gown and having a maid set her hair in a con-coction of braids and twirls so tightly elaborate it pulled at her scalp. Feeling appropriate and beautiful and *alive*, she opened the door to her room and found Darri waiting outside.

So much for a carefree evening. Callie said flatly, "You look nice."

It was only half a lie. Darri's gown was a marvelous dis-play of yellow silk and black lace. It just looked ridiculous on *her*.

"I have a plan," Darri said. "And I need your help."

Callie twisted her fingers in the edges of her sleeves, wondering what the odds were that what Darri needed help with was her hair. "Why?"

"I need you to tell me where to find the Guardian."

So much for that. "Why?"

"Because," Darri said, "he's the only one who could possibly kill the Defender."

Burial plots. Callie stepped out into the hallway and

closed the door behind her. "No. He couldn't. You heard what the Defender said, what he is. He can't be killed."

"If there's any chance—"

"Then I have to spend every moment of my existence chasing it down?" Callie found herself suddenly on the verge of tears. Her hair pulled painfully at her head. "And then face my death again, and again, every time it doesn't work? No."

Darri was silent for a moment, her fingers working at the lace on her skirts. Then she said, "You're giving up."

"I have no choice."

"You *do*." Darri reached out for her, an almost beseeching motion. "Callie, I understand. I mean, I don't—I could never understand—but I know this is not your fault. I know you're trapped. And if there's anything that can save you, anything at all—"

"But there isn't!" Callie started to turn away, then whirled. "Spirits, Darri. Do you know why I brought you to the caves?"

"To show me where you—" Her sister couldn't get out the word. And all of a sudden she couldn't meet Callie's eyes.

"Where I died," Callie finished. "So we could talk about how you could help me take vengeance on my killer. Because I wanted your help, yes; but also because I knew that was the only thing you *could* talk to me about, now that I'm this."

"That's not true," Darri whispered, but she said it weakly. "Callie, I'm not . . . I don't hate you. . . ."

"You just hate what I am."

"But so do you." Darri pushed her hair away from her face. "You begged the Defender to free you, back in the caves."

"I don't want to be what I am. But I don't hate it the way you do. I can bear it, if I must."

"Can you?" Darri said harshly.

Callie looked away. When she spoke, her voice was a whisper. "They all bear it. All the rest of the ghosts. They're as content as they can be. They laugh and dance and paint and . . . and sometimes, they're happy."

"They believe they're happy," Darri said grimly.

"What's the difference between believing you're happy and *being* happy?"

"The difference is that it's not real."

"Because *you* say it's not. But it's not for you to decide whether they're happy, Darri. It's not your choice."

"It's not a choice at all. It won't last, Callie. They'll be like the ghosts in the caves, in the end. They won't even remember they're human anymore."

"But that's in the end," Callie said. "In hundreds of years."

"And in the meantime, you can pretend along with the rest of them. Is that what you want?"

"Enough!" Callie hissed, with such force that Darri actually stepped back. "Of course I don't want it. I don't want any of this. I never did. But I'm here, and I had to accept that, and now I'm dead, and I have to accept *that*, because there is nothing else for me." She pushed herself away from the door, stalking past her sister and several steps down the hall. She had intended to keep going; instead she whirled in a swirl of green silk. "How dare you lecture me on what I should do. It's not *you* who's trapped in death! You're the one who stayed behind."

Darri went completely white. They stood there in the narrow hall, staring at each other, and Callie knew—with sudden, helpless humiliation—that she was going to cry.

"What are you talking about?" Varis said.

Both sisters jumped, and Callie flickered translucent as she turned. Varis was standing several yards behind her, dressed in black silk and purple velvet. How much had he heard? He was looking at them half-quizzically, half-suspiciously, but with no horror on his face. Perhaps he had thought her flicker was a trick of the light.

"Nothing," Darri said. "I mean—um—at the banquet—we were thinking that—"

"I'm dead," Callie said.

Darri choked. Varis kept looking at Callie, giving no indication that he had heard what she said.

"I'm a ghost," Callie said savagely, wanting to wipe that blank expression off his face. Being angry at Varis was so much easier than being angry at Darri; her rage was clean, uncomplicated. "I was killed a few weeks before you arrived. Probably *because* you were about to arrive. I can't leave with you. After tonight, I'll never see you again."

Darri drew in her breath, but Varis just stood there. Then he walked past them, turned into the stairwell, and disappeared.

He didn't look at Callie as he passed them; didn't even move slightly to the side to give her space. It was as if she had ceased to exist.

No—not *as if*.

"Why did you do that?" Darri said angrily.

Callie shrugged, suddenly weary. "Why not? All I've been thinking about, all I've been caring about since the moment I died, is how you would react. You and Varis. Now you both know, so I don't have to worry about it anymore." She lifted her chin. "I can spend my time with the people who don't care."

"You'll still care," Darri said, her eyes flinty. "No matter how much they don't."

Callie tried to think of something cutting to say, and

couldn't. She was relieved when Darri broke the gaze and, without another word, turned on her heel and walked away in the opposite direction from Varis. Her shoes hit the floor like hammer blows.

Callie felt a prickling behind her eyes, which she fiercely willed away. This was it, now; this was what she was. Neither of her siblings would ever look at her without disgust again. Soon they would leave, and it wouldn't matter. She would be surrounded by people who thought there was nothing wrong with what she was.

And she would let them convince her. It would be easy, once Darri was gone.

The Ghostlanders, Varis thought, had an odd idea of what constituted fun. Not that *that* should have come as much of a surprise to anyone.

He sat in a room full of crowded wooden benches, watching a play called *The Betrayer*. King Ais had decreed that the play, about a pre-Ghostdawn princess who killed all her siblings and then her father, would be "instructive and entertaining" for their visitors. Not five minutes went by without someone being killed onstage. The other spectators around Varis seemed to enjoy this immensely.

Varis could barely follow the intricate plot of treachery and betrayal. He kept seeing Callie in her elaborate green dress, grown up and beautiful and gone. He didn't imagine for a second that she had said it just to shock him. She had told him the truth. She was dead. And the ease with which he accepted it told him that he had suspected it for some time, without even knowing it.

That was a shock, almost worse than what his sister had become. Everything depended on his discernment and judgment now, but his horror of the dead had caused him to stumble. Even the sharpest of minds couldn't pick up on a reality it was trying not to think about.

The reality was his dead sister, who still walked and talked and looked at him with wide, angry eyes. He should think about what it meant, how it affected his plans. If he was truly his father's son, that was what he would be doing.

Varis watched the play without seeing it and thought about nothing at all.

When the play ended, the audience streamed out toward the banquet hall in a frantic rush, as if they had all suddenly discovered that they were on the verge of starvation. Varis remained where he was for several moments, watching the empty stage, until someone coughed softly at his shoulder.

He turned around to find Clarisse standing behind him, pale as—well. The green eyes that met his were as large and liquid as ever, but tonight their brilliance seemed both faded and fake.

He stood and bowed to hide his expression, not sure whether it would be pity or triumph. Either way, she had best not see it. "My lady. I did not expect the honor of your company tonight."

"Why not?" Her laughter was carefree and forced. "I do enjoy a ball."

She was lying, he thought, and she didn't even know it. Once, perhaps, she had enjoyed balls. Now she was just remembering that enjoyment. She had no idea what she had lost.

He wondered if he should pity her. If she didn't know, did it matter?

Clarisse moved closer to him, with a rustle of silk and a waft of spicy perfume. He looked down at her flirta-tiously tilted head and said gently, "Lord Cerix will be here tonight."

She went so still she stopped breathing—stopped for far longer than a living girl could have. Then she said, "Why are you telling me that?"

The scent of her perfume was suddenly overpowering. She had to be doing that on purpose.

Varis's heart pounded. He wondered why Cerix had killed her: a real plot she had been part of, a plot she had been pretending to take part in, or just because she had taunted him once too often? He supposed it didn't matter.

"I thought, rather than stay here and see him, you might be willing to meet me in my chambers. The wine would be better, and we could enjoy it in private."

"The wine is tempting," Clarisse said. "But I do want to dance."

"So will Cerix."

Her eyes went hard, and for a moment he thought she was going to attack him. Instead, she smiled. "I can stay away from him. I have excellent self-control. But after the first few dances, I would enjoy some wine. . . ." She lowered her lashes and brushed her fingertips across her lips.

Varis bowed again, and when he straightened she was gone.

Chapter Fifteen

Callie, watching her brother walk out of the makeshift theater, didn't realize Jano was behind her until he tapped her shoulder. She turned, then went still when she saw who it was. They stared at each other in silence for several moments. Jano looked incongruously genteel in a brocade green overcoat, ruffled sleeves, and a high pleated collar—like a child playing dress-up.

"Well," Jano said finally. "It seems there's something you forgot to mention to me."

So Clarisse had told him. Callie drew in her breath and tried to think of something to say. Finally she whispered, "I'm sorry."

"Why?" Jano said, with genuine curiosity.

"For not telling you. It's not . . . it's not that I didn't want

you to know. I just didn't want to say it out loud."

"It will get better, you know." Jano gestured to a passing serving girl, snatched two pastries off her tray, and offered one to Callie. "You'll learn to pretend. We do it so well, here in this castle. We busy ourselves with parties and hunts so we have no time to think. It's the only way we can bear being what we are."

He was smiling at her with calm pity, and suddenly she was angry; a hot anger that dried out the tears. She took the pastry from him and bit into it savagely, her mouth filling with spicy sweetness. Even though she was dead and shouldn't be able to taste anything.

"Are the living so different?" she asked.

"No." Jano popped a pastry into his mouth. Flaky dough trickled from his lips as he spoke. "No, not at all. But the living don't have to justify being here. They belong here."

"So do we," Callie said defiantly, after she had swallowed. "There's nothing wrong with being a ghost." She had never said it before, and the words felt wrong leaving her mouth. She didn't believe them.

But she had better start believing them.

Jano laughed. "Oh, you have been here awhile, haven't you? Long enough to believe what they all spend so much energy pretending." He wiped his mouth with his sleeve. "Let me tell you what you will know, Callie, when you've been dead for hundreds of years. Dead is *dead*. Every second that you're dead, every second that you know it, you die all over again. Watching your life escape from your grasp, over and over and over. Parties and banquets will only distract you for so long before you have no choice but to face it. And that's when you go mad."

"Which, apparently, you have," Callie snapped.

He laughed even longer this time. "Oh, no. I'm close, but not quite there. When I go mad, Callie, you'll know. I won't be able to hold onto this human form anymore. I won't be able to bear the presence of the living, when I hate them so much for having what I never will again. I'll disappear, but I won't be at peace, I won't be at rest, I won't be free. I will be hiding beneath the earth, with the other ghosts, dying again and again and again." He stepped so close she could feel his breath on her face; except of course he didn't have to breathe, so he was doing that on purpose. "That's where the spell is, chaining us here no matter how badly we want to go. That's where I'll be, close to the spell, clinging to my chains because they're all I have left."

By the time he finished speaking, she was yards away from him, her back pressed against a round table. She dropped the rest of the pastry to the floor. He didn't move closer, but he pinned her with his gaze. "Did I ever tell you how I died, Callie?"

Mute, she shook her head.

"My mother did it."

"Your—"

"I fell off a horse, and the wound got infected. The doctors told her it was too late to save me . . . but she didn't want to lose me. So she killed me."

Callie tried to step even farther back, and the pastry crunched under her foot. "But . . . if she was the one who killed you, and you knew it, then didn't you want to . . ."

"Yes."

So much anguish filled that one word that Callie felt a surge of pity. She said, very quietly, "Did you refrain for her sake, or for yours?"

"For hers." Jano watched another servant go by with a tray of fruit, then turned back to her. "I never asked her to make me a ghost. But I was all she had. And then when she died, my chance was gone."

"I'm sor—"

"I should have realized it sooner," Jano said. "I could have had my vengeance and died in truth, if I hadn't clung so tightly to the illusion that I loved her. This is what death is: not having to love anyone." He grimaced. "It's why Clarisse is so glad to be dead. More than anything, she wanted to be free of the people she once loved. And the living are never free."

Callie's fingernails dug into her palms. "The dead are?"

He smiled, faintly and bitterly. "Not noticeably."

After that, they stood in silence until Jano spotted another tray of pastries and headed after it. Callie let out a long, shaky breath. She pressed the back of her hand to her eyes, and when she uncovered them, Jano was nowhere to be seen.

I won't be at peace, I won't be at rest, I won't be free. Callie grabbed a goblet of wine from the table behind her and downed it in one long swallow. It didn't help.

Dying again and again and again.

She would rather he had lied to her. She would rather he had let her become one of the unthinking masses, believing what everyone else believed. He would have, if he were truly her friend. But he was too long dead to be anyone's friend.

He didn't kill me on the hunt, she reminded herself. But that was when he had thought she was alive, that she could be killed, or saved. He had, she realized suddenly, not turned away because he didn't want her dead. He just hadn't wanted her to become *this*. What he was. What she was, now.

What she would be forever. And no one, not even Darri, could change it.

It didn't matter that Callie wouldn't help her. It was better, in fact. Darri had a plan, and it was one that Callie wouldn't like very much.

248

She watched Kestin, who was standing near the dais smiling graciously, exchanging greetings with the stream of nobles who came up to him. He looked very regal in gold-trimmed black velvet, his stance as carefree as if this was just another of the castle's endless parties. As always, he looked more alive than most of the people around him, with a glowing vibrancy that made it hard to believe he could no longer walk in sunlight.

Even so, Darri could barely manage to keep her focus on him, to keep from looking around the banquet hall for Callie. She couldn't wipe from her mind the expression on Varis's face when Callie told him the truth: the blankness of disbelief, the refusal to recognize something too horrible to be true. She had felt the same way when she first found out the truth about her sister.

She still felt the same way.

"My lady Darriniaka," someone said behind her, and Darri turned to face a lanky man with over-oiled red hair and a fine sheen of sweat covering his face. "I have long looked forward to meeting you."

And Darri had long wondered when Cerix would make his move. He could not have chosen a worse time. "My lord," she said politely.

He smiled at her, coming far too close and giving Darri an up-close view of several newly erupted pimples.

She resisted the urge to back away, and the even stronger urge to stab him in the stomach. "You are as beautiful as they say."

You've known what I look like for days, you idiot. Darri suddenly changed her mind about being polite. This could work for her, if she played it right. "As who says?"

He blinked. "I'm sorry?"

"If there's someone in this court who thinks I'm beautiful, I'd like to know about it."

"*I* think you are beautiful, Lady Darriniaka." He actually put one hand over his heart. "The most beautiful woman I have ever seen."

"Then there's a problem with either your memory or your eyes."

Momentary anger marred his ardent expression. People within earshot were starting to snicker. "Do you not know who I am, my lady?"

"Of course I know." Darri copied his moonstruck expression as best she could. "You're Prince Kestin's heir."

The snickers stopped. People were listening more closely now. Darri glanced across the room and saw Varis scowling at her. Apparently he didn't approve of her taking sides.

Which was merely a side benefit.

Though if he was that upset *now*, she would have to make sure to sneak another look at him in a few minutes.

"Prince Kestin is dead," Cerix snapped, loud enough to be heard halfway across the hall. "I am his father's heir, not his."

Now many more people than Varis looked angry. It was unfortunate for Cerix's faction, really, that they had to back *Cerix*. This was why the Raellian method of confirming new leaders through combat made so much sense.

"Prince Kestin is not dead," Darri said, as loudly and stupidly as she could. "He's standing right there. And I wish to dance with him." She turned her back on Cerix and marched across the dance floor to Kestin, whose dark eyes were fixed on her. Unlike the other people in the hall who were watching her—which was, by now, most of them—he looked amused.

He also, fortunately, had picked up enough of what was going on to bow and hold out his hand. She took it without thinking, and it was warm and callused in hers; warm enough to let her pretend it was a living hand. Darri followed him onto the center of the dance floor and realized abruptly the first flaw in her hastily conceived plan: she didn't know how to dance.

Considering what she was about to do, the prospect of looking like an idiot in front of the court shouldn't have bothered her. Nevertheless, it did. She considered asking Kestin for help, and realized that looking like an idiot in front of him would bother her even more.

Well, *that* was going to be a problem.

She concentrated on moving in more or less the same direction as the prince. That was just about all she could manage; the same speed was out of her reach, and moving her feet the way he did was completely beyond the realm of possibility.

Kestin raised his eyebrows, and she was mortified to feel herself blush. Then he stepped forward and put one arm around her waist.

That was better. She barely had to move at all, with him guiding her so closely. But she was unbearably tense, and she couldn't even tell if it was because he was dead or because he felt so alive.

Kestin smiled at her. From mere inches away, his smile was devastating; and Darri's heart, which seemed to have forgotten that Kestin was dead, sped up. "Thank you. I was hoping for a dance."

"With me? Or with Clarisse?" The smile vanished, and Darri bit her lip. "I'm sorry. I didn't mean—"

"You should warn your brother." Kestin was clearly trying to sound dispassionate, but the words came out biting. He lifted her into a turn, then set her down on the floor. "Clarisse likes to play games."

The thought of Varis needing to be warned should have

been funny. Instead, it made Darri irritable. "So does he. And unfortunately, women find my brother irresistible."

Kestin lifted an eyebrow. "Unfortunately for whom?"

"For the women."

He laughed, clearly despite himself, and almost missed the next turn. Darri staggered very slightly when he put her down, and glanced around for her brother. She was just in time to see him leaving the hall. Which was probably just as well.

"Clarisse can take care of herself," Kestin said. "And it would be hard for her to take your brother seriously. She'll be around for centuries after his corpse has crumbled into dust."

Is that what you're hoping? This time, she didn't say it; she had no reason to be cruel to Kestin. But he must have seen her thoughts on her face, because his lips thinned as he followed the movements of the dance, pushing her away from him and then pulling her to him again. His hands were firm around her waist.

He's *dead*, Darri told her heart, which ignored her. Deciding to ignore it in turn, she said, "I'm sorry."

"I'm not," he said, so low she might not have heard him if he wasn't pressed so close to her. "It makes it easier, to let her go . . . again. It's just difficult, when I thought I was done grieving for her years ago."

His mouth was right against her ear . . . and yet she couldn't feel his breath. Suddenly there was no escaping the fact that he was dead, and it was all she could do not to pull away with such force he would go spinning across the floor. She waited until the dance pulled them apart before responding. "You didn't know then that she was still here."

"No, I didn't." Kestin leaped, bowed, and grabbed her waist, all at the same time. Darri didn't even try to follow that step. "But now that I know . . . it shouldn't cancel out all the grieving. It shouldn't be so hard, all over again. She's a part of my past, except she's still here." They stepped sideways, three times, and then turned. When he let go of her waist, his face was drawn and tired. "That's what all the ghosts are, truly. Memories made flesh, our dead forbidding us to forget them. Their presence is not easy for the living."

Your presence, Darri thought, but luckily the dance turned them away from each other just then, so Kestin didn't see her expression. When they faced each other again, he was smiling forcefully, and she knew the subject of Clarisse was over. She couldn't say she regretted it.

"I mean it, though. These have been the most enjoyable few minutes of the ball." His smile widened, and it was just for her, driving all thoughts of Clarisse from her mind. "Cerix will now be your lifelong enemy. Should I thank you for your support?"

"Probably not," Darri said regretfully.

The smile turned into a chuckle; he thought she was being coy. The music swelled, making the moment suitably dramatic. Darri turned out of his arms, stepped back, and, with a flourish more graceful than anything she had managed thus far, drew the dagger hidden within the folds of her sleeve.

Chapter Sixteen

The night was well underway, and Callie was still spending most of the party fighting tears. Jano's glum pronouncements, Darri's occasional half-angry glances, and Varis's refusal to look at her all made it impossible to pretend this was just a party. She felt centuries old.

She tried not to think about Darri, now stumbling around the dance floor in Kestin's arms. Darri, who didn't understand and didn't want to. Darri, still trying to change what couldn't be changed.

It didn't work. She kept catching herself looking at Darri, and wrenching her eyes away, until the moment she saw her sister draw a blade in the middle of the dance floor.

The dancing came to an immediate halt. Callie dropped

her goblet, and was dimly aware of wine soaking through her dance slippers. Darri stood there, slim and deadly in her lacy yellow gown, her face set and her dagger pointed straight at Kestin's throat.

The music stopped. The movement stopped. *Everything* stopped, including Callie's heart. *Oh, graveyards. Darri...*

Darri said, loud enough for the whole court to hear, "Summon the Guardian."

Kestin stared down, puzzled, at the blade resting on his throat. At first glance, it looked like steel, but there were uneven patches where silver clearly shone through. When he looked up at Darri, he still didn't look frightened. He looked . . . hurt. "What makes you think he would come? I'm not alive, remember?"

"Clarisse said he would come if you called." Darri's arm was rock steady, the dagger unwavering. "Let's test that out. Call him."

Kestin's eyes narrowed. "Or what? You'll kill me?"

"That about sums it up, yes."

"I don't believe you," Kestin said flatly.

"Why? Because we dance together so well?" Darri's face was all lines and angles, brown skin stretched taut over jaw and cheekbones. "You have no idea what I'll do, Prince Kestin. Especially considering the fact that I wouldn't be killing you. *You're already dead.*"

She hissed that last sentence with such viciousness that Callie felt it like a slap. So, judging by the way his head jerked up, did Kestin.

"You would be killing me," he said, his face tight, "no matter how hard you tell yourself otherwise. You wouldn't be dancing with me, or talking to me, if my being *dead* meant the same thing in this land as it does in yours."

Darri moved the blade closer to his throat, not enough to touch, but enough that a deep breath would bring his skin into contact with the edge.

Kestin acted as if he hadn't noticed. "I'm here now," he said fiercely. "If you move that blade much farther, I no longer will be. I'll be gone. Because you'll have killed me. I don't believe you want to do that."

Darri's face twitched. "It doesn't matter. I'll do it anyhow."

"For your sister? I am sure you would." Kestin's eyes narrowed into slits. "So allow me to point out that it won't help you. Once I am dead, I cannot call the Guardian."

Their eyes met. Kestin's face was rigid and strained; Darri's was frozen, for just a moment. Then she leaped away.

A dozen men drew their swords, but not one of them had guessed where she was going. Cerix drew a knife, too late; Darri snapped it out of his hand with one swift arm thrust, her sleeves flaring. It was a move Callie recognized. Varis had taught it to his sisters years ago, on a long rainy day.

Cerix lunged for the knife as it spun across the floor, a big mistake. Darri hit him on the side, sending him sprawling to the floor. With another deft motion, she grabbed the dagger by its hilt and pressed its edge to the side of Cerix's neck.

"I'll kill *him*, then," she said. "Unless you summon the Guardian now."

Kestin stared at her, mouth slightly open. Cerix made a high-pitched gasping noise, his arms splayed against the floor. Her sister, Callie reflected, had certainly succeeded in confusing everyone.

Kestin glanced across the dance floor. Callie followed his gaze and saw Clarisse, standing with her back to the wall, perfectly still. Kestin's voice broke the silence. "Don't."

Darri lifted her eyebrows mockingly. "Really? You don't want your rival dead? It would be a fitting punishment for killing her."

"No," Cerix gasped, craning his head to look up at the dead prince. "Let her do this, and you kill Clarisse more permanently than I did. You're doing it for *her*—it will be her vengeance."

"That seems debatable," Darri noted.

Kestin looked at his cousin with naked hatred, then

transferred his glare to Darri. "What makes you think I don't want her gone?"

"If you do," Darri said flatly, "then do nothing. And in a moment, she will be. Deep down, this is what she really wants, isn't it? To be avenged?"

Kestin looked across the dance floor again. Clarisse's face and form were so blurred that it was impossible to make out her expression. Callie felt a moment of mean satisfaction: obviously, Clarisse didn't dare get close enough to intervene, for fear that she would give in to the urge to kill Cerix herself. She was helpless. She could do nothing but watch.

"She doesn't want to be gone," Kestin said finally, his eyes still on Clarisse. "It doesn't matter what I want. Or what I think she should want. Let him go, and I'll do what you ask."

"Call him first," Darri hissed, and all at once the Guardian was there, swift and silent despite his heavy armor. He pushed two gaping men to the side on his way to his prince—one started to shout in outrage, then stopped short when he realized who had pushed him. The other hit his head on a table and lay crumpled on the floor.

Darri straightened as the Guardian approached, though she kept her dagger trained on Cerix. "Thank you," she said, so politely that the people around Callie relaxed slightly, assuming the crisis was over.

Callie knew better. When Darri got polite, that was when things were at their worst.

Cerix spluttered and rolled to the side. Darri glanced down, tracking him with her knife, then looked up at the Guardian. "I will release him for the answer to a question."

"I don't want you to release him," the Guardian said. "He's a murderer. And his rabble-rousing endangers us all."

Kestin made a strangled sound. The Guardian said, without looking at him, "She's not doing it for *you*. It's not vengeance; it won't end Clarisse's existence."

"You don't know that," Kestin said, spitting out the words. "It's not your life you're playing games with. You have no right to take that risk for her."

"It's not a *life* I'm playing with at all." The Guardian looked at Darri and inclined his head. "Kill him, and then I'll answer your question."

Darri's face set. The crowd around Callie drew back; for all that they were surrounded by death, for all that they stabbed and poisoned and murdered, a cold-blooded slaughter in the middle of a ball was too much for them.

But Callie, like her sister, was a plains barbarian. She watched without flinching as Darri turned and slashed with the dagger, as the blood spilled out across the white marble floor and crept up the hem of Darri's pale yellow gown. And even before the echo of Cerix's scream had died, before his corpse had completely stopped writhing, Callie turned away. She slipped between the tables and out the door, making her escape while everyone else watched Cerix die.

For a ghost, the way from the banquet hall to the upper halls was easy: straight up through the ceiling. Several had been shooting up and down for fun, hoping to catch someone in an illicit assignation and then shout the news to the assembled crowd. Callie took the long way: through the crowd to the side doors of the hall, down the marble hallway where several assignations were in their beginning stages, and up the wide spiral staircase. It gave her time to think, but she didn't take advantage of that. When she reached the door to Varis's room, she rapped on it fast and hard, before any last-minute hesitations could change her mind.

Varis opened the door instantly. He had taken off his cloak, and looked rakishly disheveled in a black tunic. Behind him, in the center of his room, he had set up a small table with two goblets of wine.

"Expecting someone?" Callie said.

Varis gave her an unfriendly look, then—suddenly

remembering what she was—turned away. Callie saw him swallow hard and slowly turn back, his eyes coming to rest somewhere on her forehead. She made herself stand still, pretending she didn't care.

"What are you doing here?" Varis asked finally.

Callie walked past him and sat defiantly in one of the two chairs he'd set out, knowing it wasn't meant for her. She stretched out her legs, not quite sure why she was posturing, trying to ignore the way his eyes skimmed away from her face as he turned. "Darri just killed Lord Cerix."

Varis's eyebrow twitched—for him, the equivalent of his face going dead white. "She *what*?"

"In the middle of the dance floor. It was quite the attraction."

"Spirits," Varis muttered.

Callie took a deep breath. "She did it to get the Guardian's attention, because she thinks he can defeat the Defender. You have to help me stop her. She's going to get herself killed."

"You think I can stop Darri from doing something crazy? Things haven't changed that much since you left." Varis drummed his fingers on the wall behind him, then finally looked directly at her—for just a moment before his eyes skittered away. His voice was oddly subdued when he said, "Is *she* still . . . around?"

Judging from the hint of shame in her brother's voice, "she" meant Clarisse. "Yes."

Varis's shoulders relaxed, though he tried not to let it show, and Callie sat up straight. Maybe he didn't care about Darri, but Cerix's death had to have repercussions for whatever Varis was planning. Varis had never placed any person above the greater good of his tribe; Callie, unlike Darri, had always understood that about him. It made no sense that he suddenly cared more about an assignation than about their father's plans.

Unless this particular tryst was connected to those plans.

An awful suspicion blossomed in her mind. Keeping her eyes on Varis, she crossed her ankles, lifted the nearest goblet of wine, and swirled the dark red liquid in the glass.

"I know Clarisse is beautiful," she said. "But everything she says is a lie. You have no idea what she really wants from you." She raised the goblet to her lips.

With a speed she hadn't seen in years, Varis was at her side, lifting the goblet from her grasp. One red drop splashed over the side and landed on her sleeve; the rest of it sloshed wildly, barely missing the rim. By the time Varis put the goblet back down, his hand perfectly steady, the wine had settled into a gentle swirl.

"I didn't pour that for you," he said.

She tilted her head up, and their eyes met. He was angry, and irritated, and a little bit afraid. But behind all that, too implicit to even be noticeable—except that she would have noticed its absence—was a sense of kinship.

She was still his sister. And he knew it.

Varis wrenched his eyes away, and Callie was glad for that. She didn't even want to guess what might be in her own.

"How ungracious," she said. "Don't worry, I was just leaving. I wouldn't want to miss the coronation."

She got to her feet, thinking about Clarisse; about her first miserable year here, when she had sought so desperately for Clarisse's attention and been so scornfully ignored. Not a crime punishable by death . . . and she knew, as Varis did not, how alive the dead could feel.

So she thought instead about the fact that Clarisse owed her loyalty to Callie's killer. And that this was as close as Callie would ever get to taking vengeance for her murder. Her Ghostland and Raellian instincts merged for one savage moment that was blissfully free of doubt.

"Enjoy your company," she said as she turned to the door. "I'm happy to leave you to it."

Clarisse entered Varis's room by walking through the closed door rather than by opening it. That was Varis's first clue that this meeting was not going to go exactly as he had planned. The second was when Clarisse looked at the two goblets on the table and laughed.

The third, and worst, was when Jano stepped through the door beside her.

Varis was sitting on a wooden chair, a book open in his hands. He turned a page, set his thumb on the text, and looked up, making no effort to hide his annoyance. "I don't recall inviting anyone but you."

"And quite flattering that was," Clarisse murmured, still visibly amused. "Nevertheless, Jano has something to add to this discussion. And he does have a taste for good wine."

Varis's brow creased. While he was staring at Clarisse hard, trying to figure out how much she knew, Jano walked past both of them and plopped inelegantly on one of the chairs.

"Your sisters," he announced, "are both crazy."

"Astonishing insight," Varis said. He looked back at Clarisse. "Is this another ambush?"

"No." Clarisse sighed. "You need to stop harping on that. Tonight we want to help you."

Varis closed the book with a thud. "Help me with what?"

"With conquering Ghostland, of course."

Varis put the book down on the table, allowing no

expression at all to cross his face, mentally checking his weapons. He had a coated dagger in his boot and several silver ones hidden within easy reach.

Clarisse walked across the room toward him. Her eyes measured the space between them, as if he was prey. "That *is* your plan, isn't it?"

"Right now," Varis said, "I'm more interested in what your plan is."

"My plan," Clarisse said, "is to do something about being only the second most powerful creature in this castle." She stopped several yards from him and brushed a stray curl away from her forehead. "I've had just about enough of that position to last me for eternity."

Varis slid his hands onto his knees. "How can you do anything to the Defender? He's immune to silver and sunlight."

"That was a lie." Clarisse held out her arm. "Stab me."

"What—"

"Just do it."

He hesitated for only a second. Then he said, "With pleasure," and lunged forward.

The silver knife sliced through Clarisse's skin. Clarisse smiled and jerked her arm upward. The blade went through her forearm and out the other side; Varis staggered slightly before he straightened, the ridges of the dagger hilt pressing into his palm. Clarisse's arm remained upraised, whole and uncut. Her smile was a bit strained, but triumphant.

"We can become so insubstantial that even silver won't touch us," she said, running a finger proudly over the unblemished white skin of her arm. "We can do it to only part of our body at a time. Some of us, that is."

Jano brought his chair back down with a thud, then leaned forward and stared at Clarisse with his mouth hanging open. "I don't know anyone who can do that."

"I know," Clarisse said, a bit smugly.

Jano looked at Varis, and Varis met his gaze. It was oddly difficult to do; there was something about the boy that sent chills up and down his arms.

After a moment, Jano transferred his attention back to Clarisse. "How long have you been able to?"

"This was my first time." She laughed, her teeth flashing white. "I'm glad it worked."

Jano slapped his hands down on his knees. "How did you know it was even possible?"

"I've seen the Defender do it. Many times. He does it with sunlight, too." She laughed again, in sheer delight. *Now*, unlike in the banquet hall, she looked truly alive. "That reminds me. I'll have to try sunlight next."

"But I cut you," Varis said. "In your room. And it hurt you."

Clarisse's fingers froze on her arm. She looked at him through narrowed eyes; he was prey now, no question about it. "Because I wasn't ready for it. I can't defend against silver if I don't know it's there. . . ." She stopped, lips parted, and looked at him.

"What?" Jano demanded, sitting up straight.

"So," Varis said, watching Clarisse. "The Defender, too, could be killed by silver. If he didn't see it coming, and didn't know to defend himself against it."

"My prince." She let her arm drop, and he found himself returning her smile. "I am so very, very glad you came to this country."

"What are you two going on about?" Jano demanded, his eyes narrowed. He folded his arms against his chest and gave Varis a sulky, unfriendly look. "This is nothing new. We know about your coated silver daggers. Give one to us, and we'll use it against the Defender. You won't have to worry about his opposition, and we won't have to obey him anymore. Everybody gains something."

Clarisse tilted her head back. "Let's seal it with a drink," she said. "There are only two goblets, which does present a problem, but I'm sure we can—"

Jano reacted, predictably, like a child. He snatched up one of the goblets and lifted it to his mouth.

He was still smirking when he vanished.

It was that quick: one second he was there, the next he wasn't. The goblet fell to the floor, but Clarisse's slender hand snatched it up a second before it would have hit. She must have started moving even before she had finished talking.

"Now you know it works," she said, quite calmly. "What was in it, by the way?"

Varis looked from the empty space where Jano had been to her face. "Silver powder," he said.

"A poison that would kill only the dead. Ingenious." Clarisse straightened the goblet—some of the dark red liquid had already splashed onto the wooden floor—and placed it on the table, exactly where it had been. "Were you planning to use it at your sister's wedding feast? For the toast, I'd imagine, so that we would all drink it at once."

That had been the plan, treacherous and base and dishonorable; but there was nothing in Clarisse's voice except admiration. He stepped back and leaned against the wall. "Possibly. It would have to be all of you, or at least most of you, at the same time. I can't think of anything but a wedding toast that would work that way."

"And in the meantime you were going to test it on me?"

He started to flush, remembered who he was talking to, and said calmly, "You practically invited me to."

Her admiration didn't dim in the slightest. "I wanted

to know what other weapons you had brought with you. I was a little concerned that you were too taken with my beauty to seize the opportunity, but I gambled on that barbarian ruthlessness I keep hearing about."

"And you brought Jano along as a substitute?"

"It was better this way." Clarisse stretched her arms over her head. "I did Jano a favor, really. He was terribly tired of existence." She touched the rim of the goblet with her finger and sighed. "Is this *really* a Green Islands vintage? What a waste."

"I have more," Varis said.

"Well." She swiveled slowly and looked at him. "I don't think I should be accepting wine from you, under the circumstances. But I do have another idea."

Chapter Seventeen

Darri had no idea where the Guardian was leading her, but she didn't care. She probably *had* just started a war, but she didn't care about that either. She didn't even care—much—about the horrified looks that followed her as she walked out of the hall behind the Guardian, blood sticking her gown to her calves. It was clear that if not for the Guardian, they would be dragging her across the marble floor in the direction of the dungeons.

The only one who didn't seem upset was the man whose existence she had just threatened. Kestin's face was cool and relaxed as he followed the Guardian out of the hall. Like her, he had seen Clarisse in the back of the hall, staring at Cerix's dead body. The gamble had paid off, as far as he was concerned; Cerix was dead, and Clarisse had not vanished. So despite her holding a knife to his throat, Kestin had no reason to hate Darri.

Darri did care whether he hated her—there was no point, anymore, in pretending she didn't. She had proven that she would do what she had to anyhow. But it had been harder than she had thought it would be, holding the dagger and watching Kestin's face go slack with shock. Even though she wouldn't really have killed him. Even though he was already dead.

The Guardian led them around the base of the spiral stairs, which gave Darri a chance—when the others were hidden from sight by the stairs—to stoop and dig out the coin hidden in the side of her shoe. She kept it pressed against her side as they walked through the halls into a large, gold-paneled room with a few wooden chairs and tables set out on the marble floor. Dozens of chandeliers hung from the ceiling, but only half of them were lit, giving the room a gloomy glow.

Halfway into the vast golden room, the Guardian turned around to face them. Darri braced herself, but he said nothing. His iron mask, she noticed, was crisscrossed with a thousand tiny scratches.

Somehow, that made him seem less omnipotent. She clenched her fists, curling the tiny silver coin into the curve of her fingers. It was slick with sweat. "I did what you wanted," she said. "I killed Cerix. Now I want you to fight the Defender."

"I cannot."

Darri stepped toward him, her hand swinging by her side. He watched her without moving. "Then tell me another way to set my sister free," she said. "You owe that to me. It's your fault she's dead."

And she threw the coin right into his eye.

Her aim was good; she had been practicing since the night before, when she had thought of this plan. The coin flashed sideways, right into one of the dark rectangular holes in the iron mask.

The Guardian cried out and stepped back. Inside his mask, the coin rattled – an incongruous sound, except that it was followed by silence. The Guardian lifted one iron-gloved hand to cover the eyehole, but made no sound. Even though the coin must still be in there, nestled against his skin.

Darri fell back, her arm swinging hard against her side. "You're not a ghost," she whispered.

The Guardian dropped his hand. "No."

"Then what are you?"

The spaces behind the eyehole were as black and expressionless as before. "I am the Guardian."

Kestin stepped up next to Darri, so close his sleeve

brushed hers. "The Guardian is an iron uniform," he said. "How many men have worn that costume over the centuries? You're just a living person, it seems, behind that mask. And I want to know who that person is. Take it off."

The silence stretched for what felt like a very long time. Slowly, the Guardian lifted his iron-gloved hands to his face. "You are wrong, Prince Kestin. There are those of us who don't fit your perception of what the living and the dead are. Who came before the dead and the living could coexist. You are better off not knowing about us."

"Stop stalling," Kestin said. "And who's *us*?"

But Darri already knew the answer.

"You and the Defender," she whispered, and the Guardian turned toward her as his hands came away from his face, holding the scratched-up mask.

"The spell required two," he said. Released from the iron mask, his voice still sounded exactly the same: hollow and metallic. "One to live. One to die."

A moment passed before Darri realized that what she was looking at was a face. The flesh seemed to have poured itself into the neck, the cheeks and nose eaten away, the rest of it horribly soft. It was like a wax model of a face that had partially melted.

The eyes, nearly hidden by the pasty white flesh, made

her try to control her expression; but despite herself, she made a strangled sound as she swallowed her bile. The gloved hands went back up to the ruin of a face, and no one said a word as the mask went back on. It looked at Darri, shiny and black and blank.

"You can see," the Guardian said, "why my brother preferred to be the one to die."

"Your brother?" Kestin repeated, after a long moment. The triumph and certainty had been wiped from his face, replaced by pure horror.

"There were six of us, originally," the Guardian said. He turned and strode partly across the room, stopping next to a delicate wooden chair. For a moment, Darri thought he was going to sit. Instead, he placed one iron-gloved hand on the back of the chair and turned again to face them. "Four brothers and two sisters, children of an ailing king. My brother and I were the youngest, born to a foreign wife—a sorceress from across the sea. She taught us her magic in secret, and it allowed us to survive when the factions at court chose their champions and moved with the deadliness that has always been part of our country's tragic history. Over the course of a year, my father watched both our brothers and one sister die."

"Killed?" Kestin asked, after a moment.

"We don't know. There was no way to know, back then.

That's why we did what we did. We called on dangerous powers and set our spell in stone and earth, so that it could never happen again. So that there would always be punishment for murder."

"Seems a bit drastic," Darri noted.

The empty iron eyes turned on her. "There was no other way to end it. Assassination and treachery had been our way for hundreds of years. What would you have had us do, Princess—gather the court for an inspirational speech about why it wasn't nice?"

Darri opened her mouth, then shut it.

"We gave up more than you can imagine to change the nature of death in our land," the Guardian said. "The spell could easily have killed us. Instead it keeps us alive, forever. My brother became the first of the dead, even though there was no one for him to take vengeance on. I remain trapped in life forever, so that the spell can continue to be channeled through my mind."

"Channeled?" Darri said.

"Magic is a powerful force, but it requires a living human mind to shape it." The Guardian's fingers tightened on the back of the chair, and Darri heard wood crack. "For every creation of a new ghost, every time our spell snatches a spirit away from death, it draws upon the magic that runs through me."

"Was it worth it?" Darri demanded, stepping away from the prince and toward the Guardian. "Was it worth what you did?"

The Guardian took his hand off the chair. Darri glanced at it swiftly, and saw a jagged crack in the polished dark wood. "You of all people should know, Princess, what price is worth paying for the end of violence and bloodshed."

Any price. It was what Varis had told her, in his tent long ago. Though even Varis hadn't been thinking of evil magic that twisted the natural order of life itself.

"But it started going wrong a long time ago." The Guardian pushed the chair away with a sudden movement, and it slid a few inches across the marble floor. "The ghosts were supposed to avenge themselves and vanish, not remain among us for hundreds of years. We had created creatures who were immortal, had great power, and were almost impossible to imprison or kill."

"So you became the Guardian," Kestin said. Darri glanced over her shoulder and saw that the prince was standing in the center of the room, feet braced wide, hands clasped behind his back. "To protect the living from the dead. And your brother . . ."

"Insisted that the dead needed protection as well." The Guardian inclined his head. "I believed him, for a very long time; even once it should have been clear to me that his true goal was to increase his own power until even the living would obey him."

"Then do what I'm asking," Darri said. *"Stop him."*

"I cannot. I don't know, after all this time, which of us is more powerful. And besides . . . he is my brother. Whatever he has become, we did this thing together."

This thing. He said it with such disgust that all at once, Darri knew what Callie had been brought here to do, and what she had been killed to stop.

"You want the spell to end." She said it almost in a whisper.

The Guardian's head moved, just a fraction: a movement so small Darri might not have seen it if she hadn't been staring at him so hard. Up, and then down.

Kestin's voice was barely audible. *"Can it end?"*

The Guardian kept his iron face turned toward Darri as he replied. "It is a powerful and fragile thing, our spell, like life itself. Set in stone and earth, but delicate as glass. It can be broken easily enough, if you can get to it."

"And you can't get to it?" Kestin demanded.

"Not I, nor my brother, nor any of the dead. No one affected by the spell can touch it without being destroyed." He hesitated for barely a moment. "Only someone who is still alive can do this."

Darri leaned forward. "But no one in Ghostland would

do it. They would see it as mass murder." Her fingers curled inward. "You needed someone foreign. Someone who understands that the ghosts are already dead. That's why you convinced King Ais to accept my father's offer. Not for alliances. For *this*." The room blurred. "And when the Defender figured out what you were doing, he killed Callie to make sure she wouldn't end the spell."

"I believe so. When I urged King Ais to accept your father's second offer, I overplayed my hand. My brother realized what I was after."

"And you wanted us here because Callie was no longer of use to you. Is that it?" Darri's throat closed up around her words, grief and hatred intertwined. This—*creature*—had stolen Callie's life away for his own purposes; and then, when it hadn't worked, had decided to steal Darri's life as well. "She was too young, when she first arrived. And then she was no longer foreign enough. You didn't think she would do it. That's why you advised the king to accept more foreigners into Ghostland."

The Guardian nodded.

Darri pushed down her fury with an effort; she was amazed when her voice emerged cool and composed. "And then, once we arrived, the Defender tried to kill us, too."

"He did," the Guardian agreed. "But I warned him off, and he isn't ready to attack me directly. Not yet."

Darri sucked in her breath. Nothing the Defender had said in the caves was true. He had nothing against needless killing. He hadn't killed Callie, even when she begged him, for one simple reason: because as a ghost, Callie gave her siblings a reason not to end the spell.

So he must have thought.

"I'll do it," she said.

Kestin's arms dropped to his sides as he turned toward her. The Guardian didn't move.

"I'll do it," Darri said again. "I'll do it for my sister. To free her from what your spell has done to her."

"It's not quite as simple as that," the Guardian said. "Ending the spell might not end her existence."

Darri stepped back and looked at his iron face squarely, trying not to picture the decayed remains of the real face behind it. "What do you mean? Won't the ghosts all vanish, when the spell is gone?"

The Guardian's fingers curled into fists, metal scraping against metal. "Our spell blurred the boundary between life and death. Where the new boundary would form is impossible to know."

"What does that *mean*?" Kestin demanded, striding forward until he stood beside Darri again. Darri didn't turn to look at him, even when his hand brushed hers. She stared at the Guardian's mask.

The voice issuing from behind that mask was slow and reluctant. "It means, Prince Kestin, that the ghosts *might* all vanish. Or they might stay as they are."

Darri, sensing something unsaid, demanded, *"Or?"*

"Or," the Guardian said, even more slowly, "they might stay . . . but not as they are."

Kestin drew back. "They could *live* again?"

"It's not probable," the Guardian said.

Darri could hear her heart pounding in her ears, like distant marching. Kestin whispered, "But you can't tell us it's not possible at all?"

Darri looked sideways at Kestin; his dark eyes met hers, just for a second, and then they both snapped their heads around and stared at the Guardian. For a moment, before she remembered what it looked like, Darri wished she could see the face behind that mask.

"No," the Guardian said, slowly and regretfully. "I can't."

Callie. The images flashed through Darri's mind in a cascade, fever bright. Callie laughing, Callie twirling in the grass, Callie with the falcon's claws digging into her arm. Callie's grim dead face in the dark cavern. Callie alive again. Riding beside her, sunlight gleaming on her hair.

And if it didn't work, at least her sister would be free.

"Tell me what to do," she demanded, stepping forward.

"Where—" But even as the word left her mouth, she realized that she already knew.

The older dead all come here eventually, to stand guard, Clarisse had said. This was what they were guarding. "How?" she said instead.

"The spell has its limitations built into it." The Guardian was so still he might have been a statue. "The same things that destroy the ghosts can destroy the spell that created them. Sunlight and silver." He took a step toward her. "The spell is in the caves beneath the castle, so sunlight is not an option. But we all know you have silver."

Without thinking, Darri drew the coated silver dagger from her boot. Kestin made a small sound, and she met his eyes. They were large and dark and shining. She couldn't tell whether it was with fear or hope.

And she didn't care.

"Wait," Kestin said. "You can't—not alone. That's not a place the living should go."

"I hear that a lot," Darri said dryly. "But the dead aren't there now, are they? They'll soon be attending a rather important coronation." She flashed a smile at him, and knew from the way his eyes widened that it was her old smile, reckless and heedless and uncaring.

Because she *didn't* care. The danger to her wasn't important. Only one thing was important, the same thing that had always been important: saving her sister. She felt as if she had been lost in a storm for days, and could finally see the road ahead of her again.

"Give them a good show," she told Kestin.

Then she flat out ran through the golden antechamber, down the lamp-lit halls. Somewhere to the left, she knew, was the entrance to the caverns, but she didn't trust her memory of those labyrinthine passageways. She turned right instead, into a straight, wide hall of polished marble, heading for the stables.

Clusters of people stood in the hall, sipping wine and laughing. They turned in astonishment to watch her go, and she caught a glimpse of her reflection, wavering in the polished steel that lined the hall. Her face was set, grim and determined and devoid of hesitation. She recognized the expression: she had seen it on Varis's face, dozens of times, when he set off for battle. She had seen it that night in his tent, when he told her that Callie was being sent away and there was nothing she could do to save her sister.

She looked straight ahead and ran faster.

Chapter Eighteen

The underground passageways felt different this time, vaster and murkier. They felt, Varis realized as he followed Clarisse past a cluster of bulbous rock outcroppings, empty. Even the long dead had ventured back among the living tonight, to watch one of their own become king.

It should have made him feel better. It did not. There was a ghost *with* him, after all, leading him farther and farther into the narrowing passageways, the hem of her violet gown going right through the rocks he kept stumbling over. The light of his torch cast moving shadows that played tricks on his mind. Curved hands, elongated arms, and grotesque faces slid past the walls, wavering over the curves and cracks in the rocks. None of which was helped by his knowledge that there was another ghost following them through the caves, watchful and angry.

I know which way to go, to catch his attention, Clarisse had said as she filled a glass flask with wine from his goblet. *He would never let me go into these caves completely alone. He doesn't trust me.*

An example, Varis suspected, that he would do well to follow. Which didn't make it any *more* sensible for him to be following her into the realm of the dead, certain that she hadn't told him everything.

Fortunately, he hadn't told her everything either. He was helping her because he was fairly certain that he knew how to control her. If she had been anyone else, he would have been completely certain.

Clarisse came to a stop, so suddenly that he had to grab her shoulder to keep from colliding with her. Her shoulder was firm and solid beneath his palm, so he knew she had intended for him to grab her. She half-turned so that his arm was around her, then looked up into his face, lips half-parted.

Varis knew she was trying to distract him from *something,* so he dropped his torch at the first crack from above. Then he turned and ran.

The stalactites fell from the ceiling in a cascade of sharp stone, slamming into the ground in a thunderous cacophony. One hit his uninjured shoulder, and he hissed and stumbled. But he didn't have attention to spare for the pain. He crouched low and ran, and when the second stone shard grazed his hip, he lunged low and threw himself as far forward as he could.

A falling stone thudded hard against his foot, and then he was rolling on pebble-strewn ground. The cavern was suddenly silent, the crash of stone gone, and aside from two painful bruises, he was fine.

An ice-cold hand grabbed him by the back of his tunic and pulled him to his feet. All at once the caves were filled with light; he saw Clarisse standing in the center of a cavern filled with broken rock, one of which had fallen point first through her. It was still standing upright, quivering in the center of her translucent body. Clouds of dust rose around her legs, and her eyes were alight with exhilaration.

Varis kept his gaze on her, not bothering to struggle or try to look behind him. His only move was to grab the neck of his tunic to keep it from digging into his throat. The scent of decay seeped through the air around him, like clammy fog against his skin.

"*This* is your offering?" The voice was low and gravely, nothing like the unearthly rumble he had faced down with the Guardian. "Your reason for triggering the spell's defense?"

Clarisse lifted her eyebrows. "Would you have preferred

his sister? I think it's safe to say he's the more dangerous of the two."

"He's not the one speaking to the Guardian," the Defender snapped.

Clarisse smoothed down her flawless hair. "He figured out the truth about the spell, and that the Guardian brought him here to break it. I had no choice."

Varis let go of his tunic and lifted both his arms above his head. The silk neck dug into his jugular; he jerked his head back before he could choke and snapped his shoulder blades together. He dropped right out of the tunic, rolled as he hit the ground, and came up with his back against the jagged wall.

The Defender looked like a man, as Clarisse had predicted he would. She had also said he looked like a different man every time she saw him. Tonight, apparently, he was a thin, dark-skinned man with a face that was all smooth lines and angles. The man didn't turn to look at Varis; he merely let the tunic drop disdainfully to the ground.

"Are you more comfortable now?" Clarisse asked Varis.

"Yes," Varis said, taking a deep breath. "Actually, I am."

"Well, good for you." She looked again at the Defender, whose lips were curved upward. The expression had the appearance of a human smile, yet there was nothing human about it.

He likes to act alive, in front of the living, Clarisse had said. *He pretends it's for their sakes, but it's really for his.*

So far, she had predicted everything correctly—except for the minor matter of the stalactite trap, which she had neglected to mention. Varis's heart pounded with fear and excitement both. The stone's edges were sharp against his bare skin.

Clarisse walked through the broken stones toward them, her hair sparkling with rock dust. Her eyes blazed in the dusty gloom. "Do I get to kill him?"

"If you wish," the Defender said.

Clarisse swung her head around to look at Varis, whose breath tangled in his throat. He truly had no idea which one of them she was going to betray.

"If I do," Clarisse breathed, "he'll come back." Her eyes looked like they were on fire. "That should make for an interesting few centuries. Do you think I can stay a step ahead of him?" She uncorked the flask, took a swig, and lowered it; the swift, unsteady movement made the wine swirl through the glass flask, sediment whirling up into the liquid. She grinned as she extended it to the Defender. "It's good wine. You should reestablish trade with the Green Islands, once you're in charge."

Varis might have spared himself the effort of controlling his expression. The Defender didn't even glance at him. He

kept his deep-set eyes on Clarisse as he accepted the flask. "I haven't had wine for years."

"Well," Clarisse laughed again, so easily even Varis almost believed she didn't care, "it's not a bad vintage to start with."

The Defender's smile was a tiny bit closer to human this time. He took the flask from Clarisse, tilted it back, and drank.

The Guardian's scream echoed through the corridors: hollow and endless and terrible. It froze the courtiers milling in the marble hall outside the throne room. It froze Callie, who was leaning against the wall being ignored by the courtiers.

It didn't even slow Darri down.

Callie turned her head just in time to see her sister racing down the marble corridor, the hem of her yellow skirt still dark with blood, the Guardian's scream following her down the hall. The courtiers watched her go, wide eyed. No one was sure what was happening, and no one stopped her.

Callie didn't know she was going to do it until she did: reach out with one hand and grab the trailing edge of Darri's silk sleeve. Her sister could have easily pulled away and kept going. Instead Darri stopped and whirled.

"What did you do?" Callie demanded.

"I don't know," Darri said. "He didn't start screaming until I left."

"And what," Callie said, aware of all the eyes on them, "did *he* do?"

"Nothing. We chatted." Darri, too, glanced around at the courtiers. For the first time, none of them faded, even though many of them were dead. Taunting the foreigner, apparently, was less fun now that they had seen what she was capable of. "Why should he do anything to me? I killed Cerix at his request. And this country is a better place without him." She grinned, suddenly and savagely. "This country will be a far, far better place by the time I'm done with it."

"What are you—" Callie began, but then a murmur rippled through the corridor. She looked up and saw Kestin approaching the main entrance to the throne room. The prince met Darri's eyes, and it seemed to Callie that something flashed between them. Darri's grin widened, and Kestin gave her a small, sharp nod.

"We should begin the coronation," the prince said, his voice raised to reach the courtiers, his eyes still on Darri's face. "There is no reason to keep the dead waiting."

"I couldn't agree more," Darri said, still with that grin.

Kestin walked into the throne room. The courtiers,

after a moment of confusion, followed him.

Darri looked at Callie then, and Callie realized she was still holding her sister's sleeve. She dropped it, but Darri still stood there, looking at her. A slow, sick fear swirled through Callie as she waited to hear what Darri had to say to her.

Darri smiled at her—an open, brilliant smile. Then she strode past Callie and disappeared through one of the doorways lining the corridor.

The unexpected smile stunned Callie. She almost turned to go after Darri, to—demand? yell? plead? cry? She didn't know, so she followed the courtiers. She was tired of worrying about what Darri thought and what Darri felt and what Darri was about to do.

The throne room was large, old, and imposing. Thick stone pillars filled the vast space between marble floor and arched ceiling, dwarfing the dais and the king's golden throne. Callie, whose father's proclamations were usually made from horseback in front of a tent, still felt awed every time she walked in.

By tradition, the floor space was reserved for the living, while ghosts twined about the intricately carved pillars. Callie started to float a half inch off the floor, and stepped heavily down on the black and white marble. No one else noticed, but the impulse alarmed her.

She didn't want to feel dead. Not yet.

Kestin walked through the crowd, and the spectators tried to bow, but most of them had no room. The room was crammed with people, living and dead. He stepped onto the marble dais, where his father was waiting, and bowed.

There followed what seemed like an hour of talking. King Ais publicly imparted words of wisdom to Kestin, then someone else spoke about Kestin's virtues, then someone else said pompous things about Ghostland, and finally Kestin made a dozen long-winded vows.

When he was done at last, anticipation stilled the restless courtiers. King Ais stepped forward, lifted the crown from his head, and held it out. Kestin bowed once, reached over, and took the crown from his father's hands.

All at once the air was full. Callie, along with the rest of the crowd, looked up. The dead were layered one upon another, filling the space above the living, gray and translucent. Some of them appeared barely human; Callie fought an urge to look away, to avert her eyes from forms too grotesque to bear. Yet she couldn't have said what, exactly, was wrong with them.

The cavernous room was abruptly silent. The living—and many of the recently dead—cringed away, ducking to get that much more space between themselves and the apparitions hovering above them.

The dead did nothing. They simply *were*, waiting, filling

the space all the way up to the high-arched ceiling. They outnumbered the living, and the ghosts who still had the form of the living, at least tenfold.

The silence was dreadful. Callie blurred, her body fading, proving to the dead that she was one of them. She couldn't stop herself.

Without sound, the ghosts all bowed their heads to Kestin, who looked at them without expression on his ash-white face. King Ais let his hands fall helplessly to his sides, and the first dead prince of Ghostland lifted the crown and placed it on his head.

A sound like wind rushed through the throne room, though there was no wind; a vast, approving murmuring. It was low and unearthly, and it was the only sound in the room. There was no clapping or cheering from the living. They stood as if turned to statues, watching the dead who outnumbered them so vastly.

And just like that, the coronation was over. The crowd around Callie began streaming toward the door—whether to get away from the ghosts, or to get to the food and wine still waiting in the banquet hall, Callie couldn't tell. She only knew what *she* wanted: to escape from those gray forms as fast as possible. She went solid and forced herself to move with the crowd, pushing her way between the richly dressed nobles, pausing only when one of the dead refused to move aside and she went *through* him. She took a moment to swallow her bile, aware of the glares around her. Walking through a person was extremely rude.

She went more cautiously then, sliding gingerly between the crowd until she made it to the banquet hall. Only then, with the edge of her panic faded, did she feel the tears at the bottoms of her eyes.

That, above her in the throne room, was her future. She was not going to grow old, was not going to develop aches and pains and rough skin and lose her teeth and then die. Instead she was going to forget that she was human, little by little, and become one of *those* things, and be one of those things forever. Because there was an end to life, but not to death.

She had known that for a long time; but everything about tonight—the pain on her sister's face, the shock on her brother's, Jano's hissed warnings, the goblet she had left in Varis's room—stripped away her defenses, the four years' layers of sophistication and confusion she had wrapped around herself. She felt the spell holding her down, felt the anguish that had torn through her when she first realized she was dead and not gone—an anguish not blunted or faded, but merely buried, over the past weeks.

You'll learn to pretend, Jano's voice echoed in her ear. *It's the only way we can bear being what we are.*

She *would* learn to pretend; it was better, or at least less frightening, than vanishing into the unknown. Than being nothing. She would watch how the others did it, and be like them. Like Jano, and Clarisse . . . her throat clenched as she remembered the expression on Varis's face as he snatched the goblet from her hand. Varis, at least, still thought she was his sister, no matter what else she was.

Which should have helped, at least a little bit. But all she could think was, If he can accept it, why can't *she*?

She knew the answer even before her mind had formed the question. Darri couldn't accept it because Darri cared too much. Because it wasn't enough, for Darri, to *accept* Callie; she had to love her. And how could anyone love a ghost?

All at once Callie knew what had been bothering her about Darri's smile, about everything that had passed between them in the hall. Darri had met her eyes easily, without the faintest reservation, something she hadn't managed to do since the night she learned Callie was dead. As if there was nothing disgusting about Callie at all.

Callie finally had exactly what she so desperately wanted. For Darri to look at her, even though she was dead, the way she had when Callie was alive. And now that it had happened . . .

She didn't believe it.

Not so long ago, she herself had been fully Raellian, had

felt her skin shrink from the very sight of a ghost. She knew there was no way Darri could look at her dead sister as if nothing was wrong. Callie couldn't even look at *herself* as if nothing was wrong.

Darri had just gone back to what she had thought when she first rode into Ghostland, a rider with a mission. That what was wrong with Callie was something she could fix.

Callie swore, using a word so filthy that a passing nobleman blinked. She turned her back on him and raced through the hall and into the throne room. If anyone had been left there, she would have gone right through them without the slightest hesitation.

But there was no one left—not at floor level, anyhow.

Prince Kestin stood alone on the marble dais. The crown, a heavy circlet of ruby-studded gold, looked like it belonged on his head. It was also in danger of falling off. Kestin's head was tilted far back as he watched the gray mass of translucent forms that still filled the air.

The dead were in no hurry.

Callie was. She skidded to a stop and gasped out, "What did the Guardian tell you?"

The prince jerked his head down and looked at her. For a moment he just stared, his eyes shockingly bright. Then he said, "Leave us."

At once the throne room felt echoingly empty. Callie

didn't have to look up to know that the ghosts were gone—but she did anyhow, and felt a lightness in her chest at the sight of the clear air around the stone pillars. Kestin didn't look up. He kept his gaze where it had been: on Callie.

"What did Darri ask him?" Callie demanded. It was unthinkable for her, foreign nuisance that she was, to talk to the crown prince in this tone of voice. She stepped toward him, fists clenched at her sides. *"Where did my sister go?"*

Kestin hesitated, then shrugged and bit his lip on a smile. "Your sister," he said, his voice low but clear, "is ending the spell."

Callie froze in place. "Ending?"

Kestin sat down carefully, placing both his hands on the golden arms of the throne. "This is what the Guardian has wanted all along: for the spell to end. It's why he convinced my father to bring you to Ghostland. It's why your siblings are here. So that death in our country can finally happen the way it's supposed to."

Callie opened her fingers slowly, pressed them hard against the sides of her legs. "But what will happen to . . . to the dead? The ones who are already here?"

"We don't know. We might vanish." He leaned forward, and suddenly there was nothing regal about him; he looked like a hopeful child. "Or we might live. *Really* live."

The hope that sang through Callie then was sudden, and

sharp, and it hurt more than anything had since . . . since the moment she had seen her own corpse bloated with water and smeared with mud.

Graveyards. She had forgotten how much the living cared, and how much it hurt.

And until this moment, she hadn't realized that she had forgotten.

She drew in a breath so sharp it should have hurt too, but didn't; and she let the hope go. She knew, as the Ghostlanders did not, what a stark difference there was between life and death.

"It's not possible," she said.

Kestin sat back, eyes still alight. "The Guardian said that when the spell is broken, it will once again change the boundary between the living and the dead."

Callie shook her head, so violently she felt her hairstyle shift. "The dead are dead."

"But what if we don't have to be?" She heard in his voice the same pain that thrummed through her. "She might end our existence, yes. But she might give us more than mere existence. She might give us *life.*" He aimed his dark eyes at Callie. "We don't know what will happen when the power in that spell is released. We could be what we were, not the hollow monstrosities we are now."

Hollow monstrosities. If his adoring subjects could

hear him now. Callie's fingernails dug into her palms. She released them slowly. "Where is the spell?"

"In the realms of the dead."

"She went alone to those caves? They'll kill her—"

"Don't be so melodramatic." Kestin carefully adjusted his crown. "The dead aren't there. Not tonight. For the first time in centuries, they have something to celebrate." He glanced up at the empty ceiling. "Even if they went straight back, they won't get there in time to stop her."

Stupid, stupid, stupid. But hope could do that to even the smartest people.

Kestin was silent, his lips smiling but his eyes guarded. Callie took another two steps toward him and stopped right at the foot of the dais's velvet-coated stairs. "Don't you see, Your Highness? The Guardian lied. He offered Darri something she wanted so desperately she would believe the impossible. My life."

"You don't know that." Kestin shook his head. "You're just guessing."

"So are you." She pointed a finger at him. "And you're guessing with the existence of every ghost in this castle."

Kestin stood up. His crown shifted backward on his head. "Why do you care? You're Raellian. You think the ghosts shouldn't exist. Your thinking that is the reason the Guardian brought you here!"

You can pretend along with the rest of them, Darri's voice whispered in her mind. Callie stared at Kestin. He was right. She didn't think the ghosts should exist.

But they did exist; she knew that with a bone-deep certainty that Darri could never understand. She thought of Jano, of his bitterness and pranks, of the sly jokes that had helped her survive her first year here. She thought of Lady Velochier with her arm around her daughter's shoulders. She thought of Clarisse, heady with her newfound power, fighting to remain in this world. And then she looked at Kestin, dead and regal, glaring down at her with eyes like black fire.

This was why the Guardian had brought Darri here. Because he had known Callie could never destroy her friends and acquaintances, people she had known for four years. People who shouldn't exist, but did.

"You can't let her do this," she said.

"Yes I can," Kestin said. "If you were dead, you would understand."

She didn't even flinch at that. She said, "I would. But not all of them do. Nobody is asking them if they want to vanish and be nothing."

Kestin's lips thinned. "Nobody asked them if they wanted to be here in the first place."

Callie stepped back. She was wasting her time. He wouldn't accept what she was telling him. Not when he had just accepted hope, for the first time after weeks of hopelessness.

He would come around to it eventually; he was too smart not to. Maybe in a few minutes. Maybe in a few days, or weeks, or months. It didn't matter. She didn't have that time.

"All right, then," she said, angry despite herself. "I'll stop her myself."

She half-expected Kestin to try and prevent her, but the dead prince didn't move or utter a sound. He stood and watched, his eyes bleak, as she whirled and ran across the marble floor.

Chapter Nineteen

Varis's first move, once he and Clarisse were alone in the cavern, was to retrieve his tunic and slip it over his head; not out of modesty, but because the simple, practiced movement made his hands stop shaking. By the time he turned to face Clarisse, he was able to appear perfectly calm.

Until he saw the stone shard in her hand, and realized what should have been the obvious answer to the question of who Clarisse was going to betray.

Both of them.

Clarisse lifted the shard and threw it. He whirled to the side, and the pointed stone whizzed past his ear and ricocheted off a rock. Clarisse knelt, picked up another, and stepped closer.

Varis drew his silver knife, and she shifted her hold

slightly, so that she could use the stone to block a throw. When he just stood there, the knife small and useless in his hand, her lips curved into a smile.

"A dilemma, isn't it?" she said. "Throw it, and you lose your only defense. But I don't intend to get close enough to let you use it any other way, before I kill you."

"I don't think," Varis said, "that you're going to kill me."

"You don't?" she said, pleased. "Spirits, I'm good."

Varis's stomach twisted. *You have no idea what she really wants from you*, Callie had said. "What would you gain? You have what you want. The Defender is gone, and the way is clear for you to be the leader of the dead."

Clarisse's smile was sharp and hard-edged. "That did work out quite well, didn't it?"

"Then why kill me?" Varis said.

Her eyebrows arched. "The correct question is, why not?"

"It's not that simple. You tried to kill me before, on the hunt, and I don't believe it was just because the Defender ordered it." He risked a step toward her. She didn't move back. "I think it was because if I was killed in Ghostland, my father would direct all his effort toward vengeance. Between that and the succession dispute, it would be years before we recovered sufficiently to cross the Kierran Mountains."

Clarisse moved then, her hand tight on the stone; and for a moment he thought she had thrown it. He stumbled to the side before he realized that she had only raised it defensively, as if it was he who had thrown a weapon.

"And why," she said, her eyes like green fire, "would I care about that?"

"You're trying so hard to care about nothing," Varis said, "that there must be something you really do care about. Someone, would be my guess."

She lowered the stone shard, just low enough to give him a clear view of her face. She was so furious she couldn't hide her anger, and all at once he was sure he was right.

"I used to care about nothing." She stepped forward, sliding her feet over the rough stone ground, until she stood right before him. "It's not as easy as you would think, but I did it. I broke off all connections with everything I ever *had* cared about. I died, which was rather extreme but did seem to work. And then you came."

He lowered his knife, not too far, but far enough that it wasn't directly in her line of view.

"I didn't even realize, at first, why I was so fascinated by you." Her face went flat. "You're something I've spent my whole life guarding against. A threat to him."

He nodded. "To your brother."

She actually flinched. "How do you—"

Varis met her fierce, dead green eyes. "The portrait in your room. His daughter looks just like you."

Clarisse's eyes widened. She was motionless for almost a full minute. Then she said, "Why would any of this stop me from killing you?"

"Because eventually—sooner rather than later—we will cross the mountains, and we will conquer his land." Varis took a deep breath. His father was not going to like this. "If I am alive, I will see to it that your brother lives. I swear. He and his daughter both." He waited a beat, then added, "I say nothing about his wife, you understand."

She wasn't even pretending to breathe; her chest didn't move at all when she spoke again. "You also say nothing about why I should trust you."

"You've traveled through the plains. You know my people's honor." He lowered his knife all the way, and knew she noticed the motion, though her eyes never moved from his. "All you have to do is let me go. I'll be out of your kingdom as fast as I can. And I'll see to it that your brother is safe."

Something flickered in her eyes when he said "your kingdom." She stepped back and lowered the stone shard, and he forced himself to keep his breathing even. "All right," Clarisse said. "We have an agreement."

"Shall we seal it with wine?"

Her lips formed a straight line; well, it hadn't been a particularly funny joke. "However, it applies only to you."

"Only to—" And then he understood. "No. Leave my sisters alone."

"Too late, Your Highness." She tossed the stone to the ground, and it rolled into a dark crevice. "It won't benefit me much to be ruler of the dead if neither I nor they still exist."

"What are you talking about?"

She blew out a short breath. "The Guardian brought you and your sister to this country to end the spell that keeps the dead here. I'm not going to let that happen."

"*I* won't let it happen," Varis said. "I'll take Darri with me, as soon as I leave—"

"Too late, I'm afraid. After her dramatics during the dance, I assume she found out from the Guardian where she has to go, and what she has to do." Clarisse lifted an eyebrow at him. "Why so distressed? She was never anything but an inconvenience to you anyhow."

"She's my *sister*." He had no doubt that Clarisse was telling the truth: that Darri was down here in the caves, that she was trying to end the spell. And that she was about to die. "If you kill her, I'll tear this country down. I'll grind silver into the soil. I swear it."

Clarisse blinked at him, completely unconcerned. "Why? You don't love her."

"I don't like her," Varis snarled. "I *do* love her."

Clarisse drew her lips back, and behind them, her teeth were curved into fangs. For a moment she stood poised, staring at him. Then she turned and walked right into the wall to their left. The hem of her gown was the last thing to disappear, a trail of violet on the dark rocks.

Varis swore loudly. He sheathed his dagger, then reconsidered and drew it again.

The spell's defense, the Defender had called the falling stalactites. Which meant Clarisse had been leading him in the right direction. Her walking through walls might have been just a flair for the dramatic, or a shortcut through these labyrinthine caves. And obviously, Darri was headed to the spell by some other route. But if he kept going the way they had been headed . . .

He knew immediately that it was a foolish thought. He could so easily get lost. He could wander down here forever, and die where there was not even the faintest breath of wind to carry his spirit away. Already he felt the terrible silence closing in around him. His heartbeat sounded like the march of an army, somewhere far above where the living belonged.

Besides, there were probably other defenses. And even if he did get to the spell, he would be far, far behind Clarisse; too far for Darri to stand a chance.

He swore again and strode forward, kicking broken stones out of his way as he walked through the darkness and toward his sister.

Being dead, Callie found, had one more advantage she had only just discovered. Now that she knew what she was looking for, she could feel it pulsing through the dusty air of the tunnels: the source of the energy that was keeping her here, giving her strength and will, allowing her to squeeze through crevices and scramble over rockfalls and drop down a dark precipice without knowing how far below her the ground lay. Now that she knew the spell was there, she could feel a part of herself struggling against it, wanting to go . . . wherever it was the dead went. But the other part of her was pushing between rock columns and walls as fast as she could, desperate to keep that energy from stopping. To keep herself from ceasing to be.

We could be what we were. Kestin's voice sounded in her mind, over and over, impossible and impossibly seductive. Maybe it could be true. Maybe she should let Darri try.

But every time she thought it, every time she tried to believe that the irreversible could be reversed, she remembered her body in the water, a bloated, inanimate thing. And she knew, deeper than hope or fear or even despair, that it couldn't be true. The dead were *dead*.

And maybe they should be dead. Really dead. Freed from the painful pretense of living, from the fear of nonexistence that kept them here. Maybe Darri would be doing them a favor by ending their torment. Maybe Callie would be the one hurting them, if she tried to stop her sister.

Or maybe she would be saving them, to make their own decisions, one by one. Even if they would mostly make the wrong decision.

The source of the spell was a beacon, a tide in her blood. The passages Clarisse had led them through last time had curved and twisted; Callie was going in a straight line toward her goal, with a speed that would have been impossible had she been alive. Darri would probably be going aboveground, because the way from the lake was much simpler than the way from the castle. Despite Darri's head start, Callie might beat her there.

She wasn't yet certain what she would do if she did.

Chapter Twenty

The night air whipped through Darri's hair as her horse emerged from the forest trail and broke into a gallop. The torch on the pommel, even in its protective casing, was no match for the sudden gust of wind; it flickered wildly and went out. The moon faded in and out of the swift-moving clouds, and the grass bent ahead of the wind in dark waves, making the whole hillside shimmer. She felt like a figure from legend, an avenging goddess. A heroine who would conquer death itself.

And who might ride like this again tomorrow, with her sister at her side.

No one but Kestin knew where she was going, or what she was doing, or how the world would change tonight. She pushed the horse forward recklessly, her breath whistling past her into the wind they made. Power and possibility thrummed through her, a heady feeling that made the blood sing in her body.

It took her a few false tries to find the cave entrance, in a darkness that confounded her sunlit memories; and a few more to retrace her steps through the caves she had last walked in the company of hostile ghosts. Now they were echoingly empty, hollow and silent.

When her relit torch finally showed her the glint of metal dust on the rocky ground, her whole body was tense with impatience. It had taken her longer than she had thought it would. She followed the sparse trail to the spot where the Defender had confronted them.

Clarisse had taken them straight to him, so she had known where he would be. It must be close to the spell.

That was as far as her thinking had taken her. Somehow she had assumed the source of the spell would be evident once she got here; but as she turned around, the light of the torch illuminating patches of rock, she saw nothing she hadn't seen last time. The dark passageway from which she had come; the clustered stalagmites; the bare patch of rock, deep in shadow, where the Defender had been . . .

Been what? She remembered suddenly how the Defender's voice had come from behind them, startling even Clarisse. If he had been waiting for them, he should have been in front of them. So what had he been doing there? Darri frowned, picked up a loose rock, and threw it at the shadows.

It dropped right through the bare ground, leaving behind a faint ripple. After several seconds, Darri heard a thud far below.

The ground was still and apparently solid. Darri tried not to imagine what would have happened if she had just walked straight onto it. She reached for a thin stalagmite, broke it off with a snap, and heaved with all her strength.

The crash below was much louder this time, the ripples more violent. Darri found an already broken stone, thicker and heavier than she could have wrenched off herself, and threw that, too. She was looking for another when the ground undulated violently and was gone.

Darri cautiously approached the edge of what turned out to be a craggy plateau, the edge of a sheer rock face at least forty feet high. She put the torch down. Below, the rocks she had thrown lay smashed into jagged pieces on the bare earth. The cliff face below her was unnaturally smooth, with not a single crevice or ledge she might use to climb down. Across from her, the walls were covered by a cascade of white rock, like a waterfall frozen in time. It drew her eyes down, to where spray should have crashed, far down below. . . .

Set in stone and earth. A cluster of stalagmites grew from the ground and from the wall, and met together in a swirl of colored rock, coiled together so tightly she couldn't tell where one began and the other ended. The pink and red and mottled gray were twisted together, both beautiful and obscene. There was something distorted about it, connecting different coils of rock in ways that didn't make sense and that her eyes couldn't follow. At first glance, its beauty took her breath away; after a few seconds, Darri felt nausea spiraling through her fascination. But it looked so much like she could make sense of it, if she just stared hard enough. . . .

"Look away," Clarisse said.

Darri shrieked and turned. For a moment she could see nothing but the afterimages of coiling lines and serpentine rocks. She blinked hard, and her vision cleared. Clarisse stood a few yards behind her, her hair blowing about her face in a nonexistent wind.

"Hypnotic, isn't it?" she said. "You would have stared at it until you died of thirst. It's the spell's last defense."

Darri couldn't stop the shudder that rolled through her. She turned her back on Clarisse, keeping her eyes averted from the structure while she leaned over the edge of the cliff. "Thank you for warning me. Should I assume that you're here to help?"

Clarisse laughed. "You should assume I don't have the patience to wait for you to starve to death." She took one step forward, leaned back slightly, and kicked hard at the small of Darri's back.

It was intended to send Darri over the edge, but Darri had been ready for an attack. She ducked, and Clarisse's foot skimmed along her back—painfully, but not hard enough to throw her off-balance. She stepped backward under the kick, grabbed Clarisse's leg, and yanked it up, using Clarisse's own momentum to throw the ghost forward. Clarisse flailed, screeched, and went tumbling into the cavern below.

After only a second she shot back up, her hair writhing around her shoulders, her eyes spitting green fire. Literally. She looked like a demon, a creature of nightmares, but Darri wasn't afraid. Her blood pounded through her.

Clarisse snarled, revealing pointed teeth, and flew through the air faster than any living person could have moved. Darri had no time to react before the dead girl hit her in the chest, and she found herself flying backward.

She stretched her body out instinctively, grasping desperately for something—anything—to keep her from slamming into the far wall. One of her outstretched arms hit a cluster of stalagmites; the rest of her crashed against the rock-strewn floor, skidding diagonally as the impact threw her sideways. For a moment, half-stunned on the floor, her arm a vise of pain, she couldn't move.

Then she heard Clarisse say, "Well, that was disappointingly easy," and she leaped to her feet. Her arm ached, but when she used it to push herself off the ground, it worked; so she shoved the pain aside, shoved the fear aside, and drew herself up.

The stitches of her sleeves were tightly woven, but they were just thread. With several violent yanks, she tore them from her gown and let them flutter to the ground, leaving her arms bare and unhindered. She drew her silver dagger and crouched.

"How quaint," Clarisse said, and flew straight up into the air.

She probably expected Darri to run, but Darri had seen enough falcon kills to know how quickly a swoop from above could outdistance a ground run. She flipped the dagger and threw it.

Clarisse dodged to the side. The blade hit the ceiling above her and plummeted. Darri ran for it, and Clarisse plunged down on her, turning solid as she went. They collided a few yards from where the dagger lay, and Darri turned on impact, so that she fell on her back instead of her hands and knees. From that position, it was the work of a second to flip them over so that Clarisse was pinned beneath her.

Clarisse laughed in her face. "I could turn to mist and float right up through you, you know."

"Then do it." Darri tightened her grip on the seemingly solid wrists.

"So you can grab the dagger in the meantime?" Clarisse went translucent, but remained where she was, so that Darri's hands went through her arms and hit the stone floor.

Darri lunged for the weapon; but she had to gather her feet under her first, and Clarisse didn't. The ghost simply lifted up off the floor and flew sideways, spinning as she went, her gown twirling around her. One slipper-clad foot hit Darri's already injured arm, and Darri yelped in pain and fell back—but not before she had reached out with her other hand, grabbed Clarisse's hair, and yanked.

Clarisse faded at once, her hair turning to mist in Darri's hand. But Darri's yank had already jerked her off balance, away from the dagger. Darri rolled across the rocky ground and closed her fingers around the hilt a moment before Clarisse rammed into her.

By now Darri had figured out that when Clarisse was solid, she was vulnerable. She struck with the dagger, putting all her strength into it, and felt a surge of triumph as the silver blade slid into flesh.

But she must have missed—somehow—because next thing she knew Clarisse was standing over her, apparently unharmed, and laughing. The laugh enraged Darri. She rolled backward and used her momentum to leap forward onto her feet, landing right in front of Clarisse.

"I apologize," Clarisse said merrily. "But this is just *so* fun. And you still haven't realized that this battle is not winnable."

"It seems winnable to me," Darri snarled. "You're not very good at fighting."

That was designed to enrage Clarisse, but it didn't work; instead, Clarisse laughed harder. "It's true. I had other skills. Fighting wasn't something I ever had to learn."

"Too bad for you," Darri said grimly.

Clarisse lifted her eyebrows. "It doesn't matter; I thought I had demonstrated that. Do you really think you can fight a ghost?"

She lunged at Darri, who crouched, the hilt reassuringly heavy in her palm; but Clarisse surprised her by ducking low, going flat, and shooting forward right above the ground so that her arms went easily around Darri's legs. No living person could have made that move, and Darri had no idea how to defend herself against it. She flew backward, her head hitting the ground with a crack. The dagger flew out of her hand. Dimly, she heard it clatter on stone.

She rolled to her feet, blinking away tears of pain, trying to think. Clarisse was right. How could she fight someone who could fly, who could move without fighting the pull of the earth?

Clarisse landed near the dagger. She lifted her eyebrows at Darri, grinned gleefully, and used one foot to roll a stone over the blade.

The answer was obvious: she couldn't fight. Instead Darri turned, almost blindly, to the precipice. There had to be a way down, something she hadn't seen before; something she could find before Clarisse stopped her. There was nothing she could do but try. Just run, and hope.

She lunged forward, and rammed headlong into a plate of iron.

Pain reverberated through her face and head, and for a moment she couldn't see. Then her vision cleared and she gaped at the Guardian standing in front of her, right at the edge of the precipice, his eyeholes black and empty in his scratched-up mask. There was, she thought, a slight dent in his iron breastplate.

"My brother is dead," the Guardian said.

Darri remembered the scream, raw and anguished, that had followed her down the corridor. She hesitated for a moment. Then she said, "So is my sister," and dodged around him.

The Guardian grabbed her arm. His iron fingers dug into her skin, so painfully she bit her lip on a scream. "Did you kill him?"

"I was with *you*," Darri gasped, then realized that he wasn't speaking to her. She twisted in his grasp and followed his gaze.

Clarisse's form shimmered and changed, and then wasn't there at all. A silver fog, shot through with flashes of light, coiled upward within the dark cave.

"I did," her voice whispered, from within the fog. "I am the Defender now. Shall I call you Brother?"

"I wouldn't advise it," the Guardian snarled, and let go of Darri's arm. It felt numb, as if he had compressed her very bone; the imprints of his fingers were deep and white on her brown skin.

The Guardian reached up and, with one smooth movement, drew his silver sword. The blade flashed inches from Darri's face as he held it in front of him. "That was a mistake."

The fog swirled lazily. "Should I pretend to be afraid?"

"You should *be* afraid." The Guardian took one step toward her. "Even my brother wouldn't fight me."

"And why do you think that was? Because he was afraid of you? Because he loved you?" The Guardian went very still, and the fog writhed with Clarisse's laughter. "You did think that, didn't you? That there was still feeling left between you, even after he had been dead for hundreds of years? He didn't kill you for one reason only: because the magic that feeds the spell is channeled through your mind. If you died, there would be no new ghosts for him to add to his host, no way for the dead to eventually outnumber the living. You are alive because you were useful to him, and for no other reason."

"I don't believe you," the Guardian said, but he didn't move. "And even if that's so, you need me for the same reason."

"I don't think so. I'm a bit more imaginative than your brother. The dead who exist are enough for me." The fog coiled around itself, forming a thin smokelike column. "Not that I wouldn't prefer to increase my subjects, and let you alone. If you'll do the same. We can come to an agreement."

"You killed my brother," the Guardian said.

"Yes. And I'll kill you, too, if I must." The fog thinned, and suddenly Clarisse was in the center of it, dressed in a violet gown, her golden hair still tumbling in arranged curls down her back. "It should be easier. There's nothing immortal about you, after all. All you have to protect you is a suit of armor."

"And this sword," the Guardian snarled.

Clarisse floated downward, laughing. Her feet were inches from the ground when something slashed through her from behind, and she screamed and crashed the rest of the way to the rocky floor.

The man behind her slashed the silver dagger again, this time through her back. Darri wondered wildly if she was hallucinating.

Varis's other hand shot out; Darri reached out and caught a second dagger by the hilt, almost before she realized that he had thrown it. She stared at it, at the undisguised gleam of silver.

"*Go,*" Varis snapped. "Before she recovers."

The pit yawned behind her. Varis, of course, didn't know how deep it was. Or that there was no way she could survive that fall.

No way anyone could survive that fall.

She glanced quickly at the Guardian, the creature who had started all this, who had dragged her sister into it. *I remain trapped in life forever, so that the spell can continue to be channeled through my mind.*

Maybe there was more than one way to end the spell.

Darri didn't hesitate. She threw herself sideways, into the Guardian, and the two of them plunged over the edge of the cliff.

For a moment there was only the rush of the air, the

shock of terror. The Guardian flailed, his iron arm hitting her in the head and knocking her away, so she was falling alone. The wind whipped up past Darri's ears and streamed her hair straight up above her. Her scream caught in her throat, the ground rushed up to meet her, and then two thin arms wrapped themselves around her.

Darri's scream ripped loose just as the sickening impact of iron on rock thudded through the cavern. Her hands closed instinctively on the arms that had grabbed her, stopping her fall only yards from the ground. Her fingers closed in on themselves, nails digging into her palms, as Callie's arms turned insubstantial. Darri dropped the last few yards to the ground and pitched to her hands and knees.

For a moment she couldn't move; she couldn't even breathe. Her whole body felt bruised, her head still rang from its impact with iron, and the fiery pain in her arm was bone deep. Then she looked up at her sister, who was staring past Darri with her blue eyes wide.

Darri got to her feet, ignoring the stinging in the knuckles of her right hand, which was still clenched around the dagger's hilt. She turned to follow Callie's gaze. The Guardian's armor had broken when he fell; the iron mask had come off, and rolled into the corner. Blood seeped slowly away from the crushed white thing that had been behind the mask. Darri was glad it was too dark to see much of it.

"Are you crazy?" Callie gasped. She edged farther from the spell as she spoke, her jaw clenched, as if just being this close to it was hurting her. "You would have died!"

"I thought killing him might end the spell," Darri said, turning back.

"Well," Callie said, her voice brittle, "I guess it didn't, since I am still here. Sorry to disappoint you."

Behind Callie, the streams of white rock cascaded down from the darkness, so convincingly Darri thought at first they were actually moving; but the wall was eerily still and silent, motion frozen in time. Darri met her sister's eyes.

"It's not too late," she said. "Not now that I'm still alive. Thank you for that."

"Darri—" Callie's throat worked. Her face twisted, and Darri couldn't tell if what was causing her pain was the spell, or the words she was trying to say. "Darri, you can't. The other ghosts don't think like we do. They're here, and they don't want to vanish."

"Here and unhappy." Darri shifted her grip on the dagger's hilt. "What was done to them was wrong. No one asked them if they wanted to be brought back like this."

"Are you asking them if they want to be ended like this?" Callie shook her head. "What was done to them is already done. It was done, and they are here, and they cling to the semblance of life they have. It's not your place to rescue them." She took a deep, almost sobbing breath. "Or me."

"I have to—" Darri stopped. What was the point? She couldn't change her sister's mind. It wouldn't matter, if she changed something far more fundamental.

She turned and walked up to the spell.

Up close, the spiral of rock lost its beauty and became merely grotesque. As she walked, the air around her grew thicker, and her nostrils flared at the smell of rot. She could see clearly where the strands of rock had twisted together, coiled around something. Something they were protecting. The smooth rock glowed with a faint light, casting eerie shadows around the already eerie structure.

The silver dagger was heavy in her hand. Darri swung with all her might. At the first stroke, the colored rock seemed to shudder, and a hairline crack spread along the length of a black-speckled gray coil. Behind her, Callie gasped.

Powerful and fragile, the Guardian had said. Like life itself.

Darri's breath caught in her throat. She lifted the dagger to strike again, and a hand closed around her wrist and pulled her back.

It was so unexpected that only the tightness of her grip kept the dagger from flying across the cave. Darri whirled and yanked her arm out of Callie's grasp. Her sister stared up at her.

"Don't do this," Callie said.

Her face hadn't changed: it was still small and round, wide blue eyes and coiled blond hair. Perhaps it was Darri who had changed, had learned to recognize what was in front of her eyes. Because for the first time, Callie truly looked dead.

"I'm doing it for you," Darri said.

"Because you think I could live again." Callie stepped back, letting her hand drop. "It's not true, Darri. The Guardian lied. I'm gone."

"You don't know that," Darri said. "You're just afraid to hope. Don't you see, Callie? This could change everything, make it like it should have been. This could bring you back. You—and all of them, all the ghosts—you could *live* again."

"And if we all just vanish instead? You'll be committing mass murder."

"A mass murder of people already dead?"

"They exist," Callie whispered. "They think and speak and feel. If you cause them to cease to exist, you've murdered them."

For a moment, the only sound was the hiss of Darri's breathing. Callie wasn't breathing at all.

"You're doing this for me," Callie said. "I know you are. And I'm asking you not to. I don't want to bear this guilt."

"It's not your guilt," Darri said. "Because you can't stop me."

Callie drew in a deep, shuddering breath. This time, when Darri turned her back on her, she made no movement. Darri took a step sideways, out of Callie's reach, and held the knife steady.

Her hand looked strange to her, brown and bony, inhuman. The hand that would wipe a plague of the dead off the face of this earth. It didn't matter if they might all stop existing because of what she did. They shouldn't exist in the first place.

But they do.

She thought of all the ghosts in the castle above her, going through their pretenses of life: eating and drinking and dancing and talking. She thought of all of them suddenly ceasing to be, plates and goblets crashing to the floor, dancers staring at their suddenly abandoned arms, sentences cut off to never be finished. Of the empty spaces that would stud the castle, where the ghosts used to be.

Where they never should have been.

But where they *were*. Right now. Until the moment she swung her dagger.

She thought of Callie alive beside her again. Of the two of them racing across the plains, her sister's joyous laugh floating back on the wind.

Her hand moved back, ready to strike. It hovered there for a second, shaking. Then she stepped back and let it drop to her side.

Behind her, Callie drew in a deep breath. Darri took another step back. Her fingers were clenched so tightly on the dagger's hilt that they hurt.

Everything hurt, her heart worst of all. She had just betrayed her sister for the second time. Callie's existence here was a gilded cage, warped and twisted and inescapable.

But still real.

"Darri?" Callie whispered.

Darri looked up, barely seeing Callie. Her sister, now gone forever. Her eyes swam with tears, and even as she struggled against them, she heard them drop one by one onto the dry earth. And then she heard the first of her own wrenching sobs.

It was over. Every step she had taken, from the moment in the plains when she mounted her horse and turned east, had been for this: to save Callie. From Ghostland, then from death itself.

"I'm sorry," she whispered finally. She could barely get the words out.

Callie reached for her hand and said, her voice steady, "I'm not."

As her sister pulled her up past the waterfall of stone, Darri's tears fell past her feet, down down down. If they made a sound when they hit the bottom, Darri never heard it.

Chapter Twenty-One

The packhorses were ready and waiting down in the stable-yard, but Darri sat on her bed with her saddlebag in her lap, rearranging its few contents over and over. She didn't know why. Callie had vanished last night, the instant they had landed on the cavern floor to find Varis and Clarisse still locked in battle; and she hadn't reappeared when Clarisse disappeared in a swirl of smoke, or on the long, silent walk back to the castle, or through the sleepless day that had followed. She was hardly likely to come say good-bye now, when Darri should already have been at the stableyard.

All the same, when her door slid open, she stood up so fast her saddlebag spilled onto the floor. But it was Kestin, dressed in a diamond-studded doublet, who stood at the entrance to her room.

"So," he said, stepping inside and closing the door behind him. "You are returning home?"

She nodded shortly and bent to gather up her scattered belongings. Before she had finished, Kestin was crouched beside her, helping her. She looked up, startled; and when he turned to meet her gaze, his eyes were dark and hollow, like a skull's eyes in bone-white skin.

Whatever he saw in her face, it made Kestin rise and step back. Not until she had finished, and risen to her feet as well, did he say, "I wanted to give you one more thing to take with you."

Darri recognized the parchment as soon as he held it out. She made no move to take it. Instead she met his gaze and said, "Why?"

"For all the reasons I told you before," Kestin said. "And because it's not really over. Unless we have a clear basis for alliance, your brother will be back."

Darri smiled tightly. "Even if you do . . . I wouldn't trust him. Conquest is safer than alliance."

"I have no intention of trusting him," Kestin said. "But I'd like to trust you."

She lost the smile. He extended the parchment to her. "You would, after all, be in a position to try and stop him. Even if you never accept, the offer will give you power."

Power over her father and Varis. Not much . . . but

enough, perhaps, to make her indispensable. If she used it wisely, it might be enough to make her life her own.

She reached out and took the parchment from the dead king's hand.

It felt just as thick and dry as it had the first time she held it. She thought of the endless plains, of the wind that roared across the grasses, carrying the spirits of the dead. Of the empty space that would always be beside her, the space where Callie should have been.

She swallowed the lump in her throat, got to her feet, and slipped the parchment into her saddlebag. Then she turned. Kestin was still watching her.

"I won't ever come back here," she said. "I won't spend my life among the dead."

He smiled very faintly. "I know."

She turned away so he couldn't see her face. As if from a distance, she heard herself say, "Thank you."

Some seconds later, she heard the door open and shut. She stood staring at the saddlebag in her hands. Then the door opened again and Varis said, "We're ready."

She slung the bag over her shoulder before walking with him to the courtyard near the stables. She walked warily, and so did he, keeping their steps in sync even as they descended the stairs.

But no shadows reared at them from the corners, no iron

mask appeared to watch them accusingly. The Guardian would not be coming back as a ghost; nor would anyone else, now that new magic could no longer flow through his mind to fuel the spell.

It should have made Darri feel better, to know that she had at least accomplished that. That she had saved people she didn't know, or care about, and would never see again.

The horses were already saddled in the dark courtyard. Darri slung the saddlebags into place and mounted. She felt numb. Vague images of stalagmites flitted through her mind, and her head still hurt from the day's sobbing, an ache that started in the back of her eyes and wrapped around her head, twisting and coiling like . . .

She swore, shaking her head, just as Varis said, "You know, there's a bright side. Father will be very unhappy with me."

Darri turned and stared at him, startlement forcing the images of the spelled stones from her mind. Varis smiled at her crookedly. "Once everyone realizes how badly I've failed, my position back home won't exactly be secure. I'm sure that will make you happy."

Would it? Darri considered for a moment, not just what Varis had said, but the prospect of being happy; of letting herself be happy. She said, slowly, "Not really. It's not as if Father will ever understand why you failed."

Their eyes met. Darri saw on her brother's face a weary acknowledgment: that back on the plains, among their people, only the two of them would ever understand.

The castle loomed behind them, the yellow light from its windows giving more illumination than the moon. Darri wondered if Callie was watching them go, if the dead were ranged translucent against the torch-lit windows. She imagined their skull-like eyes, trapped and accusing, but she didn't look back. To Callie, this castle was home; and to Darri, it was a place of grief and sacrifice.

She was not done with grief; she probably never would be, not truly. But she rather thought she was done with sacrifice.

"Let's go," she said, her voice rough, and loosened her reins. She wasn't going to look back. She was going to ride away, and maybe she couldn't keep herself from feeling guilty, but she was not going to let her guilt trap her. And she was not going to look back.

Hoofbeats clattered on the cobblestone behind her, and she whirled.

Callie walked across the courtyard, leading a horse. Her hair was aloft in an elaborate Ghostland style, but she wore practical Raellian riding breeches. When she got to the spot where they were mounted, she swung herself easily onto the horse's back.

"Callie," Darri whispered, and then didn't know what else to say.

Callie took a long time gathering the reins. When she looked up, her face was serene and frightened at once. "I'm coming with you."

"But—" Darri stopped, swallowed. "But you can't—"

Callie gave her a tiny smile. It was not the unrestrained, exuberant smile of the girl Darri had come looking for, but it was brave, and unfaltering, and real. "You should welcome this."

She should. But it was suddenly completely obvious to Darri that she didn't. That the important thing about Callie was not what she had become, but what she had always been. Darri's sister.

"You could stay here," she said. "You told me you could. That you could be the same as . . . as the others."

Callie laughed, and it sounded almost like her old laugh, free and joyous. Almost. "Is that what you want me to do?"

"It's not about what I want," Darri said. "It's your choice, Callie. Your . . ." She stopped. She couldn't say "life."

Callie's laugh faded, and she stroked her horse's neck. "I'm not sure I ever could be like them. And besides, I was trying so hard to be the same as them, I failed to notice that I have something none of the rest of them have. I can ride away, far enough that the spell won't touch me anymore."

"And they can't?" Varis snapped.

"They can," Callie said. "There's nothing stopping them." She looked over her shoulder at the brightly lit windows. "They might realize that, now."

Darri swallowed hard. She couldn't think of anything to say.

"But what will happen to you when we ride over the border?" said Varis, who apparently had no such problem.

Some of the laughter faded from Callie's face. "I guess we'll find out, won't we?"

"Actually," Varis said, "*you'll* find out."

Darri's hand curled into a fist. But Callie just smirked.

"I'll find out in a few nights," she said. "You'll find out . . . eventually."

Varis muttered something under his breath and kicked his horse into a trot. Darri and Callie exchanged a wordless glance. Darri grinned; Callie nodded.

Varis yelped as they raced past him, but his words were lost in the pounding of hooves and the whistling wind. Neck to neck, streaming black hair beside bound-up gold, the sisters rode like the wind across the courtyard of the castle and into the dark forest beyond.

Acknowledgments

To everyone I thanked in the first book. (Um, yes I can. It's *my* acknowledgments page.)

And specifically:

To my editor, Martha Mihalick, for her dedication, thoroughness, and insight, for putting up with "the Dark Whatever" for so long, and for taking it in stride when I said after three rounds of revisions, "Hey, guess what I just figured out about my main character?"

To everyone at Greenwillow and HarperCollins, especially Virginia Duncan, Lois Adams, Michelle Corpora, Robin Tordini, Patty Rosati, Emilie Ziemer, and Laura Lutz.

To Paul Zakris, because I was worried the second cover couldn't possibly be as good as the first, and instead it topped it.

To my family, for their continual excitement, support, and Internet obsessing so I don't have to (not that it stops me); and especially to Aaron, for putting a brake on the obsessing . . . or trying to.

To my agent, Bill Contardi.

To Cindy Pon and Caragh O'Brien, for lengthy e-mail exchanges.

To the Tenners, the Class of 2K10, and the Inkies.

And finally: one of my regrets with *Mistwood* was that because it was written over the course of eight years (and three e-mail programs), I wasn't able to thank all the people who read and critiqued it for me. With *Nightspell*, I'm thrilled that I can. Thank you: Tova Suslovich, Leah Clifford, Kay Cassidy, Pattie Lawler, Sara Fishman, Melissa Hollingsworth, Kelly Cruz, Tarah Nyberg, David Siska, Kat Otis, Laurel Amberdine, Christine Amsden, Alena McNamara, and Kim Zimring.